The words swirled around Raya Fahmi. But she was not listening to this soldier's talk of Rommel, tanks, wounds. She was listening instead to the music which came from one of the back rooms. A song about a young girl who was leaving Marseilles and going to the country. The girl would miss the city, and the lights, and one sailor in particular.

Raya liked this kind of song. She believed that the heroes and heroines actually existed. . .

But Raya had yet to meet David Chalfin, who would nourish her belief—and then allow the war to bring her to the brink of destruction. . .

Raya

FRANK KING

CHARTER
NEW YORK

A DIVISION OF CHARTER COMMUNICATIONS INC.
A GROSSET & DUNLAP COMPANY

RAYA

Copyright © 1980 by Franklin King

An ACE CHARTER Book

Published by arrangement with
Richard Marek Publishers

First Ace Charter printing August 1981

Published simultaneously in Canada

Manufactured in the United States of America

2 4 6 8 0 9 7 5 3 1

For all those who stopped the Beast
on the Western Desert.

Prologue

Scotland. July, 1942.

It had been an astonishing event, a bad, almost a filthy omen. Samuel Chalfin had been sitting on the ground, resting from his walk, smoking. He had been dressed in his fashion, as a successful fifty-two-year-old Austrian-Jewish emigré to England should have been dressed. One could tell from his stiff leather boots that he had learned the language fluently. One could tell by the expensive, baggy knockabout trousers that he had mastered even the most intricate Anglo-Saxon behavior patterns.

He was thinking of nothing. He was doing something, however, besides smoking. He was listening to the beat of his heart. It was odd that in the country he could always hear the beat. He could stop anywhere, on any terrain, and he could hear the regular thump.

Then, suddenly, he heard a much louder thump from off to one side. Since Chalfin had also assimilated the peculiar Anglo-Saxon custom of forthrightness, he walked quickly to the sound, to investigate.

On the sparse ground, twenty yards in front of him, was a peregrine falcon. Lying between the falcon's broad talons was a dead, small bird. The falcon was mantling over the corpse, spreading its wings like a cape, the head shoved forward. The blank killer's eyes were visible—black and gold marbles that turned in the sun.

Samuel Chalfin was rigid with fear. He was a cosmopolitan, a man who had survived the violence of cities because he understood the logic of cities. He could not fathom the natural creature which seemed to ignore him. He could not deal with hideousness unless it came from the hands of men.

The falcon ate the eyes of the dead bird as the corpse lay on its back. Then the falcon split the breast open, pulling out the

7

flesh in quick jerks. But always, amidst all that bone and blood and feather, the falcon was fastidious. It was a physician operating on a patient.

Chalfin suddenly broke and ran, stopping only when he could no longer catch his breath. He gathered himself, looking around, ashamed of his behavior, and then started the slow walk back to the inn.

Once inside his room he sat down by the small table and put a pen and piece of paper in front of him. He would write another letter to his son David and tell him about the falcon. It didn't matter that his son hadn't answered any of his previous letters. Samuel scratched a few words on the paper and then stopped. He wondered why the powers that be had presented a falcon to him. Perhaps, he thought, in all of England that day, he was the only man who had seen such a sight. Perhaps no Englishman had seen a peregrine feeding for years. Omens, after all, were as reasonable as reason itself. For if all was random, then everything had a meaning. Everything!

He got up from the table, shaky, not feeling well, and lay down on the bed. His feet had swelled and his toes ached from the pressure of the boots.

Why does the falcon lay the corpse out like that—so serenely, so mathematically?

Why had his son David turned his back on England? It was a land unlike any other. It was a country where the beast had never been triumphant. Never. Oh, once in a while it would raise itself and peer about and utter a few curses, but then the wisdom of the English people would force it back, and all one could see were the bubbles where it had vanished.

He sat up suddenly, making a strangled noise in his throat. What would happen if he died without ever seeing his son again?

No, that couldn't happen. No, that would never happen. No matter his own sins, and there were many, the God of Abraham, Isaac, and Jacob, and the gods of the British Isles, would never permit that.

He reached forward and tugged at the cuffs of his trousers, nervously, compulsively. He should have married again, he realized, after his wife died. He should have married and had three, four, five more children, a hundred children. He should have had twenty sons and twenty daughters, and all of them should have been different, and liked different things, and wore different clothes, and thought different thoughts. That was the way to avoid omens, the way to confuse the powers that be. He lay back again, but he was crying.

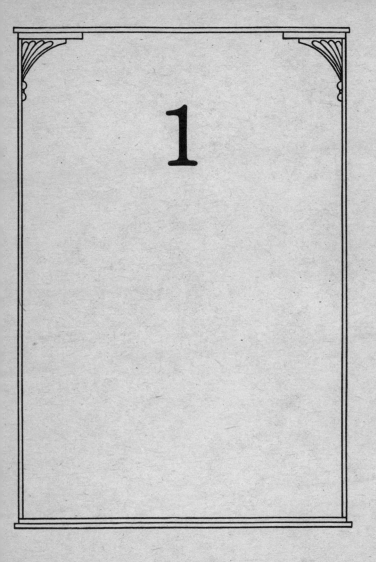

1

Cairo. October, 1942.

Cairo festered as it had always festered, in the shadow of the noose. As it had festered before the Persian conquest and the Roman conquest; before the Arab conquest and the Ottoman conquest; before the Napoleonic conquest and the Anglo-French conquest.

One hundred miles to the west, Rommel had been stopped at El Alamein. The bedouins of the Western Desert now hovered at the fringes of the graveyard, picking clean the weapons and the corpses. They worked quietly and quickly, seemingly without rancor or greed. They collected everything because here was *gadid*, the new: canteens, pistols, mirrors, razors, cans, cartridges, wallets, rings, shoes, unnamed pieces of metal and aluminum. The objects were often splintered and crushed and burned, but they were desirable because they were *gadid*—the new objects of the new world.

Hundreds of miles to the east, in the Sinai Desert, and to the south, in the Arabian Desert, monks of the Coptic orders maintained their gardens and their manuscripts. They were oblivious to the man-made conflagration of Alamein; they lived eternally in a divine conflagration.

Within the festering city, new wagers had to be made, new contracts drawn, old wagers hedged, and new strategies developed by a hundred desperate factions. The Moslem brotherhoods. The cabals of Egyptian officers. The Government bureaucrats. The British overlords.

For David Chalfin, however, words such as Rommel and El Alamein had little meaning. They denoted large historical events, and his concern was with small details—with a particular scar on the face of a certain cobbler, or the sudden disappearance of a man from a stall that sold red leather, or the origin of a perplexing newspaper report.

Tall, thin, a bit hunched, he looked very much the garden-variety dissolute Englishman out for a night in the twisted streets of Arab Cairo.

He seemed older than his twenty-five years because the sun had dried and drawn the skin around his eyes and mouth. His brown hair was parted on one side and cropped unevenly in the back. The brown suit and white shirt he wore were too large for him now, though they had fit at one time.

He strolled, keeping as close as he could to the irregular building line, avoiding the crush of donkeys and surly *fellahin*, coughing vehicles, drunken British and Canadian soldiers, and exiled Europeans in dirty linen suits and dark *fezzes*.

The sun had gone down but the hawkers kept up their incessant chants.

There was no rush. Winokur had given him those typically vague instructions: "Spend a few hours in The Trunk. Enjoy yourself. See what is going on there. Tell me."

The Trunk was a raucous club, deep in the old city, so deep that one could see the Mokattam Hills, the quarries from whence Cairo had begun.

See what is going on there. Chalfin smiled as he sauntered.

It was always difficult to understand precisely what Winokur wanted. And that was understandable because they came from different places.

Winokur had journeyed from Poland to Jerusalem to avoid death. Chalfin had journeyed from London to Jerusalem to escape nothingness. But their goal was the same: Jerusalem reborn. And this goal had led them both to Cairo under the sometimes benign, sometimes malignant aegis of the Jewish Agency.

A brace of Egyptian policemen passed him, their tan uniforms faded, but the leather and metal of belt and buckle shined to a triumphant dazzle. They twinkled in the dusk. One was swarthy and the other very light and thin, almost Circassian.

Chalfin recalled what Winokur had once told him: "There are three kinds of slaves in Egypt. White, bronze, and black. There are three kinds of free men. White, bronze, and black."

That was the entire speech. It was Winokur's often brilliant crypticity that made him, Chalfin, lean forward to listen. It was the wisdom of the Lodz Ghetto.

He strolled until his conscience rankled, then walked resolutely toward The Trunk. He entered from a vestibule off the street and was immediately thrust into a jumble of chairs and tables and a fog of smoke. Easing himself into a chair, he fingered the remains of a *bettai* cake on the small table. The Trunk was a brothel, he knew that. The room widened into a network of small draped rooms. A glistening Nubian appeared, smacked the remains of the cake off the table, and extended a large black hand. Between the first two fingers was a bottle of brandy. Between the last two fingers was a bottle of gin. His other hand held glasses.

Chalfin nodded to the brandy and dropped paper bills on the table. The Nubian placed the bottle and two glasses on the table, lifted the money, and vanished.

Chalfin's mind began to absorb the room. He was here

because Winokur wanted him to *see*. So he saw, registering, cataloging, categorizing in his brain—silently and continuously.

. . . No bar. Whiskey brought to table. Waiters black and ugly. Voices speaking in English, French, Greek, Arabic. British and Commonwealth soldiers all over the place. Officers and enlisted men. Whores circulate from table to table. They wear blue skirts and white blouses—glory to the English school tradition. Coffee served if requested. Two men at door. One circulates. They look Armenian. Prices outlandish. Whores pick up from table and take client to back rooms. Whores above average. Hear some music. Probably from a back room. Soldiers crazed in smoke and brandy. Chairs rickety. Tank crew in corner table. Sandy-haired sergeant has face burns. Purple and black. Ugly and beautiful. From El Alamein? Like Liverpool gone mad. Or like Oxford become concrete? Brandy watered but not much. Just around the fringes. Bogus label on bottle. Bogus weight. . . .

He blotted out the process, knowing that he could recall when necessary, and concentrated on the bottle. Suddenly a whore sat down at the table and pulled a glass toward herself. Chalfin poured for her. She was young and strongly built. Her hair was black and cut short. She wore a small fake birthmark on one high cheekbone.

Half and half, he thought. Half Greek, half Egyptian. Or half Maltese, half Berber. Or, half Turkish and half English.

It had to be half and half because she had those peculiar Cairo qualities—appearing both sluggish and alert at the same time. The cliché is true, he thought—"hooded, darting eyes"—but he didn't remember the source.

"English?" Her obligatory question was asked in a slow, tired voice.

"Chinese," Chalfin replied.

She smiled, tilted her glass just a bit. "Soldier?"

"Sheep herder," he replied.

This time she didn't smile. She nodded and then looked

around the room as if aware that he would not be a productive event.

"Is there anything you want?" she asked matter-of-factly.

"A bit more brandy, and that's all," he said.

She drained her glass, smiled at him politely, and left.

He watched her circle the room and finally sit down with the British tank crew. Then he pushed the bottle of brandy and his glass to the center of the table, rose to his feet, and left The Trunk. He should have stayed longer, he realized, he should have seen more.

Chalfin walked west, toward the European quarter. At the second intersection there was a crowd pressed into a small pocket. He edged closer and peered over the heads. A recalcitrant donkey was being worried, pushed, pleaded with. The beast's ears were laid back. An aged *fellah*, desperate at being caught in the hated city after the sun had set, increased his efforts with each shout of encouragement from the crowd. Dozens of blankets jounced on the donkey's back, and trinkets were slung over the withers. Finally the ears relented, the doleful eyes seemed to gather purpose, and the donkey moved. The crowd parted and man and beast passed by Chalfin. Suddenly, without any thought, he called out. The old man and the donkey came to a halt. Chalfin quickly flipped the top blanket forward onto the donkey's neck. Emblazoned on a corner of the next blanket was a palm tree on a swastika—the copper-brown insignia of the Afrika Korps.

Chalfin stepped back, cursing himself for stupidity. What happened to be on the backs of donkeys meant nothing. He stared at the old man, who was now afraid, who grinned and cocked his head. The old man's *galabia*, his long-sleeved loose cotton gown, was soiled and stained.

I am afraid, thought Chalfin. I am afraid of the simple insignia of the Afrika Korps.

The old man's grin became wider.

"*Alkhof baraka*," Chalfin whispered to him. Fear is a blessing.

17

The old man and the donkey moved off. Chalfin waited where he was for a few minutes; one leg was trembling slightly. He would tell Winokur everything about The Trunk, but he would never, he knew, tell Winokur about the blanket. Then, once again, he walked west.

The words swirled around Raya Fahmi. But she was not listening to them. She no longer listened to soldiers' words, they were all the same: bits and pieces of England, Rommel, tanks, names, wounds. She was listening instead to the music which came from one of the back rooms. A song about a young girl who was leaving Marseilles and going to the country. The girl would miss the city, and the lights, and one sailor in particular. But in the country there was fresh cream, and large trees, and safety. It was a slow song, in French, and the words were sad. Raya liked those kinds of songs. She believed that the heroes and heroines actually existed.

The British soldier seated next to her slipped his hand under the table; it crawled up her thigh. She let it crawl.

Raya Fahmi drained her glass and the hands of six Eighth Army soldiers reached out to fill it. She drank only once during an evening, and that was before her first customer; only the first customer was difficult.

Seated across the table, she knew, was that first customer. Not the one whose hand was still crawling under the table. It would be the soldier across the table, the one the others called Peters. The light-haired man with the horrible burn on one side of his face.

Next to Peters was the one they called Tomlinson. But Tomlinson's face was lying on the table. He was mumbling. From time to time Peters would pull his head up, and then lower it gently.

Peters kept looking at her. He would address a remark to his comrades, then look at her. He would move his hands, describing an event, then look at her. He would puff up his

18

cheeks and mimic an explosion, and then look at her. Whenever he looked, Raya Fahmi smiled.

She felt healthy compared to them. She felt as if she lived on fresh fruits and vegetables. All the desert soldiers were sickly. Their skins were burned brown but they had a pallor. Their lips and fingers were cracked with running sores. The backs of their necks were leathery and rubbed raw.

Peters pulled up Tomlinson's head. Tomlinson murmured.

"What did he say?" asked a soldier.

"Petrol, he was calling for petrol," said Peters.

They laughed, almost hysterically.

"Petrol?"

"Yes, petrol."

"He really meant water," said Peters, glancing at Raya, shyly, this time. He slowly brought his hand to his cheek to hide the scar.

"Yes, he meant water," Peters repeated. "He meant Kipling: 'You can talk of gin and beer when you're quartered safe out here/And a serving of Her Majesty the Queen/But when it comes to slaughter/You'll do your work on water/And you'll lick the bloomin' boots of him that got it.'"

"He meant *petrol*." This was said by the soldier sitting next to Raya. He removed his hand from her thigh. He stood up menacingly, wrapping his hand around the gin bottle, glaring at Peters.

"Perhaps he meant petrol," Peters admitted. And they all relaxed.

Peters grew silent. He drank. He gave up his attentions to Tomlinson. He began to curse. Then he shook his head from side to side, the overhead light dancing over his burn. Suddenly he stood. He looked around as though the panzers were coming for him. Then he extended a hand toward Raya Fahmi.

A soldier guffawed. "But he can't do it, luv. They shot it off! They shot it off old Peters. It's hanging now in Berlin. Ask anyone. They shot it off old Peters!"

Peters flushed. Raya Fahmi rose from the table and walked toward the rear of The Trunk. She could hear Peters stumbling behind her. She could hear his comrades laughing. She could hear them calling out, "Petrol, petrol . . ."

They passed into a room. Raya closed the sliding rattan curtain. There was a bed, next to the bed was a table. On the table was a bowl of water and a kerosene lamp, burning.

"What a small room. Why do they make these rooms so small? Why aren't they large and airy? Why are there no large windows?"

Raya shrugged. She unfastened her blue skirt and draped it over a hook on the wall. There was nothing under her skirt. She unbuttoned her white schoolgirl's blouse but did not take it off.

Peters looked at her, at her legs, at her open blouse, and then looked away. He pulled some notes from his pocket and threw them on the table without counting. Egyptian pound notes and British pound notes, crumpled together. He waited.

Raya touched his belt. He stepped back. Yes, he knew he had to undress, but he would do that himself.

They were all like that, the British. They were all awkward between the time they put the money on the table and the time they touched her. They could not fathom whores. They could not fathom a body for purchase. Their bewilderment made them awkward. The French were not like that, nor the Egyptians, nor the Greeks, nor the Russians, nor the Turks. Not even the Australians were like that. Only the British were awkward in that small space of time. The time in which they could not fathom the event.

Peters unhooked his belt and stepped out of his khaki shorts. He took off his shirt. His boots stayed on. He stood there, his head slightly turned from her. Raya reached for the sponge in the bowl of water and quickly brought it between his legs.

Sound exploded in her head, and then she felt pain on one side of her face. His slap had sent her across the room, to the foot of the bed where she lay now, stunned. When her eyes focused, she saw Peters in a crouch. He was glaring at her, and his hand held a long knife that he had slipped out of his boot. Suddenly he relaxed. He speared the sponge on the point of the knife and held it up.

"What were you trying to do?" he asked evenly.

"Wash you. You must be washed," she answered.

"I'm sorry I hit you. I didn't know what you were doing. It was so sudden. The sponge was cold."

She simply nodded. She watched him as he carefully washed himself, then took off his boots.

Raya Fahmi stretched out on the bed, close to the wall, leaving space for him. She kept her eyes on the ceiling because she had learned that many customers did not wish her to look upon their naked bodies. He would not want her to use her mouth, few of the British did. He would not want her to get on all fours, or bite him. When they came to her, the British wanted wives. So she would lie there, keeping her knees up and slightly apart. She would wait for him.

Peters lay down beside her. He angled his face in a gentlemanly attempt to keep from her his burn scar. This had nothing to do with vanity. He slid a hand beneath her open blouse, onto her breast. She murmured. Customers expected their whores to make accommodating sounds. What she felt on her breast was a hand that was afraid, and also astonished.

He will try to kiss me, she thought. She did not want to be kissed.

He did not kiss her. He withdrew his hand. A woman lay beside him! He found this difficult to believe. His hand had been upon her breast! He found this difficult to believe. He trembled slightly. His head spun. Probably he had had too much gin.

Swiftly he flung himself on her, his body tautly desperate as he entered her. He was there for but an instant, his hands grasping alternately the sheets, her hair, her shoulders. And then he rolled off, finished. For a while he couldn't catch his breath. He pulled at the sheets. Finally, he whispered, "You said something."

"No."

"Just a moment ago you said something, in Arabic. I heard you."

"I don't know," Raya replied.

Involuntarily, she had said something. She had said what all whores in Egypt had been taught to say. She had said: *"Fedwa Aleyk."*

It could mean: "I am prepared to die in your place." It could mean anything because lovers said that to one another. Whores had been taught to say it the moment their customer ejaculated in them. So that the customer would believe that his orgasm had been sublime, that it had given pleasure to the whore, that the act of sex had been an act of love; that, with him, it had been different.

Peters began to dress. Suddenly they heard laughter and loud voices just outside the rattan curtain. A hand holding a gin bottle shoved the curtain aside. "Petrol! Petrol!" And in a moment, all of Peters' comrades were in the room.

"Didn't I tell you, luv, didn't I tell you they shot it off!"

But abruptly there was an absolute silence. They were staring at Raya Fahmi. Her body. The color of her skin, the birthmark on her cheek, the open blouse, her half-covered breasts, the place between her legs where Peters had been. . . . They stared. Their faces were utterly sad.

Raya sat up, with no effect on the sadness of their faces.

"Now you must take care of *him,*" said a soldier.

Tomlinson was dragged to the bed and sprawled by her lap.

"She must take care of him. Am I right, Peters?"

Peters nodded.

Crumpled notes were tossed onto the table as they filed out, muttering, "Take care of Tomlinson, take care of Tomlinson. . . ."

The evening had started badly. The slap from Peters. Now

this: Tomlinson. He was handsome. His eyes were large and blue. A religious medal hung from his neck and she played with it absent-mindedly. It wasn't the gin alone that had made him collapse, she thought. There was something else. She took the young soldier's head into her lap. He whispered, "Petrol, petrol . . ."

Winokur lived in a modern flat on Gezira. Gezira was that large island in the Nile which had absorbed the British move away from the old city. On Gezira were the Turf Club, and the more opulent cabarets, and the headquarters of the various army groups. No longer was it the westernmost oasis of Cairo—the Europeans had long since colonized the West Bank, north and south—but it was the most stolid. As Rommel had catapulted toward Alexandria, all of Cairo had begun to pack, to burn papers and hide gold, to write wills—but on Gezira there had been calm. For it was British, and the Empire had taught the inhabitants to proceed with calm. To view fate with a cool clarity. So, when Rommel was stopped at Alamein, Gezira did not return to normal; it had always been there.

Chalfin stood by the window, absorbing the morning sun, waiting for Winokur to finish his paperwork. The older man worked swiftly, pulling a sheet from the pile at his left, reading it, initialing it, then placing it on the pile at his right. He worked with great enthusiasm and speed, the pile at his left shrinking rapidly.

Winokur seemed made out of a piece of scrap iron. His nose was a beak, his hair amounted to three or four wisps, his frame was small and twisted. He dressed like a businessman, which did not hide the fact that he was a piece of scrap iron, that he would survive burning and corrosion; that his death would be inexplicable.

He had been a communist in Poland. And then, when Hitler and Stalin decided to give each other a Polish gift, he left the communists and joined one of those small, desperate

23

splinter groups of Jewish revolutionaries which managed to do exactly nothing. When the invasion came, they ran. They killed communists and fascists and Poles and Jews, striking out in lunatic gestures of defeat. They fired pistols that blew apart, threw grenades that happened to be music boxes, built firebombs that could only toast bread. They fell down and broke their legs. They spoke Polish at the moment they were supposed to speak German, or Yiddish when they were supposed to speak Polish. But some escaped, from border to border—in ships, in trucks, by foot. And they went to Palestine. It was the only place to go. Winokur was one of those who survived. He wasn't particularly smart or particularly imaginative; he was good scrap iron.

Chalfin was afraid of him, and he loved him, and he longed for his respect. Chalfin was too civilized to make an outward show, to say a word, but every assignment given him by Winokur was fulfilled with the conviction that Winokur would notice. To Chalfin, he was the most admirable sort of Jew. He was all the gangsters of Odessa, the caravan trekkers, he was all those who survived because they were made out of scrap iron. Yes, he was admirable. And sometimes, when Chalfin was drinking, Winokur took on a slightly different guise: he was transposed into the hero of Chalfin's youth: the Elizabethan sea dog, bandanna blowing, cutlassed, crazed, barefooted, scurvied: triumphant.

"Good," said Winokur. "Very good." He had just taken the last paper from the pile at his left and placed it on top of the pile at his right. "You made your visit last night?"

Chalfin nodded. "I had to shoot my way out," he replied sardonically.

Winokur, grinning, walked to the table that supported all his coffee-making apparatus. He made coffee like a bedouin. He ground the beans, boiled the water, poured, mixed. Chalfin found it undrinkable.

"You are still angry," Winokur said to Chalfin between sips. "Still angry because the Agency does not let you jump into

24

Europe, kill fascists, and bring out half-dead Jews. Still angry."

Chalfin noted that Winokur had used the word fascist instead of German.

"Sit down," said Winokur. Chalfin sat down on one of the three wooden folding chairs placed in a semicircle in front of the desk. Winokur brought his coffee to the desk and lit an Egyptian cigarette. "We are waiting for someone," he said.

Chalfin simply watched the billowing smoke.

"Do you know who we are waiting for?" asked Winokur.

"No."

"Colonel Malorange."

David Chalfin leaned forward in the chair, his hands instinctively coming together and squeezing. His face tried to fight his surprise.

Malorange! He had heard of Colonel Malorange. The name was like a murderous undercurrent. Malorange. The name was one of those gray specters in British Intelligence. The name was one of those anonymous legends which seemed to radiate throughout Cairo. Malorange was supposed to have been responsible for the assassinations, thefts, double-crosses, and everything else that could not be pinned to a specific source. Malorange was everywhere and nowhere. Malorange was a lunatic and a saint. Even in Palestine they had heard of Malorange.

Winokur sipped his coffee. "Do you know why we are waiting for him?"

"No."

"Because it has been decided that from now on, as long as the war is being fought, the Jewish Agency will cooperate with British Intelligence."

Winokur picked up the pile of initialed papers and stuffed them into a desk drawer. He slammed the drawer shut. "Don't you think that's funny, my young friend?"

"Not funny, not sad."

"Spoken like a good English Jew. But I say it's funny.

Because after this war, there will be another war. And in that war, you and I will be shooting at all the Colonel Maloranges."

Winokur ground out his cigarette, crossed the room to get more coffee, returned to the desk and lit another cigarette. When they heard the knock on the door, Chalfin got up and opened it. He ushered in Colonel Malorange. There were handshakes all around.

Chalfin felt stupid, inpotent, unable to function. He was not prepared to meet a legend. But the awe vanished quickly, as soon as the legend grinned.

Colonel Malorange was whiplash thin, wore civilian clothes, smoked American cigarettes, carried a manila envelope. He was concerned and he was confident. His face was curiously flat; the features seemed to have been compressed for function. Yes, coffee would be fine. Might he smoke? What a fine flat. How nice for Winokur to live here. He was gentle and persuasive. He was almost patronizing, but never quite. Malorange was what Chalfin's father had aspired to. Malorange was what he, Chalfin, had been meant to be, to think as, to look like. Malorange was brave, literate, soft-spoken, loyal. Malorange was the model and dream of the rich English Jew. Chalfin despised the model. He had thrown it away, gladly. It was a model that young English Zionists mocked and mimicked and paraded after three brandies were consumed. His friend Matthew, who worked for the Jewish Agency in Palestine, was so obsessed by the model that he had developed a twenty-minute burlesque based around a Malorange-type character who notifies his superiors that he has just learned both of his legs and one arm would have to be amputated. It was a satire whose aesthetic had been overwhelmed by hate.

David glanced at Winokur. The older man was smiling. He was reading him. He was reading him correctly.

Malorange asked for a bathroom and was directed to one.

Winokur and Chalfin could now hear the man urinating.

The Colonel returned and opened the manila envelope.

"First, some background information. We stopped Rommel at El Alamein. Now we are going to destroy the Afrika Korps. Within a short time, the Eighth Army will go on the offensive. Of course, we want Rommel to remain ignorant of the date, the direction, and the scope of the offensive."

"That is common knowledge," said Chalfin, contemptuously noting his brief patronizing catalog of events, as if the world was simple.

"So it is, so it is. Well, shall I continue? One of the reasons we think this offensive will be very successful is that we are now able to read virtually all the German codes. In other words, to a great extent, we know what Rommel knows, as he knows it."

Malorange lit a cigarette. So did Winokur. The Colonel played with the envelope's open clasp, but he removed nothing.

He continued: "However, a short time ago we began to monitor a new transmission. Obviously a German operator within Cairo. We have been unable to break the code. The set transmits about twice a week from a houseboat on the Nile. We know the location and, in fact, we know who the German operator is."

Malorange pulled a photograph from the manila envelope. Chalfin followed protocol and handed it first to Winokur. Winokur looked at it briefly, then handed it back to Chalfin.

"His name," continued Malorange, "is Brian Quinton. He's an Irish National, and a physician at the Daughters of Mercy Hospital."

"If you know who he is, kill him," said Winokur.

"When the time comes we will kill him. But we don't wish to stop the transmission. We want to control it. Firstly, *what* is he transmitting? We need his cipher book. If we had more time, we could break the code without his cipher book. But

27

there is no more time. We need the cipher. Then we will take over the station and transmit what we want Rommel to hear. It is as simple as that."

"Perhaps," mused Winokur, "he's transmitting weather information."

"Perhaps. And perhaps it's something else."

"And you want us to obtain the cipher, without his knowledge."

"Precisely. And we'll take over from there."

"Why us? We have no special talents in this area," Winokur said dryly.

Malorange said, "Aah." He leaned back in his chair. "Quinton is a bit of a profligate. He frequents a seedy place called The Trunk."

Chalfin glanced at Winokur in confusion. It was the first time Winokur had ever lied to him. Winokur must have known about this for a while. The order to go to The Trunk had been given days ago.

Malorange took another photograph from the envelope and laid it on the table. "Her name in Raya Fahmi. She works in The Trunk, with much success, I am told."

Chalfin swiftly turned the photo toward himself. A three-quarter face, in dim light. The fourth quarter, with the birthmark, was missing. Nevertheless, it was the face of the whore who had sat at his table.

"She's a Jewess," Malorange added softly. He looked at his shoes for a moment and then glanced up to catch their response. Neither Winokur nor Chalfin made a response. They were looking at the photograph.

Winokur shifted his chair and said: "How do you know?"

Malorange lit a cigarette.

"I don't remember how. We obtained the information from any one of a dozen Egyptians who keep feeding us tidbits so they can stir sugar into their coffee. We call if the Sugar Trade. A pound of sugar for a pound of gossip. Fair trade."

Sugar. Chalfin could visualize the staff of British Intelligence in Cairo measuring out spoonfuls of sugar to the natives. He could no longer contain his hatred.

"Have you ever been to Woburn Abbey, Colonel?" He asked.

"No, I don't think so."

"The moment I saw you," Chalfin went on, "I was reminded of a portrait in Woburn Abbey. A portrait of the Earl of Essex."

"The Earl of Essex," Malorange repeated, studying Chalfin's face to see if a joke were coming. Chalfin's face revealed only an ironic hostility.

"Yes, you remember, surely you remember, the Essex who rose against Elizabeth in 1601, and was destroyed."

"I've never seen a likeness of him. Anywhere."

"A remarkable man, Essex. He was responsible for the death of Lopez. Do you know of Lopez, Colonel?"

"No, I can't recall."

"He was Elizabeth's personal physician. A Jew. Essex trumped up charges of treason against him because he, Lopez, had diagnosed Essex as a syphilitic. Do you recall if Lopez was hanged or beheaded?"

"I don't recall, no, I really don't recall."

Winokur stopped the childish baiting. "More coffee, Colonel?"

Malorange rose to his feet. He smiled at Winokur, he smiled at Chalfin. He turned and walked toward the door. Halfway to the door he paused, turned, walked back to Winokur, and handed him a small envelope. "I had almost forgotten these. We know you are anxious for them."

Then he was gone. On the table lay the two photographs. When Winokur opened the envelope, half a dozen other photos fell onto the table. He arranged them so that Chalfin could see them. He lined them up above the face of Raya Fahmi.

They were all poorly focused and all of a single "action." Probably Poland. SS Troopers stood in small groups, smoking. Behind them lay naked bodies. Six photographs, one "action." The faces, both of the executioners and executed, were not clear. They were not in focus.

"How nice of British Intelligence to provide us with documentation," said Winokur with venom.

Then he pushed all the photographs toward Chalfin.

"Take them," he advised. "You are about to recruit a whore."

When the night had been ground out, ground to a finish, the whores, if they wanted, could gather in a small room and listen to gramophone records. There was also a plate of sweets, of small candies and cakes, some good wine, and some hot water.

This was also the room where they stored the residue of the evening, the trinkets the customers left through forgetfulness, or because they wanted to discard the item. Lighters were the most prevalent. Lighters that burst into bright flames or dull flames, lighters with grotesque wicks, and lighters with long, snaky wicks that hung out—all the way out of the object. By tradition, these trinkets belonged to the whores and not to management, so they were dumped in the small room for the women to take, if they wished.

Raya sat there, alone, She stared at the trinkets. It had been the worst of nights, and she only came there when it was very bad. Not for the trinkets or the sweets, but for the small battered gramophone which occupied a dusty corner. Stuffed between the machine and the wall were the records—seven of them.

That soldier they called Tomlinson had made her physically ill. He was crazed. He did not know where he was or why he was there. He had looked at her and not known what he was seeing. He had called her strange names. He had fallen onto the floor and crawled. He had spat on her. He had cried over her.

Raya stood up and walked slowly to the table which held

the plate of sweets. Her body ached and her eyes hurt from the smoke. One of the cakes had a pistachio border. Raya flipped it over and walked to the gramophone.

She touched the machine. No matter how many times she was in its presence, she felt a sense of awe. The machine was magic. It was the most beautiful and wondrous machine she had ever seen. The disc was placed on the top, it began to spin, and then the music came out.

Raya reached behind the machine and extracted the records. She shuffled through them until she came to the Marseilles song. She placed the record on the machine and reached for the start button—then pulled her hand back quickly. No, she really didn't want to hear any music, not even her favorite song. She walked back to the chair and sat.

It was time to go home. Another whore walked in, ate the pistachio-bordered cookie, and began to flick the trinkets with her fingers.

It is time to go home, it is time to go home, she kept telling herself, but she was too tired to stand up. She watched the whore by the table, dully. Raya had already forgotten Tomlinson's face. In a few moments she would forget the color of his hair, and then whether he was short or tall, and then whether he was from England or Australia. And then the last thing would be forgotten—the pressure of his body. But it will take a little longer for that—because Tomlinson had made her sick.

"Look," said the woman by the trinket table, holding up a tiny golden medal. She held it high against the light and laughed, dangling it by the small pin which was designed to be attached to a chain. She threw it to Raya, who watched the thing in the air, who watched it come toward her and bounce against her lap and then fall to the floor.

She cursed Raya for letting it fall, then promptly forgot all about it, and started the gramophone.

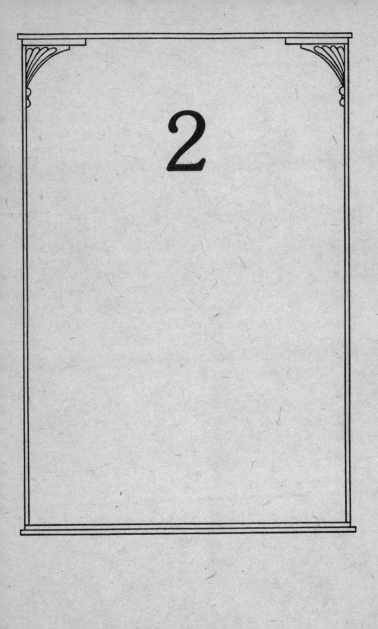

2

The street was paved with bleached cobblestones, rising and falling in random patterns. The muzzein's call to morning prayer seemed to fall from the sky and skip along the stones. On the north side of the street, near the mosque, an old man squatted against a low wall, a donkey loosely tethered to his foot by a rope. There were blankets on the donkey's back, and the old man also held a blanket, cradling it in his arms as though it were a small child. The old man appeared to be half asleep, rocking slowly back and forth on his heels.

On the other side of the street, near the corner, stood Moussa Tmai. He was a short man, anchored to the ground by cascading layers of fat. He wore a brown silk suit, a white cotton shirt, and well-kept sandals. His face was very large, almost chocolate in color, and kindly, with wide, perplexed eyes. Although the morning was cool there was perspiration on his bald head. The stubby fingers of his left hand dexterously opened and closed a linen handkerchief—white linen with a border of red herons. His fingers bunched it together, released it, fluttered it in the quiet air.

Moussa Tmai was a talented man. Everyone said so. And they also said he was great-hearted. His talents lay in the realm of procurement. In the vast multilingual city, he was able to bring together buyers and sellers. And furthermore, he was able to identify mutual interests that were not readily apparent. For example, if Moussa knew a man who had good meat to sell, and knew another man who wished to buy refitted weapons, Moussa could find a reason for the two to deal, in spite of the fact that there seemed to be no points of convergence. He would suggest a third item, that perhaps one desired and the other wished to dispose of, and thus consummate something from nothing. As for his great-heartedness, many people could attest to that. He wept openly and copiously for all the petty injustices in the world, that is to say, he wept for their victims. He knew that injustice was the inviolable will of God, but still he wept.

Recently Moussa's feet had begun to ache, even in the mornings. So he had switched from European shoes to native sandals. But his feet still ached, particularly in the tendon above the heel, and he kept shifting his weight as he watched the empty street.

He fluttered the handkerchief once more in the air, folded it carefully, and put it into his pocket. Stepping back a little, he moved into the shadow of a doorway. The morning was very quiet, so quiet that he looked up above the roofs, searching for a bird, listening for the whir of a bird in flight.

A sound came from the corner. He pressed back against the building. The click clack click of boots on cobblestones sounded in his ears.

Two men came into view. The first, Colonel Quaffid, took long rapid strides. Behind him was an aide. Quaffid kept swinging one hand as he walked, as though he held a riding whip. He was speaking to his aide, who nodded, from time to time observing the arc of the riding whip.

Moussa watched Colonel Quaffid with admiration. Quaffid was the shiny sword of the new Egyptian Army. Tall and straight and disaffected, and difficult. Everyone said he was difficult and everyone said he was plotting.

The two men entered the mosque for their morning prayers.

It is good, thought Moussa, that men of such power continue to pray. He removed the white handkerchief with the red heron border from his pocket and began to play with it again.

Across the street the donkey started to amble off and the old man cursed it sharply and yanked the rope. The beast made an awesome sound and stood still again.

Moussa held the handkerchief by two fingers and watched it billow in the slight breeze.

Twelve minutes after they had entered the mosque, Quaffid and his aide emerged. The Colonel lifted his chest and looked around, as though contemplating all the myriad possibilities in the Cairo morning. He slapped his hands together once as though applauding his fate. With a little nod he brought the attention of his aide to the old man and the donkey. Quaffid and his aide both smiled. The old man raised his blanket in deference. Two small objects dropped from the blanket and began to roll down the cobblestones toward the mosque. They made almost the same sound the Colonel's boots had made—only a bit softer.

But a few seconds later they made a different sound. The smiling Colonel and his smiling aide were blown to kingdom come.

"I have been reading a lot lately. But all I have read seems only to confirm what I know. What do I know? That the peace which follows this war will mean nothing. That no place can have any meaning anymore to intelligent people. That you should forget everything—and after the war come back to England. Maybe I am saying that the only thing a family can do is die together, David. Do I sound unbalanced? I am not. I have been thinking about this. Maybe I should stop reading. After all, we always got on very well when you took me to task for not reading; when I played the Jewish businessman and you played the Jewish intellectual."

David Chalfin didn't read any more of his father's letter. He folded it carefully and put it in his coat pocket, next to his wallet. The letter was more than three months old. It had been sent to the old address in Jerusalem, then went through a series of misadventures, and turned up finally in the Agency mail.

And there really was no reason to finish it. Every step he had taken in the last six or seven years had infuriated his father—the abandonment of Cambridge, the refusal to hold a job, the Zionist affiliation, the decision to go to Palestine. Now his father wanted a reconciliation, which was fine. He loved his father. But there were no grounds for it. The breach was wide and treacherous, and neither knew what was required to cross it.

Chalfin was sipping cold coffee. A few other solitaries sat at tables in the small coffeehouse near his flat. On the table in front of him, in a tidy pile, was a stack of newspapers. Every morning, about eleven, he came here to have coffee and to look through all the newspapers available in the city. It was part of his professional duty to do so. He would wait until arriving at Winokur's office to clip those items he thought important. Then he would go through the dispatches that came by pouch—from a man called Neurath in Alexandria, from a man called Louis in the Gaza, and from men and women with no names at all. He would open a folder, date it, and fill the folder. The dispatches which requested money or information came first, then the important newspaper clippings, then all that was left. The folder was placed prominently on Winokur's desk. That was his job.

Last night had not been a good night and the morning was no better. Something was gnawing at him, stiffening his neck, making him listless and sleepless and unable to eat. He ordered another coffee and stirred in the sugar. Suddenly he arched his back and planted his feet firmly under the table. I am acting like an ass, he thought.

Chalfin knew what was bothering him. It was very simple. He had an assignment to carry out. The assignment must begin to be carried out this evening. The assignment was to recruit a whore. And after all was said and done, after all the grand strategies had been formulated, there was only way to commence: pay your money and get into bed with her.

He beat a gentle tattoo on the table top with his fingers. There it was. Simple, pathetic. At twenty-five years of age, David Chalfin was not chaste—but he had never slept with a whore. He had never bought a woman. He never would. But now he was required to.

He had thought of alternatives, other modes of procedure. But Chalfin was not a fool. If he wished to do his job well he had to act correctly. The correct procedure was to first buy her body. To participate in her execrable trade.

I am not a prude or a puritan, he thought, but I despise whores. And this one was Jewish! He rolled up a newspaper and used it now instead of his fingers, rapidly tapping the table. Of course, he would do what he must.

Chalfin retrieved his father's letter and read it through. Slowly, deliberately. As he put it back in his pocket he found the photograph of Raya Fahmi. He drew it out and set it on the table, quickly pulling back his hand as though he had done something illicit. He stared at her image. He found it incomprehensible that in a few hours he would be lying beside her.

Slowly, sadly, Chalfin shook his head. The world was in

flames. His people were systematically being destroyed. To the north, to the east, to the west, men and women were gambling with their lives as rag peddlers gambled on a single piece of trash.

But he, David Chalfin, was preparing himself to sleep with a whore.

At the front gate of the Daughters of Mercy Hospital, a nun sat on an aged folding chair. She was reading a small religious pamphlet, from time to time forming the words slowly and silently with her lips. When she turned a page, she did so reluctantly, as though the page might never be seen again. Her habit was simple. Her small face, enclosed by the flared cap, appeared delicate and childlike.

Moussa Tmai stood for a moment, marveling at her. Such a gentle thing she was; and what an abundance of good grass on the hospital grounds; and the driveway which led from the gate to the administration building was so neatly raked. In all, a lovely scene.

The nun felt his presence. She closed the pamphlet, marking her place with a finger, and inclined her head in a greeting.

Moussa bowed.

Europeans perplexed him. They killed each other with ferocity and then built beautiful hospitals for those who survived the killing. And many other aspects of their lives seemed to him incomprehensible. But in spite of the perplexity, he was devoted to them.

"I am here to see Doctor Quinton," said Moussa.

She nodded and returned to her pamphlet. Moussa walked up the neatly raked gravel drive and passed through the dull white doors. The floor, recently mopped, astonished him by its sheen. Gazing down with pleasure at the shiny surface, he noticed a speck of blood on his right sandal. He licked a finger, bent one knee, and rubbed away the blood.

Brian Quinton, in a white smock, stood by a large French door that gave onto a garden. His hands were locked behind his back and he was leaning slightly forward, so that his face nearly touched the glass.

Moussa approached with trepidation. It was well known that persons who have red hair and blue eyes traffic with the devil. That was stated even in the holy writings.

Quinton turned to regard his visitor. "You've put on more weight, Moussa," he said regretfully. "It's no good. No good at all."

"There are many worries."

Quinton laughed. His eyes shifted to the garden again, then back to Moussa. He towered over the Egyptian, his long, thin wrists sliding from the sleeves of his smock.

"It has been a tragic day," said Moussa, turning up his large eyes.

"Tragic?"

"A great soldier is dead."

"Sad."

"He is in Paradise," said Moussa emphatically.

"Are you sure?"

"I am sure."

"Then he's a lucky man, isn't he? In Paradise, I understand, everything is as it appears."

"So the prophet says," acknowledged Moussa.

"And it is all good."

"So it is said."

"Then that great soldier must be happy. After all, he could not be happy on earth because he didn't know who his friends were."

"That is a bad thing," Moussa agreed, "not knowing who one's friends are."

"It is the surest way to Paradise," Quinton said dryly.

They stood in silence for some minutes. Finally Quinton reached into the pocket of his smock and withdrew an envelope. He handed it to Moussa who accepted it with a slight bow and put it carefully into the pocket of his jacket. Then he turned and left the hospital.

Quinton played with an unlit cigarette. He didn't want to go back to the ward. He wanted to stay for a while, gazing through the French door. He wanted to stay and worry that strange word, Paradise. Since he would never be a Muslim and had long since ceased to be a Christian, it was necessary to construct his own Paradise. But, as he stood there, the very notion of it eluded him. There would be books and music and women and alcohol—but that, surely, is not Paradise. It must be as it was described: Paradise is where everything is as it appears to be.

He lit the cigarette. It was in times like this that he mourned his intellectual isolation. Paradise was a term that should be discussed, at length, with congenial people. It was not something one could babble about with a whore, or joke about with Egyptian procurers. The word could not be bandied about with his fellow physicians who (in this particular hospital) tried to cure souls as well as bodies.

Quinton ground out his cigarette on the freshly mopped floor. The hospital must know, he mused, that the enemy is always within. As he walked back to the ward he remembered that he had forgotten to ask the exact means the assassin had used to transport Colonel Quaffid on his journey to Paradise.

Chalfin watched Raya Fahmi meander through the smoke-filled room. A few nights earlier he had refused her service, so now he thought she would not stop by him unless he made a gesture. Or perhaps she had already forgotten his face and would try anyway. He concentrated on his brandy.

She had remembered. She passed by the table quickly.

He waited until she circled the room and paused for a moment, looking vaguely in his direction. Then he held the brandy bottle by the neck, and lifted it at a slight angle off the table. She noticed the gesture and gave him a quizzical look.

Chalfin sloshed the brandy in the bottle, smiling as broadly as he could. She began to walk toward him.

He forced more of a grin and silently recapitulated his plan: I am a man about to pay for a woman; I am a hospital inspector from England; I will do nothing, say nothing, to contradict this image. I will buy her, use her, pay her, and leave.

She sat down at the small table. Her skin was lighter in tone than he had remembered it, but the phony beauty mark was still there and she wore the same schoolgirl's clothes.

He poured a glass of brandy for her. Raya didn't drink; she was already past her first customer of the evening.

He waited for her to say something. She didn't say a word. Chalfin looked around the club. It was crowded, as usual. The tank crew he had seen before wasn't present. There was an enormous variety of uniforms. One table caught his attention: Well-dressed Egyptians sat without talking, their hands folded in front of them, their eyes fixed straight ahead.

He turned back to Raya. She was moving the glass slowly back and forth across the same two inches of the table. Her shoulders were hunched a bit as though she were cold, and she appeared to Chalfin to be thinking. What did whores think about? Chalfin didn't know. He felt that he must say something to her now.

"There ought to be more light here," Chalfin said.

"Why?" she asked, casually interested.

Chalfin shrugged. He had no answer. His hand wandered involuntarily over his coat pocket, over Raya's photograph. What would she think if she knew that her face was in his pocket?

He wondered if there were other Jews in The Trunk right now, Jews other than himself and the whore. He felt absolutely no sense of solidarity with the whore, and he wondered why. She was Jewish. Why did he have such a loathing for whores?

"Do you have time for me?" he blurted out suddenly. He then leaned back in his chair, sipped some brandy, and felt a relief so great it seemed like pleasure.

She nodded—yes—and stood. Chalfin didn't care to move that fast. He wanted to wait a moment. But she walked away from the table and he got up and followed her, glancing back once at the bottle of brandy, wondering who would drink it when he had left.

He followed her into one of the small back rooms and watched as she swiftly peeled her clothes. She seemed to diminish in size and looked almost childlike.

Chalfin undressed, awkwardly. He slowly, laboriously folded his clothes as he removed them, and then didn't know what to do with them.

She pointed to the dresser and the chair. He put the garments down, then turned to face her, his hands half closed into fists at his thighs. Raya came to him with the sponge.

He could not look at her as she washed his crotch. He felt an odd sense of impotence, as though she were not a whore but a nurse who was treating a debilitating wound. He heard the sponge fall back into the basin with a little splash. When he opened his eyes Raya was lying on the bed, naked but for the open white blouse. She was smiling. Her right hand was turned palm up in a gesture that seemed to him supplicatory.

Chalfin panicked. I will not be able to carry this off, he thought. Make love to a whore? How? Should he touch her? Kiss her? Should he talk to her? What should he do? And what in the world was she thinking?

There was a time factor. He was paying for her time. His body felt stupid, felt no desire. How should he function?

He had to say something to her. Didn't men talk to whores?

"Have you worked here long?"

"More than a year."

He tried to formulate another question, but he couldn't think of a single thing to ask her.

"Small," he finally said.

"What is small?"

"The room. This room."

Now her eyes were on him, at the same time blank and keenly focused—that oddity. And he couldn't make out the color of her eyes. He sat down on the bed beside her. He touched her thigh, and waited for his body to respond.

It's a woman, he thought. She's just a woman. She lies there like a woman. She looks like a woman. Chalfin relaxed. He felt himself falling into an ordinary landscape. She could have been the young woman he met on holiday in Scotland years ago. She could have been the colleague in Jerusalem. He no longer thought. He proceeded. He touched her where she should be touched, he moved his body in the prescribed way. Entering her with the classic in-draw of breath, he felt the strength in his body and the resistance in hers. Then, he ejaculated with a suddenness that sucked the strength out so swiftly his legs trembled.

He dressed, feeling both triumphant and professional. He left the small back room, secure in the knowledge that he had initiated his mission in a proper manner.

Raya, in her usual style, waited until the client had departed before she dressed. Then she gathered the money and reentered the smoky bar. She proceeded on her rounds, now ignoring the young Englishman who was finishing the brandy that, surprisingly, no one else had claimed.

The tanks seemed to have burrowed under the sand, in scattered rows. Sheltered by logs, they did not move. Silence and stillness reigned. The long shanks of their guns looked like succulent plants which used starlight, not sunlight, for growth.

The time was somewhere before dawn. Sentries walked in crisscrossing patterns, guarding the tanks and their crew. The crews were nestled together in improvised tents, none set up in the formal manner but buttressed by barrels and rifles and assorted pieces of wood.

Peters huddled under a blanket. The tent had been so

poorly set up that its top sagged against him. He had been tossing and turning all night with visions of the whore. He couldn't sleep, but he couldn't masturbate either.

Now he peered out of the tent. The sky was brilliant! He wished he had learned to read the stars, to know the sky—but it was all too much for him. Peters was from the city.

He let his eyes rest on the surface of the ground. A desert soldier's trick, learned because the atmosphere was treacherous and undependable. Looking up and out, one might see herds of elephants and gods. Looking out and down, one might see German tanks as they approached.

There was some movement along the ground: a city of rodents, some native to the region and some imported, scampered back and forth from latrine to garbage dump. Some crawled, some hopped, some moved sideways like snakes. If, on a given night, they found no legitimate food, they ate rope and leather and canvas.

An hour, Peters thought, before dawn. An hour before the black and white panoply would dissolve. He dozed.

"Peters! Peters!"

He tensely arched his back like a cat, almost bringing the tent down around him.

Yates was squatting outside. "Get up," he said.

Peters slid out of the tent and got to his feet.

"Tomlinson is gone," said Yates.

"Gone?" Peters stretched. It was still cold and he rarely listened to anything Yates told him.

"Vanished. Gone."

"Where could he go?"

"A sentry saw him. He was going out for a walk, he said. South. Into the desert."

Peters stared at the speaker. Two more soldiers joined them.

"Did you check the tank?" asked Peters.

"He's not there. He went into the desert."

"He didn't go into the desert. Why would he go there? What are you talking about?"

46

Yates stopped talking and pulled at Peters, who finally let himself be led. The others followed. They approached the sentry, a tall man with a tattered poncho.

"Tell him," said Yates.

"Tomlinson went out there," said the sentry.

"He was going crazy," said Yates. "We all saw him going crazy."

"Cow man," said Peters, as if in explanation.

"I can't think," said Yates.

"You never could think."

They walked back to the tent area. The sky was lightening. Men were brewing tea over small fires.

"We saw it. We should have done something. We should have watched him. You saw the way he was when we went to Cairo. He's been crazy for weeks," concluded Yates.

"For years, probably," said Peters.

They squatted in front of Tomlinson's bedraggled tent.

From north to south, across miles of desert, the British Eighth Army was rising.

"Maybe he'll come back," said Yates.

"Maybe."

"He'll miss us."

"He didn't *desert*. To be charged with desertion you have to be going somewhere. There's nothing out there."

"Look here," said Keeple, who came from East Anglia and was usually mute. They turned. Keeple was holding up a piece of white cloth. One end of it was tied to Tomlinson's tent pole.

The dawn had broken, a dazzling dawn.

"Is it his?" said Peters.

Keeple shrugged. "I never saw it before."

Peters rose from his squat and approached the white cloth. Now he could see that it was a handkerchief, bone white, with a border of red herons.

"He should have taken it with him," said Yates, "to keep the sun off."

They all sipped their tea, straining out the sand.

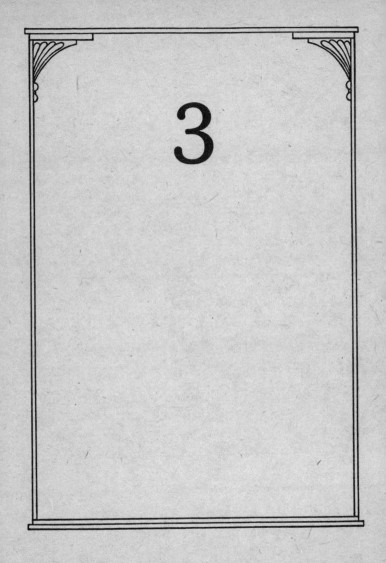

3

"Did you hear about Quaffid?"

"Yes."

Winokur slapped his hands together. "Boom. And he's gone. Gone. Boom, and you're in little pieces. Are you worried you'll get blown to pieces, my young friend?"

"Who did it?"

"Who knows? The British. The Germans. His own staff. Maybe I did it. Do you think I did it?

Chalfin didn't answer the question. He thought Winokur was capable of it, but there was no reason for the Jewish Agenty to murder Quaffid. The Jewish Agency considered all anticolonial revolutionaries in the Middle East its friends. Quaffid was difficult, but he was playing the same game as the Jews.

Winokur voiced one of his peculiar guttural exclamations which signaled that the topic in question was now dispensed with, then said: "Well, as they say in this business, did you establish contact? Establish contact. Establish contact. Establish contact. . . ."

Winokur kept repeating the phrase, as if astonished at his ability to say it distinctly.

"But what about Poland. In Poland," he continued, "they say, 'Did you *shtup* her?'"

Chalfin felt that Winokur was mocking him.

"I don't speak Yiddish," he said dryly.

Winokur laughed and slapped the pile of papers in front of him. "It was a Yiddish word only in the beginning. Now it's a word for the world. The *world*. Rio. New York, Cairo. The world."

"I established contact," said Chalfin.

"Any burning during urination?"

Chalfin shook his head.

"Funny rashes?"

Chalfin shook his head.

Winokur sat back and sighed, letting Chalfin know the fun and games were over.

"When do you see her again?"

"Maybe tonight."

"Make it tonight."

"Fine."

"What kind of woman is she?"

"I don't know yet. We didn't talk. I thought it would be best just to be a customer at the start."

Chalfin wondered why he was nervous now in front of Winokur.

"Malorange contacted me again," said Winokur, "and he wants speed. He says speed is important. He says the cipher is important. He says Montgomery's offensive is important." Winokur shrugged at his own words.

"I'll see her tonight," Chalfin reiterated.

Suddenly it dawned upon him that he wanted to see her. He looked about the room in confusion. No. He was lying to

52

himself, certainly. But yes, he did want to see her. He wanted to lie beside her on the bed again, her white blouse open. He wanted to enter her again. But no! Yes, *again*—

"Malorange said something else. He thinks money won't work. He thinks she is making a lot of money. He thinks the only way to her is through her Jewishness."

"If it's there," said Chalfin.

"Or, perhaps, her goodness?" Winokur was mocking him once again.

"I have no notion of whores as romantic heroines," Chalfin replied.

"But I thought all petit bourgeois Englishmen were prey to that notion."

"I am not, any longer, of the petit bourgeois English genre."

"And remember that you are a Jew and a Zionist," Winokur said forcefully, "and a foot soldier. A foot soldier."

"A foot soldier without a rifle."

"But you have a rifle!" said Winokur, and then laughed.

Chalfin rose to his feet and nodded deferentially, then started toward the door. He realized that he could never respond properly to Winokur. He could never summon up the right word, the right tone to match him.

"Wait, David. Wait. You must not long too much for the violence of war. It will come. It will come. And, in fact, you are already in its midst. I assure you, what you are doing is daring and violent. Much more so than shooting a Fascist in the head from three hundred feet. When will you learn this? It's a very important thing to learn. If you do not learn it you will be like my old friend, Isaac. He was a chicken thief. He stole chickens in the countryside, slit their throats, and carried them back to the city under his coat. But one day he found gold pieces in a chicken. Among the innards. He cleaned them off and then threw them away. You know why he threw them away? Because he could not believe that there would be gold in the chickens he stole. So, when he was murdered, when Isaac's throat was slit like a chicken's, he was still a chicken thief."

"You are beginning to sound like a rabbi."

"Perhaps I am your rabbi," Winokur said happily, "and perhaps you will feel better if you know there's a good chance this Jewish whore will slit your throat. Does that make you feel better?"

"Much better."

"Good. Don't forget to bring in your vouchers."

Chalfin nodded, and walked out of the flat.

Sister Charlotte often saw the bleeding heart of Jesus as a palpable presence. Suddenly it would appear on the horizon, flare a bit, overwhelm her, and then subside.

She had entered her vocation later in life than most. First there had been Ireland, then Lowell, Massachusetts, then a husband and a child, and then untold miseries which she no longer recalled.

Her duties in the hospital were now largely administrative, but not a day went by when Sister Charlotte did not make her own rounds. She selected patients she believed to be neglected, and she hovered over them, spoke to them, listened to them. This both renewed her love for her fellow creatures and brought on the exhaustion necessary to sleep.

As she grew older she craved more work. And while she was inexorably and reluctantly moving up the ladder of hospital authority, whatever spare time she could steal from her office and her rounds was spent in the receiving rooms—a network of spotless space where blasted bodies were first viewed and diagnosed. The bodies came by truck and military ambulance and donkey cart.

She was in one of the receiving rooms the afternoon they brought in Reggie Cornell.

An entire procession of strange dusty vehicles had descended upon the hospital. Almost a dozen men had carried the still-living body inside. They were soldiers Sister Charlotte had never seen before: crazed-looking, in tattered uniforms

54

and outlandish hats—some with feathers. They laid the body on the examining table. Sister Charlotte watched Brian Quinton probe through makeshift bandages, fabric, and flesh.

She had the greatest respect for Quinton as a physician in spite of his reputation as a degenerate man who frequented brothels and did God only knew what else. She had been in their world long enough to know that the natural physical depravity of men does not always extinguish their godliness.

In pairs the soldiers left the room, at five- or ten-minute intervals. They said nothing; they watched Quinton, and when they were satisfied about something, they vanished. Sister Charlotte could hear the cough of their vehicles as they started them up and drove off—to the west.

"Do you know who this is?" asked Quinton.

There were two other nurses in the room and Sister Charlotte did not know to whom he had directed the question.

"His name is Reggie Cornell," said Quinton as though the name were its own explanation.

Sister Charlotte had never before heard the name.

Quinton plucked a last remnant of uniform from the wound. He let it flutter to the floor. "Reggie Cornell is one of the luminaries of the Long Range Desert Group."

Quinton looked around at the nurses. "Rommel," he continued, "is supposed to have said that Reggie Cornell is the finest combat officer on the Western Desert. Rommel is also supposed to have said that if Reggie Cornell . . ." Quinton paused to scrutinize the wound. "Those are perhaps rumors. Who knows what Rommel says? But this is the legendary Reggie Cornell."

Sister Charlotte regarded the man's face: a peaceful profile. The peace seemed to triumph over the blood and grime. The hair was light brown, long and matted. Although his eyes were closed she felt sure they were blue—a very light and friendly shade of blue.

"He probably has about a hundred fifty pieces of shrapnel

in him, none fatal. "He's been shredded like good Irish sausage but all he needs is blood and rest."

They worked on him, staunching and cleaning the wounds. Then they rolled him into the ward, peppered with small spotless gauze patches that mapped the line of shrapnel. They screened him off and set up the blood-transfusion apparatus.

"He'll live, this time," said Quinton. He smiled at Sister Charlotte. She returned the smile, trying to let him know that she thought he had done an extraordinary job with the soldier.

Later that afternoon she stood just inside the screen and watched the blood flow into him. Reggie Cornell was breathing easily and his face still reflected peacefulness. She edged closer, curious now to find out if his eyes were in fact blue. But his eyes were shut. She looked past the bed and out of the window.

Cairo frightened her. She rarely left the hospital for the simple reason that she could not deal with non-Europeans. She felt obliged to speak to Egyptians and all the rest, and since she didn't like to make conversation, she avoided them entirely. With Europeans it was different; she could remain silent in their company without anguish. Sister Charlotte knew that she was moving toward the solitary life. She was glad; she welcomed it; she could foresee the day when she would be old and tired, sitting in a clean cell-like room, watching the sun come and go, waiting for the heart of the Lord.

She walked to her small office, closed the door softly behind her, and sat down to work. Papers were piled neatly in the center of her desk: reports, procedures, requisitions. She used an old school pen, from time to time dipping it into a bottle of blue ink.

When she finished working she ate a bowl of lentil soup and a cracker. She fell asleep at the desk, her face against the wood grain that had been polished over the years into absolute smoothness.

An hour later she woke, feeling stiff and a little foolish. She drank some water and set out on her rounds. Sometimes she gave out chocolate judiciously to those who could tolerate it, but supplies of late had been hard to come by. She gave a nod here, a few words there. Once in while she sang a song—usually an American song she remembered. She was not an angel of mercy. She was a good woman greeting good men in a very bad world. That was how she thought of herself and her rounds.

She stepped behind the screen to look at Reggie Cornell. The hero must be better, she thought, his eyes are open. She approached the bed. There was no blue in his eyes. They were brown. A deep brown. She felt as though she had made an error of consequence. Ah, well, a hero can have eyes of any color he wants. She touched his arm gently. His eyes looked startled; they were very wide. Perhaps shock, she thought. Then a sudden weakness attacked her spine and threatened to make her legs give way. He was dead. He was dead. He had brown eyes but he was dead.

She turned to the blood-transfusion bottle—it was half full. But no blood was flowing. Halfway down the tube it stopped. She ran her fingers down the tube. At the point where the blood stopped there was a small piece of tape; expertly wrapped around the plastic tube, it was choking off the flow.

Sister Charlotte sat down on the edge of the bed and began to pray.

This time Chalfin kept his eyes on her as she brought the sponge quickly and professionally between his legs. There was nothing in her face; not one discernible mood; not fear or resignation or disgust or anticipation. She does this hour after hour, day after day, he thought. And, once again, he loathed her.

But he wanted her to acknowledge him. He wanted her to make him feel different from all the others.

She put the sponge away and walked toward the bed. He stood behind her and slipped his hands under her blouse. She made a quiet murmur, a sound that might be construed as passionate. Did she murmur that way because she was a whore, or because she liked it when he touched her? Chalfin let his hands fall. Raya lay down on the bed.

Same position, he thought, three-quarters turned toward the customer.

He lay down beside her. She was the same as she had been the first time: vacuous, accessible. But he was different—he was alive; he wanted her. His hands seemed unable to touch enough of her.

Suddenly he put a finger to her forehead. "Jewess," he hissed through clenched teeth.

He saw the widening of her eyes. Was that fear? No. Recognition? No.

He kissed her, desperate to taste her. He felt the tip of her tongue for a moment—alien, exciting. But she turned her head swiftly, as though he had the plague.

He touched her thigh. Why didn't she speak? Why didn't she say a single word?

"Jewess, Jewess," he repeated several times.

When he tried to kiss her again she pushed him away. He understood that he had gotten to her somehow. She was no longer silent and still. Her eyes were searching the ceiling. Such incredible eyes, he thought. Ludicrous Oriental eyes—Arab eyes. They could see everything and see nothing.

He pushed his face between her breasts. She tried to disengage but he was too strong. He smothered himself in her chest. The oddness of place and time vanished. He was somewhere else. He was paying for nothing.

Now, he thought to himself, now.

He moved a hand beneath the nape of her neck. He had the illusion that he was guiding her, that he was conducting her movements. She gave herself up to him, simply, professionally. Chalfin felt that she was opening for *him*, and for something else. It was a miasma, a cloud that was there in the back of his head. But beneath him was a woman. A whore. A Jewess.

As he entered her and felt the shudder of them both, Winokur's image surfaced: the possibility that the Jewish whore would slit his throat.

It didn't matter, then. It was good. It was good to enter her, to feel her body expand and then contract, to catch her rhythm.

I don't want to stop, he thought. I want to keep going. I want to keep moving in her. I want to hear her cry and call my name. I want to listen to her. I want to keep going until kingdom come.

Deeper. Deeper. His body was drenched with sweat. His hands were holding Raya Fahmi's face. His body raced. Too fast, too fast. He tried to brake himself. He looked at her. Her eyes were half closed but she saw him. There was a pallor on her cheeks.

And then it was over. He fell against her, wasted. They lay there until she tried to move. He rolled away, swinging his feet over the side of the bed. His hands were trembling. The salty sweat had run into his mouth.

Taking a deep breath, he tried to speak—once, twice. Then he heard himself say, "I am also a Jew, Raya Fahmi."

She sat up, startled. "How do you know my name?" Her voice was low and slightly hoarse.

Chalfin felt a terrible thirst. His clothes seemed a mile away.

"How do you know my name?" she repeated.

He got off the bed and went to his coat, rustled through a pocket, returned to the bed.

"Now, in this time," he said, "all Jews know the names of all other Jews. Because we are all the same."

He let the photo flutter to the bed. She was staring at his face.

"Look at it," he said quietly.

She picked up the photo and looked at it. Then she closed her blouse, as though the room had become cold.

"What is this picture? Who are you? What do you want of me?"

Chalfin stood in the middle of the small room. He stared down at his bare legs. They seemed unsavory.

"That is a picture of Jews being murdered in Poland. I am a Jew—David Chalfin. I want you to help me."

The lingering softness from their sexual act seemed to have been sucked out of the room.

"It's a sad picture," she said.

He walked quickly to the bed and sat down. He took the photo from her hand. He began to speak, quietly, with great passion.

"No, it's not a sad picture. It's a picture of a natural phenomenon now. Every day they are being killed. Every day. Like the tides come in and go out. Every day they are being murdered—hundreds of us, thousands of us, men, women, children, cripples, whores, businessmen, mystics. Every day. And it will go on as long as the Germans control Europe. You can help us, Raya. You can shorten the agony. Just do one thing for us. A simple, dangerous thing. One thing. For all of us. So some shall survive. So that one day we will all be in our land—in Palestine. Not Egypt. Not Poland or England or America, but the land God gave us. If you believe in God. And if not, who cares?"

He sat back, confused by his own statement. He wanted her to be with him, and he wanted her once again sexually.

She stood up and put on her skirt. "Please, no. I am sorry about those people. I don't want them to die. But I can't help you. I don't know what you want me to do, but I can't help you. No. No, I can't."

Then she was gone. Chalfin stared at his clothes. They seemed to belong to a different person. He lay back on the bed, crushing, by accident, one corner of the photo.

"You don't try to comprehend the man, you just accept his hospitality," said the tall, strikingly handsome woman.

A glass was put in her hand.

60

The man standing beside her ignored the profundity and made his own comment: "What I'll never understand is the simple fact that while I know this is a houseboat anchored in the Nile, I never feel any movement when I'm in it."

"You mean when you're on it."

"On it or in it."

"Perhaps it's not floating on the water. Perhaps it's set in concrete."

They both looked across the room at their host, Brian Quinton. The houseboat was a many-layered space. Each room had a certain elevation, and the next room was either sunken or raised. Thus, one walked down to another room or up to another room. There were no doors, no screens. There were sofas, couches, pillows, cushions, tables, all simply designed. The walls were hung with a bewildering variety of paintings—large and small—representing virtually all schools.

Carla Boudine sipped her drink. There was a faint river stench around them. She fluffed the hem of her formal black gown as if to make certain that the stench did not linger there. Her hair was perfectly coiffed. Her makeup was impeccable. Her entire form was graceful. The small, tin maltese cross that hung at her neck was the only noticeable flaw.

"Quinton doesn't seem to age," said Martin Boudine, her husband. He complemented his wife by being breathtakingly ugly and shabbily dressed.

"Nor do you," she replied, and smiled to hide the hate in her voice.

"But there was a time," he said, "when you seemed to be infatuated with him."

"With Brian Quinton?"

"Yes! Have you forgotten? Before he returned to his ministry of the scalpel."

"I had forgotten. But then again, as you well know, I was attracted to many men."

"And that was Alexandria."

"And that was Alexandria," she echoed, and they both laughed together in harmony. A delicious sudden laugh.

They drank and talked. Having arrived at a place of comfort they were in no mood to move. And they were enjoying their conversation as only married people can, who, after the plague of constant and required intimacy, suddenly find themselves in a neutral world and discover each other to be attractive again.

They could also watch the spectacle of arrivals. Quinton had invited the Alexandrians, who had removed to Cairo when the war became difficult. Their hour was over; Alexandria was now a fueling station. Cairo was the center, but it had never been able to erect the intricate social structures of the older city. So the Alexandrians survived, but not happily. Cairo did not appreciate their cosmopolitan attitudes, or their allegiances, or their many, admitted vices.

Alexandrians were unique only in the fact that they had annihilated race. They adhered to criteria of wealth and lust. Thus, they were a heterogeneous group, their races reflecting a hundred crosses: all the Europeans mixed together on the tip of the African continent.

Carla juggled the ice in her glass and Martin shifted his weight. They knew who was who; they knew whoever it was. That was X and there was Y. And do you remember when . . . ? They watched Quinton greet them all with his impeccable manners, with his ravenous self-confidence that made guests cling to him.

Trays piled high with lamb baked in pastry crusts were being circulated through the rooms. The Alexandrians were famished for good food and quickly depleted the trays, which were just as quickly refilled.

Martin ambled off and Carla was alone. For a moment she lost sight of Brian Quinton; this made her nervous; she thought he might appear behind her suddenly, and touch her. Then she found him again in a group, laughing over a drink.

He laughs the same, she thought. Teeth clenched, eyes looking directly at his companion. Even his laugh was a challenge. He might have been a schoolboy playing soldier, or a very old man still potent.

Quinton moved away, and she also moved. He knows I'm stalking him, she thought. She grasped the tin cross at her neck. Stepping down into another room she saw on the far wall a painting of a fisherman who was dangling his fingers over the bow. A muted romantic scene: the primitive boat, setting sun, softly lapping waves.

That is where we shall meet, Carla Boudine concluded.

She was right. Their movements led them from one side of the room to the other—smiling, talking, drinking, slowly weaving across the room. And then, they faced each other, under the fisherman.

"You are still young," he said softly.

"Very young."

"And myself?"

"You look well."

"Why do you think I look well?" he asked.

"Perhaps you are no longer obsessed with politics, like you once were. Perhaps you no longer speculate on the metaphysical differences between communism and fascism and parliamentary democracy. Or, perhaps, Brian, it's because you're no longer infatuated with whores. I see few whores here."

"You are wrong. There are many whores here."

He held out a hand, and they began to walk together, slowly, greeting people as they went along. They never touched.

Quinton suddenly pushed a wall panel and they were outside on a small walkway. Beneath them was the Nile. The wind whirled into her hair.

She quickly turned to face him. Quinton, avoiding her eyes, looked down at the river.

"Do we have anything to say to each other?" she asked.

He pressed his lips against her neck, holding her fast.

Was it gloom that settled about her? Raya walked slowly toward the place where she lived, a brightly knit shawl wrapped around her shoulders. It was near dawn—the time she always left The Trunk.

Perhaps it was gloom and perhaps not; but it wasn't the usual stupor after work—the dim, dull cloud that completely enveloped her so that no voice, no hand could reach her. This was something else: a genuine sadness. Raya knew it was something else, and she walked even more slowly, tilting up her face to feel the cool air of the fading night.

One hand was thrust into her skirt pocket, holding the night's wages.

She couldn't remember the face or the name of the Englishman—there had been too many after him. But she remembered the fact of him; she remembered that he existed. And although she couldn't remember what she had seen in the photograph, she did remember that there was a photograph and it depicted something sad.

She remembered that he had talked about Jews, about the fate of Jews.

The breeze became quick. Raya paused and reveled in it, pulling back her shawl to let it move along her neck.

Her mother used to love nights like this. Even toward the end, when she would sit in a chair wearing an old, elegant French gown, surrounded by abysmal poverty—even then she would ask Raya to open the panels and let the breeze come through the tiny room, a room filled with bits and pieces of the past.

And then she would begin to speak about that past, about the houses they had lived in and the good servants who tended to them and the clothes and jewels that were the finest in Cairo. If it was very late and the breeze was very strong, she would talk about her husband, about Raya's father. He was not really dead, she would say. He was in Beirut. Or he was in Paris, or Athens. He was just taking a rest and then he would recoup his fortune and show up in all his splendor, with his dark face and his brilliant mustache and his beautiful hand-sewn linen suits. Yes, he would come back. In his train would be servants bearing beauteous rugs, the finest of fabrics, the most delicate meats and pastries and fruits—yes, even fruits they had never seen before.

Raya shook the memories out of her head. She looked around her, listening to the awesome silence of Cairo just before it stirred, and then moved toward home.

There was a sudden violent pressure in the pit of her stomach that seemed to force her breath away. She leaned forward, grabbing for air, and as she did so she realized that human hands gripped her. She saw the outline of knuckles clenched together over her abdomen.

She tried to turn, to spin, to move out of the grasp. She tried to scream but the sound caught in her throat.

And then, as suddenly as she had been grasped, she was let go. She fell forward onto the street and heard a high, manic laugh.

"It is me, Raya, it is me, Raya, it is me, Raya." The voice had a singsong madness.

Fear left her. She rolled over and got to her feet, breathing with slow deliberation.

It was the dwarf. He was grinning and chuckling and clapping his hands, all the while dancing up and down on one foot. His massive chest was perched on two spindly legs, and one shoulder seemed to be a foot higher than the other. He lived in the streets outside The Trunk, befriending the whores and the waiters, doing favors for them in return for coins and food and words of kindness. His head was swathed in a rag; his dirty, grizzled face was astonishingly white. He wore nothing on his feet; a long rope kept a black woolen blanket around him.

"You hurt me," said Raya.

He dropped his head in sorrow. Then, from under his blanket he stretched out a hand.

"For you," he said, "for you."

He dropped something into her hand. She shivered. He moved off quickly, vanishing into an alley.

There was a dirty lump of chocolate in her hand.

Suddenly she felt the old sense of loathing. She loathed herself. So many years had gone by without loathing. Now it returned, a familiar affliction. She loathed herself. She loathed the dwarf. She loathed The Trunk. She loathed the cobblestoned streets, the night and the dawn and Cairo. Then and there, in the midst of her loathing, she remembered something else about the Englishman: his hands.

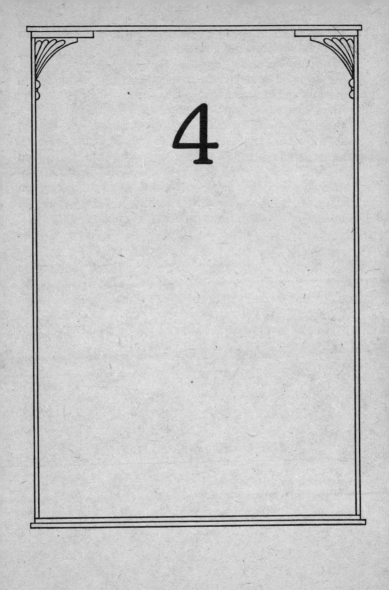

4

Tomlinson lay on his stomach in the morning light. He lay on brownish sand, peering into a tiny vortex of activity. It is a burrowing lizard or rat, he thought, and when it comes out of the sand I will bite its head off. Bite it off. He snapped his jaws open and shut.

He retreated suddenly, away from the swirling hole. What if it wasn't a lizard or a rat? What if the whore was burrowing out of Cairo? That was no good.

Tomlinson got to his feet and stamped out the activity. Then he started to walk. He had the long loping stride of a man who has walked farms and pastures as a child. When he tired of walking he ran. When he tired of running he rolled in the sand.

Something was beginning to afflict his nose, and it was worse than the thirst in his throat. He slowed down and shifted his head from side to side. The affliction was an odor.

The odor was becoming stronger. He stopped moving completely. It was the very stench he feared and hated: petrol mixed with grease, rubber and steel.

He squatted on the sand, sniffing like a dog. The odor was coming over a small rise to the west. Tomlinson started to weep. His body seemed caught in a fight or flight dilemma.

Finally he ran up the rise and vaulted over the top, losing his balance on the far side. He rolled down, until his roll was stopped by a body. He sat up. He looked around.

Two armored carriers lay on their sides, their treads blasted off, their plates mangled. The bodies of Italian soldiers lay in wheel-spoke patterns about the vehicles, their uniforms bloody and torn.

Tomlinson gazed at the scene, comprehending nothing. Then he trotted over to the collapsed supply tent behind the gutted vehicles and he peeled back the canvas. Cartons of supplies lay upended. Tins of fish and dried fruit had been flung around. He pried off the top of a wooden box that had not, oddly, been touched. Eight bottles of wine were packed in straw. He broke open a bottle and poured wine down his throat. It was warm. He drank some more, then gathered three bottles under his arm and returned to the corpses.

Tomlinson made sure each dead Italian drank all the wine he wanted. Then he sprawled on the ground, cradled his head against someone's arm, and fell asleep.

"Can you repeat that?"

Winokur's question infuriated him. "Repeat *what?*" Chalfin asked.

Winokur smiled at Colonel Malorange, who was absentmindedly drawing stick figures on a yellow pad. The smile seemed to be an apology to Malorange for his colleague's ill humor.

The smile infuriated Chalfin. Winokur was becoming too close to the Colonel. Was Winokur mesmerized by the man's reputation? Winokur was giving Malorange the respect he should be giving his comrade. *I* am your comrade, Chalfin thought—not him, not that manqué T. E. Lawrence.

"Repeat your conclusion," said Winokur.

"My conclusion is that Raya Fahmi cannot be recruited."

"Why is that?"

"She isn't interested."

"You mean the plight of her people doesn't interest her."

"That is what I mean."

"You are sure."

"I am sure."

"Why are you so sure?"

"Because I was with her. I spoke to her. I showed her the picture. I told her."

"Perhaps you didn't present your case strongly enough. Or perhaps you presented it too strongly," said Malorange with a shrug. He continued to draw on the yellow pad.

"This case you speak of is not really your province, Colonel," replied Chalfin.

Malorange smiled and inclined his head slightly, as if Chalfin had scored a point in a tennis match.

Winokur said, "Could it be a question of fear?"

Chalfin thought for a moment. "Not fear," he replied.

"Then simple disinterest. She's not afraid of danger if it's in the service of something she believes in, but she doesn't believe in Jews."

"I can't affirm or deny that."

Winokur looked up at the ceiling for a moment. Then: "Is she a good whore?"

"I don't know."

Malorange said, "You don't know?"

"I don't know."

"Well, did she service you? Did she give you value for your money?" asked Winokur.

Chalfin could detect a rising anger, rigorously suppressed. That he was making Winokur angry made him, Chalfin, unhappy.

71

"Yes," he answered.

"Good," said Winokur.

"If she is a good whore she will be a good operative," Malorange noted.

"Has anything happened between the two of you that might have compromised your ability to recruit her?" asked Winokur.

"I don't understand your question."

Winokur and Malorange smiled. Their faces are in collusion against me, he thought, they are mocking me.

"Do you wish to be relieved of the assignment?" asked Winokur.

"No," Chalfin replied.

"Are you sure?"

"I am sure."

"Then we must continue, mustn't we?"

"Yes."

"And we must find out why you have been unsuccessful and change the pattern. Am I correct?"

"You are correct."

"Do you have any suggestions, Colonel Malorange?"

"I am sure your young friend realizes the gravity of the situation and will do all he can to achieve what is necessary."

"Do you like her?" asked Winokur.

Chalfin stared at him, trying to read the meaning of the question. And how was he to describe the way he felt about Raya Fahmi?

"Yes, I do," he said simply.

"What type of woman is she?"

Malorange resumed drawing stick figures.

"I know little about her. She is quiet, very quiet. But there's something, how shall I say, *authentic* about her."

Malorange laughed first. Winokur followed.

"*Authentic!*" Chalfin seemed to hurl the word at both of them.

"Then bring this authentic woman," Winokur enunciated

slowly, "into an authentic relationship with her authentic past."

"I would second that," said Malorange.

"What is the English verb I am looking for, Colonel Malorange? The English verb for David."

"Intensify."

"Ah, thank you. Intensify, David. Intensify the assignment. Since Raya Fahmi is so authentic, and such a fine whore, why, she must be with us. She must."

The hero lay stitched in a canvas sack. An identification tag hung from one end. Presently the sack would be placed in a coffin and the coffin placed in the earth.

Sister Charlotte, her eyes closed, was praying for the peace of his soul. She opened her eyes with a start. She didn't know where Englishmen were buried. Were they sent back to England to lie in their own land? Or were they shoveled into some amenable piece of Egyptian desert. . . .

It had been a frightful death for her. The hero had needed blood, and blood had been flowing into him, bringing him back to life. And then, all of a sudden the blood had stopped; the life had stopped. It was the worst, the most horrible, the most inexplicable death because it was not *fair*. And she, Sister Charlotte, was responsible, and the entire staff was responsible. It was a death that should not have happened.

Sister Charlotte was very agitated, and she walked down the hall with quick, small, purposeful steps.

She had not slept during the night. Blue eyes, brown eyes, the calm face of the hero kept her awake. What also kept her awake was the thought of a stealthy hospital hand cutting off the blood flow in the tube. And the thought that the hand must have belonged to Brian Quinton. But how could that be? How could a physician kill? Why? What was happening to her that she should lose her trust in a man who was ultimately on God's side?

Sister Charlotte reached the end of the hall, turned down

73

another hall, then another, and then another one after that. She was obsessed by the fact that on a floor beneath her, beneath her walking feet, the body of Reggie Cornell lay in its canvas sack without movement, without regret, without . . . anything.

"I am walking over him, we are all walking over him," she whispered to her feet; then she quickly crossed herself.

Turning another corner, she stopped abruptly, one foot away from a fat brown face.

Moussa Tmai smiled and bowed ever so slightly.

Frightened, Sister Charlotte took a step back, looked around, then brought her hands to her throat. Moussa was perplexed. He forced a wider, more gentle smile. It was his ultimate effort, his smile specially reserved for frightened Europeans. It worked, as it had always worked. Sister Charlotte responded by looking at the short Egyptian in his flawless attire. She noted his very thick fingers which held a package wrapped in brown paper. She realized she had seen him before. She returned his smile.

"I am looking for Dr. Quinton," said Moussa.

"Dr. Quinton will not be in today."

"He is ill?"

"That, I do not know," replied Sister Charlotte. She was slightly irritated; she did not like to be asked questions.

Looking down, she was astonished to see that Moussa was wearing sandals.

"I have a package for him."

"If you wish, I will give it to him in the morning. Or, leave it in his office—he may arrive later on."

"Thank you. Thank you."

Moussa Tmai extended the package toward her, holding it in two hands even though it was quite small. Instinctively she held out both her own hands, as if she might hurt his feelings by not receiving the gift in the same way it was proffered.

"I will put it on his desk. He will see it the first moment he arrives," she assured Moussa.

74

He had an inclination to pat the nun's head; but he did not. After all, she might misinterpret the gesture. What he wanted to signify was that he understood her torment; or rather, he understood that she was tormented. He had watched her walk down the hall. Perhaps, he mused, it was something to do with their god. Christians were known to become inconsolable over theological questions.

Moussa bowed again and shuffled off.

Such a strange man, thought Sister Charlotte, such a strange but nice man.

She took the package to Quinton's office, opened the door, and walked in. There were shadows on the floor. She put the package on Quinton's cluttered desk, on top of all the papers. Suddenly the stillness and the shadows overwhelmed her. She sat down on Quinton's leather chair, exhausted. She stared at the package. It was badly wrapped. Just a single piece of tape on each end. One piece was already curling.

She reached out and touched the package. Her fingers fell on the tape. She froze. It had the same feel. It was the same kind of tape. The same kind of tape that had been entwined around the tube. The tube with the blood. The blood meant to keep Reggie Cornell alive.

Then Sister Charlotte laughed aloud. It was only a stupid coincidence. Cairo was held together by millions of rolls of tape and they all felt the same. She tried to flatten down the tape but it had no more stickiness. By her efforts she simply opened one side of the package.

She saw a pair of pliers. The handles were wrapped with heavy black rubber. Under the pliers was a beautifully painted cardboard box.

"Nachtigal," she whispered in awe.

It had been over two years since she had seen a box of those exquisite chocolates. Each one, she remembered, was wrapped in foil. And the taste! Rich, dark bittersweet, with a hint of nuts, a dash of brandy.

Sister Charlotte had a longing to walk through the wards

distributing Nachtigals. She desired to unpeel them one by one and pop them into the yearning mouths of her patients.

Sadly, she pushed the package away. She left Brian Quinton's office.

There was a new whore in The Trunk. From a distance she appeared to be golden-haired. But when she passed Chalfin's table he saw that her hair was actually brown. Russian, he thought, or Polish, or Slovakian. They were always in demand, he realized. Perhaps it was a historical quirk—a reminder of the Circassian Mamelukes, who were blond but not Slavic.

She passed his table again, waiting for a sign of interest, a movement, a gesture. Chalfin sat rather stiffly, his fingers frozen around his drink. She was very tall and very thin, and wore a simple brown dress. He sipped from his glass.

Only a few short months ago he had read the great historian Ibn Khaldun. Now he recalled Khaldun's characterization of Cairo under the Mamelukes as a place "illuminated by moons and stars of learning."

Perhaps, despite war and pestilence and death, secret places in Cairo were still illuminated in that manner. Perhaps . . . but he had no time.

Before he actually saw her he felt Raya Fahmi's presence. Then he turned; she was speaking to some soldiers at a table to his right, halfway across the room. Quickly he turned back to his drink. She would come to his table soon. But what if she took one of those soldiers! Anger made all his limbs rigid.

Chalfin took a deep breath. He tried to relax. So what if she took a soldier? She was a whore. That was her job.

I am becoming a fool, he thought, surely I am becoming a fool. Then he saw her walking slowly along the wall, alone, and he tried to catch her eye. She did not look his way.

He poured more brandy into his glass. Winokur had said— what? What was the word? Suddenly he remembered: intensify.

76

Raya sat down three tables away. She began to talk to a flyer. He was short, bull-necked, and he hovered over his drink as if in agony.

Chalfin made efforts to catch her eye. Raya kept up her conversation with the flyer. She did not look at Chalfin. Occasionally she ran a hand over her skirt as though brushing away lint.

What will I tell her tonight? That the entire war will be lost if she doesn't agree to my proposition? That the food supplies of the whole Middle East will be infected with lethal poison if she refuses? That the moral universe will vanish if she does not act with us? Chalfin formulated a dozen threats, all cosmic and humanitarian, all ludicrous.

In reality he was just watching her, watching her perform, watching her solicit.

Suddenly Raya and the flyer rose from the table. Chalfin tensed. What was she doing? She hadn't even walked by his table. Why was she going with the flyer?

They vanished in the hallway. Chalfin drained his glass. The vision of Raya Fahmi moving that sponge between the flyer's legs made him furious. Then weak. Then ill.

It occurred to Chalfin that he must do something for the next twenty minutes, he must focus on something in order to avoid the memory of his last visit with Raya Fahmi. He did not wish to speculate on the ways the bull-necked flyer might be touching her. He would focus on the walls. They were so evenly painted. He would focus on the next table, at which a large man kept pulling down one end of his mustache.

Sweat began to drench the back of his shirt. He drank more brandy. He waited.

The flyer came back first. He stood at the table, then decided not to sit down, and proceeded to leave The Trunk. On his way he passed close by Chalfin who felt the slightest contact would end in blood.

Raya then emerged from the hallway and stood against the far wall. How could she appear so calm, so unruffled, so absolutely in control? Her eyes roved over The Trunk. She saw him. He knew that she saw him. Chalfin raised his glass. For a moment their eyes locked.

Why is she so blank, he thought.

She moved out of his line of sight, sauntered around the far tables, and then sat down with an elderly Egyptian. He wore a wide-brimmed white hat.

The brandy was starting to make his head throb. He understood the absurdity of his situation. He must contact the whore again, he must attempt to recruit her again. The whore was ignoring him. But all of that was beside the point. The point was that he wanted her! The reality was that he couldn't bear to see her soliciting. That . . .

Her laugh seemed to cut through the noise in the room. The old Egyptian in the white hat had reached across the table and was touching her arm.

Chalfin watched her profile. She could smile without moving any part of her face but her lips. She could laugh without moving her shoulders or neck.

Then he looked away from her, up at the ceiling. It seemed to him that a great bird named Winokur was hovering up there, watching the scene.

Raya Fahmi stood up. The man in the white hat rose and slid to her side. He was both taller and younger than Chalfin had imagined.

Chalfin got to his feet and kicked the chair away. It spun across the floor. He had to catch the strolling couple before they passed the curtain. He had to stop them. Chalfin wobbled as he walked, banging into tables, receiving the curses of those seated there. He held out his arms and cut them off in the hallway.

Raya and the Egyptian stared at him. Chalfin could think of nothing to say.

Oh, God, he thought, she looks so lovely. How can a whore look so lovely? And how can she go there, again?

Then his thoughts jumbled and the heat in the hallway seemed to suck the air out of his lungs.

Raya touched his arm. He should move it. I am Samson, he thought, and I shall bring the walls down. He tried to put his palms on the walls but they slid off.

"Please," she said, "let us pass or they will hurt you."

Chalfin laughed and lunged forward against her, his face in her dark hair. She smelled of soap and water and night and fog.

Then he smelled something else—olives or cloves—and he saw the fist which subsequently smashed into his windpipe. Chalfin fell choking to the floor. Someone kicked his ribcage. He rolled over in pain. Raya and the Egyptian stepped over him and walked down the hall. Two men lifted Chalfin and carried him out of The Trunk. They let him fall to the cobblestones.

She lay on the bed beside Quinton, and thought about him. Years ago, when they had first become lovers, she had laughed at his statement, "I am the Last European." It signified an intellectual posture that she found ludicrous. But now, thought Carla Boudine, she was not sure. Perhaps he was what he had said he was.

If there was an animal such as the Last European he would have to surface in Egypt. Where else?

She reached down by the side of the bed and retrieved a glass of wine, half full. Sitting up against the pillow she sipped the wine. Suddenly she was chilled. Making love with Quinton always made her uncomfortable, or cold, or disconcerted, afterward. While engaged, there was only uncontestable joy.

Lovemaking with Quinton did not resemble lovemaking with the others. It was not a war. It was not a game. It was not an episode. Quinton, somehow, made sex lovely. Simple and lovely. Sudden and lovely. He was there, he touched her, he was in her.

The word "lovely" made her grin. She sloshed the wine in the bottom of the glass. Was it possible to say "lovely" in 1942?

Carla leaned over and kissed his shoulder.

She finished the wine and when she looked at him again his eyes were open.

For a moment she was astonished. That any man now was still alive sometimes astonished her. She had seen the long columns of the dead walking out of the Western Desert.

"Does your husband know you're here?" said Quinton.

"Probably."

"How has he been?"

"Dying by inches."

"What a strange way to die."

"He's a peaceful man."

"Cairo is an excellent place to die," suggested Quinton, "whether by inches, by feet, or by centuries."

"I thought you preferred people to die in hospitals."

"It's the appetite for death, not the place, which is really important."

"Are you imparting wisdom to me, Brian Quinton?"

"No."

"Good—because, as you well know, I am from Alexandria, and we despise wisdom there."

"Learn to like it; in a short while there may be no Alexandria."

"Is it falling into the sea?"

Quinton reached down on his side of the bed for the wine bottle and a glass. He filled both their glasses.

"You've changed," she said quickly, quietly.

"In what way?"

"Many ways."

"Name seven."

"You hesitate now."

"Hesitate?"

"You hold back just a bit. Just a bit. In your speech, in the way you greeted people at that party, in the way you make love."

"You may be right," he said casually.

"And you don't speak about things the way you used to. You don't mention things."

"I mention what has to be mentioned."

"You used to speak of books and poems. You used to describe people. All those memorable sardonic bon mots which used to roll off your tongue!"

"I don't read books anymore."

"What do you read?"

"Patients' charts."

There was a long silence. Carla stared into the dizzying sequence of open rooms.

Finally, "Is that all?" he asked.

"Do you want more?"

"Always more. I always want more. I'm essentially a greedy man. I want more and better uniforms. More and better tanks. More and better ways to administer blood plasma. More and better critiques."

"You are no longer all things to all people."

Quinton laughed. Then he leaned over and lay his head on her stomach.

"There was a time," she continued. "when you could stand in a room filled with lepers and they would see you as one of their own. Or a room full of fishermen. Or monks. Or businessmen. Or communists. Or fascists. Or birdwatchers."

"And now?" he asked, turning up his face to see her eyes.

"You have your own place."

"Which is . . . ?"

"I haven't the slightest idea, but it's political."

"What does it look like? This political place?"

"I don't know."

"How does it smell?"

"Bad."

"Who else is in this place?"

"No one. There's only you."

"Are you sure?"

"Just you. Egypt has passed you by."

"Couldn't you be mistaken? Couldn't there be hundreds, thousands, millions with me, in this place?"

"Just you."

"And what place are you in?"

"But surely you know, Brian. The aging Alexandrian beauty. The exile. The stranger in an exotic land. All that nonsense." As though ashamed of her reflections, she pushed his face away, then said, jauntily, "Do you still sing?"

Quinton raised his palms in mock supplication. He sat up and crossed his legs on the bed. He sang:

> "'At a cottage door one wintery eve
>   as the snow lay on the ground
> Stood a youthful Irish soldier boy
>   to the mountains he was bound
> His mother stood beside him saying,
>   you'll win my boy don't fear
> And with loving arms around his neck
>   she tied a bandolier.
>
> "'Goodbye, God bless you, mother dear
>   your son you'll see again
> And when he's out on the firing line
>   and the flag of truce is hung
> Remember you're the mother proud
>   of an Irish soldier boy . . .'"

"But do you have a bandolier?" inquired Carla.

"No. But I have a substitute." He left the bed and returned seconds later holding what appeared to be a large white linen handkerchief embroidered with red herons. He wrapped it playfully around her neck.

"You see," he remarked, "a bandolier."

Then he snapped the ends and Carla felt the cloth tighten. Pain and panic flooded her entirely.

Quinton loosened the cloth, then flung it over the side of the bed.

She looked at him.

"I didn't mean to frighten you," he said. "I was just showing you the place."

He kissed her hands which were now wrapped protectively around her neck, and then kissed her eyes. They made love again—more slowly, more tentatively, more reflectively.

Raya Fahmi saw Chalfin the moment she left The Trunk. Her first instinct was to approach him, to find out if he had been hurt. But she kept to her side of the street and began to walk home at a rapid pace.

After a while she felt that he was following her. She walked even faster, then slowed down. Any attempt to avoid him was futile. Suddenly she stopped and turned.

"I am sorry about what they did to you." Even in the darkness she could see the discoloring bruise on his neck and the mud on his shirt.

"I interfered with the economic arrangement . . . and that is a cardinal sin. Therefore I deserved it, didn't I?"

They stood in silence, awkwardly, surrounded by distant noises.

"May I walk you home?"

Raya shrugged, turned, began to walk. She felt confused and frightened; but she was glad he was there.

Chalfin kept a step behind her. As he walked he penned a silent memo to Winokur: Beaten, bloody, but unbowed, he was continuing intensification.

He watched her walking just ahead of him. Her gait had a simplicity that fascinated him. Everything was stationary but for her legs.

Each walked in the rhythm of the other.

Whenever Raya turned a corner she slowed, heard the steps behind her, felt both anxious and relieved.

A pair of drunken soldiers reeled across their path, spun to the middle of the street, then careened back against the buildings. Raya and Chalfin walked past them with a certain trepidation.

Chalfin no longer knew where he was; the twists and turns of their path had wrecked his sense of direction. The irregular buildings of the Quarter seemed to tumble over one another.

She opened a small wooden gate and entered an alley. He followed, closing the gate behind him.

"I live here," she said, pointing to a door.

The alley was narrow, the buildings decrepit, apparently about to fall down.

Chalfin said, "Do you have coffee?"

Raya folded her shawl and looked away from him. She was tired, very tired.

"I won't help you," she said wearily. "I won't help you. I am sorry that Jews are being killed, and Egyptians, and the English, and the French. I am very sorry. But I think everyone kills everyone today. That is how it appears. I am a Jew but I have no special feeling for other Jews. And, as for the Jews of Cairo, those who live there," and she pointed with a finger, "with their riches, and fine schools, and books, and beautiful clothes—let *them* help you."

She moved closer to him, her face, suddenly bitter and dark, turned to one side. "And this land you spoke about. This land that is ours—to the east. What does it mean to me? Nothing. This is the only land I shall inherit." She pointed down.

Chalfin listened; he believed. He felt no passion for her now, just a deep and abiding intimacy. As if he could press his lips against her forehead for days, weeks, years.

"It doesn't matter," he said.

She stared at him grimly. Then she turned, opened the door, and began to climb the steep flight of rickety stairs. Chalfin followed. She opened another door and they were in a small apartment. She turned on a lamp. She gestured to him.

Chalfin sat down on the edge of the bed and looked around. There was a mélange of styles: an English chair and rugs woven in Egypt, a few pieces of French origin and some mats from the Sudan. It seemed as though one day some things had been thrown into an empty room and there they had stayed, becoming traditional, becoming livable.

"I don't really want coffee."

"The stove isn't working."

Raya sat down on the far side of the bed and slowly peeled an orange. She watched him stare at the shuttered door which opened onto the balcony. The balcony which looked down on the alley. He seems so young, she thought. He seems like a child. She wanted to ask him if he had brothers or sisters. She wanted to ask him about his home. She wanted to ask him why he had waited for her.

Chalfin accepted half of the orange. It was bitter but refreshing. She brought him a cloth to wipe his hands.

Their fatigue had a sharp edge; they wanted to speak to each other but they couldn't. They sat there, three feet from each other, in an historical vacuum.

Language, Chalfin thought. We use different languages. That is why I can't say anything. But what do I wish to say?

Chalfin muttered something about her exhaustion. Raya made a confused comment about the long walk home. Chalfin said that he was English, an English Jew, and then remembered that he had already told her that. Raya apologized for not sitting at his table. Chalfin said that he couldn't stand the thought of her going behind the curtain with that old Egyptian. Raya laughed and said that old men were better than young men. Chalfin asked where she had gotten the oranges. Raya explained why her stove was not working. Chalfin made a comment about the city of Jerusalem and how it differed from Cairo. Raya said that one day she would like to visit Paris. Chalfin told her that there was a letter from his father in his pocket. Raya said that . . .

They muttered themselves into the dawn. Then Raya undressed and lay down. Chalfin did the same. They touched only at the knees. A great weariness and a great joy came over Chalfin. He turned his head. Raya was asleep, her breasts rising and falling in an even rhythm. His eyes seemed incapable of absorbing her. He fell asleep.

A good morning, brisk and bright, and everything was functioning, thought Sister Charlotte. The ward work was being done with dispatch, the new admissions had already been tended, and even the administrative details—deliveries of food and fuel and medical supplies—had fallen into place.

Brian Quinton would show up this morning and she walked to his office to check on the package she had left on his desk. Sister Charlotte had a lingering guilt about her brief flirtation with theft. But Dr. Quinton would see that none of the chocolates had been touched, and she would tell him that the tape had come undone because the package was so poorly wrapped. And that was true.

As for the strange death of the hero; that was receding. Brian Quinton must be trusted, or there would be no healing.

She knocked twice, briskly, opened the door, walked in, and shut the door behind her. Quinton was sitting at his desk. But something was out of order. She leaned back against the door, grasping the knob.

His face was covered with blood.

A rough hand muffled Sister Charlotte's cry. Pressing against her mouth and nose, it cut off all air. She struggled instinctively for a moment and then became still.

"The little birdie will get her bloody feathers clipped if she makes another sound—a single coo, a single tweet. Understand?"

Her body went rigid with fear.

"Understand?" repeated the voice from behind her shoulder.

Sister Charlotte nodded. The hand moved away. A man appeared. Then another. And then another. They were British soldiers. She had seen them before, the day Reggie Cornell had been brought to the hospital. She remembered them. She remembered in particular the short soldier with the rakish cowboy hat and goggles who was now standing near Dr. Quinton's desk. They all carried weapons. The man beside her, who had put his hand over her mouth, now gently placed the muzzle of his gun against her neck. "Just a little inquest, luv, a little inquest."

Sister Charlotte looked at Quinton. He was sitting perfectly still. Blood flowed from a jagged scar at his hairline and ran down his face. She moved slightly to escape the coldness of the gun at her neck. The soldier smiled and kept the weapon pressed against her.

"We brought him in alive, and you sent us back a corpse. Now, mate, that's no way to run such a glorious medical establishment. Where is your Christian love?"

Quinton nodded reflectively, and said nothing.

"So we want to know more about what happened, about why he came back to us a corpse."

"Some we save and some we lose," said Quinton.

The short soldier slammed his foot savagely into Quinton's chair; Quinton sprawled on the floor. He picked himself up slowly, pushed the chair back behind the desk, and sat down again.

They will kill him, thought Sister Charlotte, they will kill him and me. She heard an ominous click. The short soldier had placed a round in the chamber; he held the gun in Quinton's ear.

"It was no one's fault," she blurted out, "it was no one's fault. We were making blood transfusions, and something went wrong with the apparatus, with the tube that carried the blood. It was no one's fault. We don't have enough people to watch all our patients all of the time."

May God forgive me for lying, she thought, but it is permissible to tell a small lie to save a large life.

"We're sorry it happened to your friend. We're sorry it happens to so many who come here."

The short soldier withdrew the gun from Quinton's ear and looked at her. His face was marked with lines and with dirt, and there were small ridges along his chin, like imprints. He nodded to the soldier beside Sister Charlotte. She felt the weapon move away from her neck.

"A mistake," said the short soldier, as though explaining to the world. "A mistake," he repeated. Then he laughed hysterically, and so did his companions.

Then all was silence. The soldiers' odor was powerful and rank. They seemed to mark whatever they touched with it.

The short soldier began to poke around Quinton's desk with the muzzle of his gun. There was the package. The soldier grabbed the box and opened it. He unwrapped a chocolate and popped it into his mouth. Then he distributed chocolates to his comrades. They ate the chocolate thoughtfully, continuing to watch Quinton and Sister Charlotte. They threw the chocolate wrappers all over the floor.

Sister Charlotte could see that the blood had begun to clot over the wound in Quinton's head.

"A mistake," said one of the soldiers in a whisper. Then they slowly walked out of Quinton's office.

Sister Charlotte stooped down and began to pick up the chocolate wrappers. Hearing a sound, she looked up. Quinton, sitting straight at his desk, seemed to be sobbing. But there were no tears. His wound had also reopened.

She dropped all the wrappers she had picked up and walked out of the office, shutting the door softly behind her. She could not speak to him right now. The fear of those weapons and men were still with her; and the horrible knowledge that she shared their suspicions.

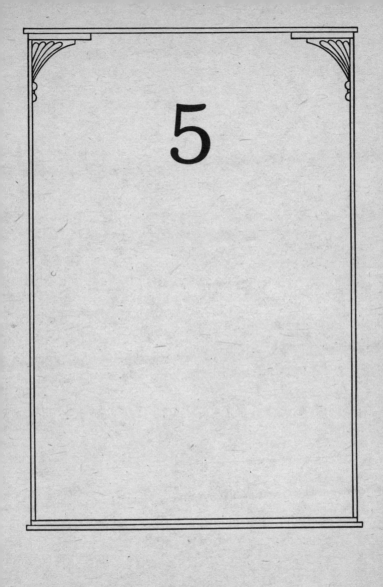

5

Raya stared down at the narrow alley, at her neighbors scurrying out through the gate to the street and market, and back through the gate with assorted foodstuffs. Some carried pails of water because the primitive plumbing in these buildings had long since ceased to function on a regular basis.

David Chalfin had left while she was sleeping. He had scribbled a note saying he would be back early in the afternoon, if he could find his way.

It was past noon; the chill of the morning was gone. Raya wore a robe. Her feet were bare.

Hearing the scraping of feet outside the door, she waited a moment, then opened the door. There was a small loaf of fresh bread wrapped in ancient newspaper, a pail of brackish water, and the jug she left outside her door each night had been filled with sweet black coffee. Raya smiled. The boy who performed these tasks for a few bright coins each week was always on time, always dependable. She left the coins in a chink outside the door, and he duly collected them.

The sun flooded the apartment through the open balcony doors. It unveiled the room with a laughing passion—shining on the broken metal stove, digging up dust from the rugs, exposing flaws in the furnishings.

Rocking slowly on the chair, she sipped the coffee and ate a piece of bread, until the sun made her head ache. She got up and closed one door. Now, as she sat in the chair, the light bisected her body—one side in shadow, the other illumined.

She chewed the bread slowly, thinking about the grain, about the many transformations the grain had gone through. Raya was not a curious woman, she always dealt with the given—except for things like grain and cloth and metal. Here, she was curious. Since childhood she had wondered about who gathers and changes and finishes them.

It occurred to her, sitting in the chair, that she wanted David Chalfin to return. She wanted it very much. And for a moment she thought about Chalfin as she thought about the bread.

What strange events had brought him to Cairo? What had he meant when he spoke about that place called Palestine? Who were really his people?

Why did he talk about Jews so much? Yes, she was a Jew. So what? There had been Jews in Egypt for thousands of years. In Cairo, in Alexandria, everywhere. Jews who sold cotton and silk and camels and leather. Jews who bought and sold. Rich Jews and poor Jews. And the poor Jews hated the rich Jews like the poor Arabs hated the rich Arabs.

She finished the bread and still she sat there. From the alley came the playful screams of children who ran from building to building, in and out of windows and doors.

If he doesn't come, she thought, he doesn't come. If he doesn't come it will be because he can't find his way back here. If he doesn't come it will be because he'd rather pay than not pay.

94

She stood up abruptly and began to clean the apartment. Every few minutes she walked to the balcony and looked down at the street. Finally she sat down on the bed, her feet drawn up under her, and watched the curve of sunlight move inexorably into the afternoon.

A dizzying spiral of reflection seemed to possess her, making her weep, making her clutch her arms across her chest. That was all there was now: the rocking chair and the bed and the few pieces of furniture. That was all there was. In the very center of her being was a hole, and with each passing day it grew, widening its jagged province.

If he does not return this afternoon, she thought, I will walk to the balcony and just drop myself down.

The image of her body falling and landing stopped her tears. She was ashamed of herself for thinking in that manner; she was ashamed of her tears. She was alive and well and had enough to eat and brought pain to no one. It was stupid, childish to weep over one's fate—God allots and determines and collects.

A dull stream of sound entered her consciousness and it was moments before Raya realized it was a knocking at her door. Then she moved quickly. Chalfin stood in the doorway, smiling, his jacket slung over his shoulder. She wondered how his shirt stayed so white—just a few sweat marks.

He had brought nuts and fruit and a small jar of milk.

He joked about the trouble he had had finding the gate. He stared at the open balcony and from time to time paced across the room.

They ate the nuts and fruit and drank the milk. Raya served what was left of the coffee.

"How long have you lived here?" asked Chalfin.

"For many years. My mother died here."

"And your father?"

"I know nothing about my father. My mother used to tell me that he was a rich man, that we were all rich once. But that was before I was born. She told me he—"

95

Chalfin gave her an apricot, breaking off the conversation to show her he didn't want to pry any further.

Suddenly she said, "What kinds of animals are there in England?"

He laughed. "Cows. Dogs. Cats. Goats. Pheasants. Geese. Rabbits . . ."

Raya was thinking: I have never loved a man, but I am going to love this man. I want him to put his hands on me. I want him to kiss me. I want him to tell me about all the animals in England and Jerusalem.

She felt strong and happy and foolish. He was like a gift that had suddenly been given to her. A different kind of gift; one that made her well. It was a mystery, like the machine that produced music.

She reached over and touched his lips with one finger. She unbuttoned his white shirt and felt his thin, muscular chest. I am doing to him what they have always done to me, she thought for a moment, with apprehension. Then she laughed and kissed him.

Tomlinson awoke. His head ached and his eyes burned. He kicked at the empty wine bottles and stumbled over to where he had lined up the dead Italian soldiers.

Their faces were covered with flies, their limbs were stiff. He leaned over and brushed the files off each face. Finally he found the face he sought; he found a particular face. He removed dirt from the officer's trousers, puttees, and sand-painted helmet. The helmet was adorned with the black stenciled silhouette which signified participation in a motorized infantry division. He blew away dross from the collar patch of the Sicilia Brigade—scarlet with two light green stripes.

Tomlinson stepped back, then squatted on the ground. He was studying his new friend. His eye dropped and caught the flash of steel. He grabbed and pulled; a 9mm Beretta submachine gun emerged from the earth. He studied the chamber mechanism intently. He fired a few bursts in the air, and then he fired into all the dead Italian soldiers except his chosen one.

"Pietro," he said, "you look sad. Why should you be sad with all this wine and food here?"

Tomlinson fired again and the bullets careened off the steel plate of the armored carriers to his right. He rocked back and forth on his heels, cradling the machine gun. The flies were resettling on his friend's face.

"There are anchovies in the tent. Are you hungry? Do you want anchovies?"

His friend didn't answer. Tomlinson started to cry.

"Pico, I'm going to make you happy. I'm going to take you to Cairo. I'm going to take you to a lady who will make you very happy."

Tomlinson stood up and ran to the tent. He flung aside crates and weapons and articles of clothing in his search. Finally he found what he was looking for: a coil of rope. He returned to his friend, knotted the rope around his ankles, and dragged him away from the other dead soldiers.

"Benito, I am going to take you to a wonderful place. Trust me."

Tomlinson lifted a hand in a gesture that bid his friend to stay still, then trotted over to the other soldiers. He removed all their boots. He then opened several tins of anchovies and poured anchovies, in equal measure, into the boots. He went back to the tent and sniffed around until he found some petrol. He filled the boots with petrol. He lined the boots up in a perfectly straight line. He put another magazine into the Beretta and fired a burst at the line. Flame exploded from the boots, snaked out to the dead soldiers who had worn them, ignited the clothes, and consumed the bodies.

"Garibaldi," he shouted over his shoulder to his friend, "I can't take all of you to Cairo."

Tomlinson grabbed the end of the rope, wrapped it around

his wrist, and began to walk, dragging his friend, feet first, behind him. The soldier's helmet thudded softly against the ground.

"I can't sing, Enrico, I can't sing. But this place where we go, in Cairo, this place has music."

Tomlinson leaned forward, pulling his friend, walking.

She had said she would meet him. She had said she would meet him before she went to The Trunk. It would only be for an hour or so. It would be nice.

Chalfin spent the morning waiting for that hour, drifting through the city. Ostensibly he was making a walking tour of the city's architecture—and so he studied building material, arches, porticoes, colonnades. When he identified something, when he could name a concept, then he recalled bits and pieces of data from all the guide books he had read.

This is twelfth century something . . . this obviously shows French influence. . . .

None of his identifications was correct. This he suspected but did not mind.

He felt physically powerful. He felt as if his body were made of steel and silk and he walked quite slowly, but with a definite catlike bounce. He softly sprang from foot to foot. He began to imagine incredible adventures for Raya and himself: desperate flights into the very center of Occupied Europe; vast archeological digs in the deserts of the Holy Land that would unearth scriptural treasures beyond compare.

Suddenly he burst out laughing. His fantasies were ludicrous; Raya Fahmi cared for absolutely nothing that he cared for. Nothing.

Better, he thought. Just us—just two anonymous, throwaway Jews.

He lifted his head. Odd, how lately, at various times of day, he would smell Europe. The scent would drift across, over him, just out of reach, reminding him of some ritually slaughtered animal. If he thought hard, he could smell an old Hasid slitting the throat and making the continent ritually clean.

He began to walk faster, as though he were pushing the time. Push Raya. Push Cairo. The tall young man springing along, pushing it all.

He reached the coffee shop and sat down. He had chosen a place close to the crossroads so that there would be a mix for Raya to see.

Five minutes early she turned the corner. She wore a light blue print dress and he stared; it was the first time he had seen her out of uniform on the street. She walked in the middle of the street and only her eyes moved from side to side, looking for him.

He wanted to wave to her but did not—the picture was too engrossing. She stopped suddenly, smiled, came toward him.

Chalfin stood up, one hand in his pocket nervously jangling coins, the other extended to take her hand.

He said, "Good afternoon."

She said, "Hello," and sat down stiffly.

Coffee came. They stirred the hot syrupy brew with small spoons. They grinned at each other.

"How did you spend the morning?" she asked.

"Walking."

"Walking," she repeated, as if he had said something profound.

The sounds of cups and saucers, sandals and boots, soldiers and animals swirled around them. Raya tossed her head and her hair swirled. Meeting the eye of an English officer at a nearby table, she dropped her head quickly.

"Do you have any brothers or sisters or cousins?" he asked.

"Many," she replied.

"Where are they?"

She laughed and stretched out a hand toward some vague point in the distance.

Where? thought Chalfin. Alexandria. Morocco. Turkey. Greece. Portugal. Syria.

"And you?" she asked.

"Many."

"Where?"

He stretched out a hand.

They sipped the coffee.

He was caught in a remarkable silence with her. Nothing needed to be said. Everything was there. He could sit happily at this table for a thousand years, watching her neck and shoulders, stirring coffee.

The English officer left his table and walked past them, his revolver swinging in a leather case from his belt. The gun jostled Chalfin's elbow. Chalfin rose halfway from his seat, staring at Raya. Her eyes were lowered into the coffee cup. The officer passed.

Now he wanted her. Right there, by the side of the street, on a donkey's back, under the table—anywhere, anyhow, somehow. She knows, he thought. She knows. With two fingers he bent the coffee spoon.

He could not have her then and there. The truth made him surrender to that adolescent despair he so despised: the little tremors that say all is lost, all is broken, all is hopelessly, irretrievably gone. Extinguish thyself.

"Tomorrow," she said.

Red-faced, he stared at the spoon and carefully corrected its alignment.

They shook hands. He watched her walk away.

If this were England, he thought, I would sit down and write a lyric. And he had written them in the past. They could tear the heart out of fools. But he no longer remembered any lines, no longer remembered even whom he had aped. Not Keats, no. Not Blake. Not Marvell. Ah, he remembered now. Hopkins. Yes, Hopkins. He had stolen the meter, gleefully removed Christ, and filled it with genteel pornography which could be construed as bohemianism by English intellectual Jews.

"I am no longer anyone special," Chalfin said aloud to himself, "I am in love with a whore."

He lingered at the table for an hour after Raya had left. Winokur was expecting him, but there was no rush. When he finally paid his bill and began to walk to Winokur's flat, he took the longest, most intricate route possible—through the winding stall streets.

As he walked she was very much with him. Her voice was with him and her smile and the way she held the cup in her hands.

A young boy almost tripped him up, then shoved a small leather clasp purse under his nose. The boy shouted the price, and he shouted that the purse was eternally magnificent, that it would never tear or tarnish or age, that it would make him a rich man by keeping his money safe. The boy kept opening and closing the clasp.

Chalfin walked past him. The meeting with Winokur was worrisome. He would have to tell Winokur that Raya Fahmi would not work for the Jewish Agency and he would have to hide what he felt.

What he felt was simple. There was no longer anything complex about it. There were no longer any little questions to be solved or any large questions to be chewed on. He did a small hop and clenched his fist, as if he had won a wager.

Chalfin froze, mid-stride. Just to his right, standing beside a pile of crates, was a girl who looked astonishingly like Raya. She couldn't have been more than fifteen. She had the same black hair and the same complexion; she wore a long, loose-fitting black smock that seemed neither native nor European. He looked around as if for someone who could explain the girl.

She pulled something out of a deep pocket in her smock. He relaxed. She was going to try to sell him something.

Something glittered at the end of an ugly leather thong. A silver Star of David. The girl let it find its own rhythm and swing at the end of the thong.

101

For Raya, he thought. He would get it for Raya. But would she like it? He stepped forward, gesturing toward the Star. The girl slipped behind the stall, vanished, then appeared at another wooden plank. She had made her sales pitch and now she was a vendor ready to bargain, ready to engage in the ritual of high price, low price, and then the golden mean.

Chalfin hesitated. But he had to give Raya something besides fruit and nuts. Why not this? He could see the Star lying exquisite on Raya's throat. He would put it on a silver chain and fasten it at the back of her neck.

Chalfin followed the girl's path.

There was a sudden numbing pain at the side of his head, an eclipse of all light. Then he was tumbling over and over and over, grasping with his hands, trying to stop the fall.

He was on his knees, then struggled to his feet and flailed out with both fists. He connected with something. Then there was another pain at the base of his neck, and his head rang with what seemed to be an explosion of dull low bells. Everything slipped away.

When David Chalfin opened his eyes, he saw a tiny bit of the sky. His head throbbed and something in the depths of his eyes seemed to be pushing forward. He realized he was lying on his back and he sat up. The pain which shot from his spine to his forehead made him gag. He was dizzy, but he did not lie down again. The pain and dizinesss increased. He ignored them and looked around in puzzlement. Then he remembered.

The girl was gone. He pulled himself up and held on to the nearest ledge until his legs steadied. Enlightenment dawned: he was not the victim of a natural disaster; someone had hit him from behind. He quickly reached for his wallet. It was still there. He checked the inside pocket of his jacket. The photos were still there.

Only one thing was missing: his father's letter. Chalfin waited until he could move away from the supporting ledge with confidence. Then he went through all his pockets again.

His father's letter was missing. How absurd. Someone had clubbed him from behind to steal his father's letter. Not possible. Had the girl been part of it? He stared down at his clothes. They were filthy. He tried to brush them off but the pain stopped him.

The walk was long and slow and difficult—two steps and then a long rest, two more steps, a long rest. Finally he climbed to the last landing, entered Winokur's flat and crumbled into a chair.

Winokur looked up from his papers, sighed, and vanished into the next room. He returned with a large wet towel which he pressed against the back of Chalfin's neck.

"You've been playing," Chalfin heard him say. He couldn't laugh because of the pain.

Winokur made strong coffee for him, then returned to his desk and watched the younger man recover. Then, Chalfin told him what had happened.

Winokur said, "They took your father's letter?"

Chalfin nodded.

"They clubbed you on the head to get your father's letter?"

Chalfin nodded again.

"Is he that good a writer?"

Chalfin's cup slammed down on the desk. Suddenly he didn't appreciate Winokur's humor. The coffee sloshed over the sides of the cup. Winokur took the coffee pot, walked to Chalfin, and refilled it.

"Do you want me to say that your life is in danger, David, that there is a sinister conspiracy against your life?"

He said it gently, but the sarcasm was there.

Chalfin shook his head. He was ashamed that he had lost his temper.

"I will tell you a great truth," Winokur continued. "Europeans who wander about in Cairo are often robbed. You see, the Arabs think Europeans carry their fortunes with them, in their pockets. And they know that the heads of Europeans are soft."

103

Winokur stopped walking and placed a piece of scrap paper on the spilled coffee, to soak it up. Then he crumpled the wet paper and flung it playfully against a far wall.

"And the whore?" He asked.

"What about her?" Chalfin asked quickly.

"Will she do it?"

"No."

He let his breath out slowly, on a line, pushing the word with his chest.

"You are sure?"

"I am sure."

Chalfin walked slowly back to the chair and returned the towel to his neck. He had done it well. He had told it matter-of-factly. But the reality was different. To fail before Winokur was a horrible thing. Winokur was the yardstick of action. Winokur was the man who had fought his way out. Chalfin was in such awe of him he couldn't hear his contempt or disgust. For the first time he wanted to confront Winokur with the past, critically. That was the only defense for his own failure. Yes, Winokur, he thought silently, you got out of Nazi Europe but how many corpses of your friends did it take? How many little betrayals? No Jew escaped clean. But Chalfin said nothing.

The two men sat in silence. Winokur seemed pensive. Then he chuckled. Then he giggled. Then he began to laugh, slowly at first like a freight train, gradually picking up speed until his whole body convulsed in guffaws.

Chalfin grinned sheepishly. Then he too began to laugh. He knew what Winokur was laughing about. He was laughing about the way things were going. About the Jewish whore who could not be recruited by Jews. About the Jewish prude who falls in love with a Jewish whore. About the young man who walks along a Cairo street and is clubbed by assailants unknown in order to steal his father's letter.

They laughed until tears fell from their eyes. Winokur opened a desk drawer and took out a bottle. Cradling it in the crook of his arm as though it were holy scripture, he carried the bottle to Chalfin.

"Polish vodka," Winokur whispered between guffaws, "Polish vodka!"

Chalfin forgot the pain in his head. He touched the bottle, wondering at the small specks in the clear liquid.

Winokur found two discolored glasses and poured. They drank. Chalfin mimicked the older man, swallowing quickly with a jerk of his head. It went down fast and scalded all the way. Winokur succumbed to another fit of laughter. He wiped his eyes and poured again.

We will drink until we collapse, Chalfin thought. The idea made him happy. He was drinking to Raya! And Winokur? Who knew what Winokur drank to? Who cared?

When they finished the first bottle, Winokur produced another bottle. They drank themselves into an exhilarating stupor. Winokur made many toasts: to the Englishmen out there—by which he meant those fighting in the Western Desert; to the Russians out there—by which he meant those fighting on the Eastern front; to all the partisans in all the hills and deserts; to all in uniform, actual or spiritual, against the fascists.

Chalfin collapsed, and then came to. Winokur lay babbling. Sometimes their moments of coherence coincided and they talked and laughed, and groaned.

Chalfin crawled to the desk and opened a drawer. "Malorange!" He shouted. But Malorange didn't appear. "The great Malorange, the mysterious Malorange is out on a secret mission. He is recruiting all the flies in Cairo and teaching them to fight the Luftwaffe." Chalfin paused, then shouted "Malorange, Malorange" into the drawers again until he pulled a drawer all the way out and rolled over on his back.

The hours drifted by; day turned to night. Winokur began to sing Yiddish songs. Although Chalfin understood not a word, he thought they were the saddest songs he had ever heard. Empty vodka bottles rolled haphazardly on the floor.

They fell into a stuporous sleep, Chalfin sprawled on a chair. Winokur lying prone in a corner of the room.

When Chalfin awoke he saw Winokur sipping a cup of coffee.

Winokur asked: "What were we celebrating?"

"Failure."

"And your broken head." Chalfin agreed with a nod.

"Some people will go to great extremes to open a bottle of Polish vodka."

"Some people will do anything."

Winokur suddenly grew animated and jabbed his fingers into the air: "Vodka should not be drunk here. The British are beginning their biggest offensive of the war—against a ghost! There is nothing left of the Afrika Korps. Nothing. The fools. They don't want to fight the real war any longer. They want to fight here. Back and forth in the desert. The war is in Russia. Drink vodka in Russia. A thousand miles of war from north to south."

He stopped as suddenly as he began, and asked calmly, "How is your head?"

"It hurts."

"Good. If your head didn't hurt you would know something was wrong with it."

Chalfin couldn't fathom Winokur's reasoning, but that didn't matter. He thought it would be impossible to wait another twenty-four hours before seeing Raya again. Other things were possible, but not that.

Winokur ushered him out of the flat gracefully, as if they had spent the afternoon and evening discussing substantive issues.

It was past midnight. Cairo at this hour was muffled. People walked more quickly and kept to the edges of the street. Military vehicles rumbled on at a slower pace, as if without direction, as if out for a night of sightseeing.

Chalfin's body ached now and his stomach was sour. His

vision occasionally blurred. Yet he felt no fatigue, and everything was bearable because he was going to The Trunk to wait for her.

The events of the past few days—the drunken scene in The Trunk, his love for Raya, the beating—had loosened Chalfin and made him more of a denizen of Cairo. He walked easily through the dangerous streets, as if he had been blooded and was in control. He absorbed the shadows rather than shying away from them. He sought to untangle the threads of Arabic, Greek, French, and other whispered languages rather than to shut them out.

At The Trunk he commenced his vigil. His expectation, need, and desire obliterated his horror at what was really going on in there. She would come out, in time, and they would walk together, and all would be well.

A tiny, dwarflike man approached, stood on one foot and then the other, studied him carefully, then made a face. Chalfin ignored him; the creature moved off.

He lost his sense of time but the loss didn't concern him. He was comfortable waiting there for her. More comfortable than he had ever been in his country of birth, England. And more comfortable than he had ever been in his country of history and adoption, Palestine.

Raya at last came out of The Trunk. He kept his distance, matching her steps across the street until she noticed his presence. Then he walked quickly to her side.

"I said tomorrow," she whispered.

It was a whore's response—sudden, quiet, firm. It was designed to put off desperate men with money in their hands. She knew it and was ashamed.

"I know."

Her face was hard for a moment, but then she smiled. They walked to her home without exchanging a word.

Upstairs, Chalfin undressed quickly, trembling so much that he could hardly stand on one foot as he stepped out of each leg of his trousers. He lay down on the bed and stared at the dark ceiling. He could hear her moving about in the darkness. How many men had she slept with during the evening? Five? Ten? Fifteen? It was academic. He didn't really care. Or did he? When he felt her weight on the bed he didn't care because the contradictions were resolved.

She lay next to him, on her side, her face away from him. He touched her thigh and marveled that she was there. He drew his hand along her spine and traced the shape of her neck. She turned over on her back.

I want to tell her what I feel, he thought. His hands couldn't tell her.

He dropped his face onto her breasts, and saw her looking at him with wide eyes. He took her head in his hands and kissed her again and again. She said something in Arabic, then in French. He heard but did not hear; he understood but did not understand. Then he felt her hands at the back of his neck.

He entered her and felt pure ecstasy. There was nothing else he wanted—he had what he wanted. It must go on, he thought, it must go on. We must stay like this! Soft and hard and lovely and wet and all the colors of the night.

But it ended, and he rolled away, very weak, very tired, very happy. They lay in the darkness, her hand on his thigh.

Suddenly he awoke. She was pulling at his arm. He sat up.

"No, lie down," she whispered, "nothing is the matter."

Chalfin lay down.

Raya said, "Listen to me."

He touched her mouth. She kissed his hand, then pushed it away.

"I am going to do what you want, Englishman."

He laughed at her *Englishman*.

"Do you hear?"

"You are already doing everything I want," said Chalfin.

"No, I mean the other thing. I will do that other thing for you. What you spoke of."

108

Chalfin gripped her hand in astonishment. She pulled away. His grip was too hard.

"No!" he exclaimed, then realized his blunder. He paused to formulate a careful response.

"Why have you changed your mind, Raya?"

She leaned over and kissed both his eyelids softly.

Unable to speak, Chalfin turned to the wall. He was frightened, he was chilled; his head hurt again. He felt exhausted and impotent and stupid. Soon he was aware of Raya nestled into his back.

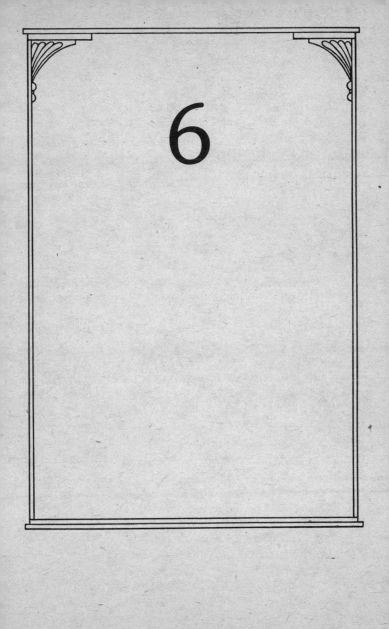

6

Chalfin began to introduce Raya. "This is —"

Winokur cut him off with a gesture of his hand. "Just sit," he said.

They were meeting in a Jewish Agency safe house, miles away from Winokur's flat, at the southern edge of the city. When Chalfin and Raya arrived, Winokur and Malorange were already there.

Chalfin squirmed while Winokur asked her if she would like tea or coffee or something stronger; while Malorange asked her if she was comfortable. They were playing out the old cliché: always treat a whore like a lady. However, Raya was neither one; she was not in their lexicon.

When the preliminaries were over, Winokur approached her, smiled his most courtly smile, and said, "Why have you decided to help us?"

She glanced quickly at Chalfin, then looked straight at Winokur. "I am a Jew," she said simply.

Winokur began to pace slowly back and forth in front of her. He looked at her from time to time in astonishment, as though she had made a startling statement.

"Raya Fahmi. Raya Fahmi," he said, drawing out the syllables.

She liked the man. She liked the way he paced and she liked the way he said her name. And because he was David's companion, she trusted him.

"What you will be doing for us is very important," Winokur began, still pacing but a little more slowly. "And it will be very easy. No one will get hurt. No one will be shot. It will be easy and fast. A few days, or a few weeks at the most. At the most."

He stopped talking, looked at Chalfin, looked at Malorange, then pulled a chair close to Raya. For a moment he touched her hand. "There is a man who goes to The Trunk. For the same reason other men go there. We want you to become friendly with him. We want you to be invited to his house. We want you to gain his confidence. And then we want you to find something for us in his house. It is very simple. And you will be safe."

He paused, waiting for her response.

Raya Fahmi simply smiled.

Chalfin felt fiercely proud of her. He longed to show support with a gesture or a word. Her face was in profile to him, open and beautiful, and he felt an immense gratitude along with his pride. But he also felt shame, a deep shame at having brought her into this.

"What do you want me to find?" asked Raya.

Winokur looked at Colonel Malorange. Malorange nodded, and said, "You will be looking for a book, or a magazine, or a printed pamphlet. The book will be underlined in a regular pattern. Or it will have writing in the margins."

"What is the name of the book?" said Raya.

"We don't know," replied Malorange.

Raya looked in perplexity at Chalfin.

114

"Let me explain," said Malorange, "the most simple elements of a cipher. He drew from his pocket two small red books, dog-eared and worn. Chalfin squinted until he could make out the title: *Schrag's Handy Guide to Nuremburg*. Malorange had two copies. He went on, "Suppose, Raya, you and I are in the same army. Suppose we are in the tank corps. Every day enemy planes fly over us and kill our comrades. We know the planes come from a certain city, but we don't know if the airfield is north or south of the city. You volunteer to find out. I give you a radio, and this little book."

Malorange handed one copy to Raya.

"Turn to page twenty-two," he said.

Raya turned to page twenty-two.

"Tell me what you find," said Malorange.

She looked down at the page for a long minute, then said, "The word *north* has a line under it."

"Now what do you find on page thirty-eight?"

Raya turned to page thirty-eight. "There is a line under the word *south*."

"So, Raya, when you go on your mission, and radio back the numbers 2-2-3-8 on your wireless set, I know that there are two airfields in the city, one to the north and one to the south—and the enemy, which monitors your message but does not have our book, will not understand the numbers 2-2-3-8."

Raya nodded. Then she leafed through the book until Malorange grabbed it from her with a laugh.

"Of course," he continued, "this is the simplest cipher there is. Ciphers become more and more intricate, based on pages, lines, relations between words and sentences, inversions, and what have you. But whatever our ciphers, they will be based on this book. So, that is what you will be looking for."

Winokur stepped in front of Malorange and waggled a finger at her as though she were a difficult schoolgirl. "Remember: the cipher book won't be near the transmitter. You don't have to find the wireless set. All you have to find is

115

the book. And the book won't be near the set. It will be in the kitchen or the library or the bathroom or under his pillow. If he has a dog it could be strapped to the dog. Once you find it, bring it to us. We will keep it for only a few hours, and then you will replace it. And that will be the end. All will be over."

There was silence. Everyone relaxed. The instructions had been given, the secrets divulged.

Malorange said, "The man's name is Brian Quinton. He is an Irish doctor."

"Let's have the picture, David," said Winokur.

Chalfin took several items from his inside pocket. He shuffled through them, found the photograph, and gave it to Winokur.

Winokur looked at it, then made a face at Chalfin to advise him that the photo should have been protected from grime and sweat. Then he handed it to Raya. "This is Brian Quinton," he said.

Chalfin knew something was wrong before the others knew. He saw a nearly imperceptible straightening of her spine. Instinctively he began to move toward her, then stopped himself.

"So you know him," said Malorange quietly.

Raya held the photograph out to Winokur until he took it back. "I know him," she said.

"Then it will be easier for you," suggested Malorange.

Raya shook her head, then looked at Chalfin. He caught a sense of despair and terrible sadness. There was nothing he could do. There was nothing he could say. What had she seen in the photograph?

"David, see that she gets home safely," said Winokur, lapsing into his "treat the whore like a lady" speech.

Chalfin approached her and waited for her to rise. She remained seated. Everything about this place was hateful to her now. Including David's companion.

"Raya," Chalfin said.

She stood up. The photographic image remained with her,

covering her lover's face but for the eyes. "Raya," said the eyes once again—and she followed them out the door.

"She can do it," said Winokur. Malorange made no reply. He appeared to be extremely tired.

There was no balcony in Chalfin's flat, but there was a window, and Raya stood beside it, sipping the tea that he had prepared.

Her response to the photograph had killed whatever sense of celebration he had had. Now he was nervous, frightened, faced with the possibility that he had involved her in something utterly horrible.

They had been in the flat for an hour and still he had not asked the question. They had said nothing whatever to each other. Once she had walked around the flat and smiled several times to show him that she approved, that she liked this place he lived in. The tension oddly canceled out desire, leaving simply concern.

"What is that?" she asked, pointing out the window.

He moved closer to her, and looked. "What?"

"There, with the red roof."

"I don't know." He realized he was close enough to touch her. So he did.

"I have to go to work soon," she said graciously, and moved away from him.

He followed, embraced her, but she pulled away again. It wasn't a question of wanting to make love to her; he wanted to assure her. Finally he said, casually, "Tell me about the man in the picture."

She shrugged, looking into her teacup. She said nothing. Abruptly she raised her head and looked at him.

This is a condemnation, he thought.

She said, "It doesn't matter."

"Everything matters."

"To Englishmen," she said.

"To Jews," he corrected.

He sensed that she was preparing to leave. "We can forget about it!" he shouted, momentarily losing control. Then he lowered his voice: "You don't have to go through with this."

"I wish to."

"Then tell me about the man in the photo."

"Why is that important?"

"Because I love you . . . and because we are working together."

"You love me. . . ." She repeated the phrase, oddly.

Perhaps, he thought, he had gone too far. Perhaps it was none of his business. Perhaps his hatred of her customers made him unduly suspicious. Perhaps her response to the photo had been one of simple recognition.

Suddenly she turned and walked to a chair. "Please, come here." He went to her. Putting her right foot on the chair, she pulled up her skirt. Chalfin stared at a small burn scar on the inside of her thigh. Coveting, possessing every inch of her body, he had missed that burn. The sight of it made him sick with anger. "Quinton," he said quietly.

"Yes."

"How? When?"

She told him the story simply—too simply, so that he had to fill in the lurid gaps.

A year ago, when she had first begun to work in The Trunk, Quinton had been one of her customers. The first time, he had only talked to her. He didn't want sex. He just talked. And because he was drunk he sang a few songs. Then he paid and left.

Weeks passed and he didn't appear. Then one night he came again. This time he wanted sex. A certain way. He wanted to be loved. He wanted her to hold him and cradle him and hum to him. And he wanted her to sponge his whole body, and kiss him. He wanted her to be his mother. She did whatever he asked. The man was kind, and time was time. She finished by making love to him with her mouth.

Again he stayed away for many weeks. When he reappeared in The Trunk she felt she ought to stay away from him. And it was her option to do so. But as the evening wore on she lost her resolve. Once again they were together.

Without warning, without a single word, he put a cigarette lighter against her thigh. She screamed. He covered her mouth with his hand and begged her not to say anything. A hundred times he told her he was sorry; he begged forgiveness.

After that he often came into The Trunk. He always looked at her apologetically, and always invited her to his table. But she refused.

Chalfin had never heard her tell a story before. She thought as she spoke, as though searching not for words but for concepts. Now, at the conclusion, her face was paler than he had ever seen it. She returned to the window to stare at the red-roofed building neither of them could identify.

He felt incapable of speech, and began to pace across the room, violence and hatred spiraling toward the top of his head.

Suddenly she said, "I must go."

He held up a hand, as if to stop her. He forced himself to speak, and his words came slowly. "Listen to me, Raya. Until this is over, we must limit our contact. Otherwise . . . it would not be safe for you."

His voice was so low she could hardly hear him.

"Do you remember that café, where we met," he said.

"Yes."

"We will meet there every afternoon for a few minutes. At three in the afternoon. If you cannot come one day, come the next day. If you miss two afternoons in a row, I will know you are in trouble. Do you understand?"

"Yes."

"Raya . . ." Stepping toward her, he sobbed once. "Next year in Jerusalem," he whispered.

She turned quickly and left his flat. Chalfin washed the teacup. Was there something else he could do? Anything else to occupy him? He turned and looked around. He saw the chair on which she had placed her foot, then lifted her skirt. He saw the burn; the burn imprisoned his eyes.

Then he vomited on the floor.

Raya and Chalfin met each afternoon at the café. They spoke to each other stiffly, almost formally, for not more than ten minutes. Then they parted. It was terribly difficult: they longed to touch. Once they succumbed, then felt even worse. Chalfin had only one question to ask: "Did he come in?" And Raya shook her head each time in answer.

Four days after her mission had clearly been defined, Brian Quinton visited The Trunk.

She had just made her fifth decision of the evening, judging quickly by the way a man held his glass of whiskey or the cast of his eyes or his seated posture. The process was not scientific but she had been right more often than not. Mistakes were occasional—such as Quinton; and she had a scar to remind her of that mistake.

He was sitting at a small table near the exit. There was too much smoke in the room for her to be certain. She took a few steps forward and had a clear view. It was Quinton. He was casually observing the scene with a look of bemusement, as though he had wandered into a zoo.

Suddenly he saw her. She became fearful, weak, and indecisive. She felt incapable of approaching his table. She noticed that his brightly flowered shirt was open at the collar. This made him seem less dangerous. Then he smiled, turned up his hands, and shrugged, as if to say he had not been responsible for the past.

Someone at a nearby table grabbed her wrist. She shook him off and walked across the club to Quinton.

"Well," he said, "you have finally forgiven me."

She sat down. He looked just the same. He had that quality of calm that she liked in men. Chalfin did not have it. But she loved Chalfin.

"Have you forgiven me?"

"Yes."

He dropped his head for a moment, then looked up, smiling.

Raya wondered if he were as sorrowful as he seemed. "You haven't been here in a long time."

"Not that long," he responded. "I've been exploring other forms of life."

"Are they better?"

"Better than you, Raya?" He laughed.

She didn't know that he knew her name; she didn't remember telling him; but perhaps she had.

Their knees met under the table. He looked at her for a confirming glance, but her expression was neutral. She was watching his face. She thought that wherever you might put Brian Quinton he would be at ease. He seemed to own The Trunk.

"More and more soldiers," he noted.

"More and more," she agreed.

"British soldiers."

He was drinking native beer, and poured some for Raya. She drank.

"Can we go?"

Raya nodded, and stood up. He sat for a moment in his chair, sloshing the beer, then got to his feet. They walked to the rear and went behind the curtain. He stood with his back against the curtain, watching her undress. She felt his careful observation.

"I have thought about what I did to you, thought about it a thousand times. I am ashamed. And I don't know what to say to you, how to make up to you. How could I have done that? Particularly to you. I am a physician! How could I willfully inflict a burn on someone?" He paused as though in exhaustion, then continued: "As for the other thing. As for what I ask of you and what you do. It's strange, I know, and you feel uncomfortable, and I can't justify it in any way.

121

Except, that is what I desire. That is what I need. Is there something you need? Something that puts the pieces together, stops the visions of butchery in your brain? For that is what I'm talking about."

Raya had long ceased listening to him. The small room was stifling. His presence was a shadow that stained her, that made her feel close to the end.

Still talking, he began to undress.

She thought of David. Of the last time they had held each other. Safe.

She was a whore, she knew. She slept with men to earn her daily bread. But she also slept with one man for love. And now she would submit to Brian Quinton for a reason she could only dimly perceive. It had something to do with her past, and the past of the man she loved. It had something to do with the war, which was everywhere, even in the water they drank. But nothing—not the past, not the war, not the man she loved—could make her happy to be with Brian Quinton. But she had promised to do something, and to do it she would have to appear happy—or fail. She turned to him and forced her eyes over his body. She smiled.

Quinton lay down on the bed and became a completely vulnerable child. His calm was replaced by eagerness.

Raya leaned over him and kissed his chest. He squirmed in delight. "It is what I want," he whispered, "it is what I want from you."

She sponged the length of his body, slowly, methodically, humming a song in a guttural voice, intensely. The room was close and filled with heat. He moved pleasurably under her hands. Sweat dropped into her eye, blinding her until she rubbed it away.

"This is what I want . . . want. . . ." His words followed the rhythm of her hands. Once, sitting up with plaintive eyes, he begged forgiveness for the burn. He asked to see it. He pressed his face against the inside of her thigh with a sob.

She would carry it through; she knew that now. She was

going to give him what he wanted and much more. She would become her Englishman's heroine. For Quinton would love her and need her and call for her in his darkest hours.

She brushed her black hair back, back against her scalp. It would be easy now. It was David there. Or it was for David.

Chalfin knew . . . he knew. He saw it in her face as she walked toward the table. She was trying to compose her face, to let her face show him that it had been nothing at all. When she sat down she folded her hands in her lap.

"Last night?" he asked softly.

"Yes."

"Did he hurt you?"

"No."

"Tell me what happened."

"There is nothing to tell."

"Did he say he would come again?"

"No."

"But he will."

"Yes, he will."

Chalfin looked past her, past the railing of the café onto the street. A tall man in a red cape was hurrying by. The cape was part of a military uniform, but he couldn't identify the branch, the service, or even the nationality. His eyes returned to Raya. "What type of man is he?"

She smiled, and shrugged. Chalfin understood that the question had been extremely stupid. She had confided all that she would ever confide about Quinton several days ago. She would say nothing else—unless something related to her assignment.

A fury began to grow in him. She was so composed! His head hurt again. Suddenly, he thought of how easy it would be to strangle her. A few moments . . . finished. This absurdity would end.

But his fury passed as he comprehended that she had simply practiced her trade to help him. That was all.

123

The classical perils of loving a whore, he thought.

They drank coffee with great concentration. His sexual longing was so intense that the cup trembled in his hands. She looked at him with sadness that was a promise.

"Scotland, Raya. You would like Scotland."

He was instantly astonished by his remark. What did Scotland have to do with anything? When, in fact, during the entire history of the Jewish people, had Scotland had anything to do with anything?

Chalfin looked at her closely. Now, he saw her as the errant Jewess, as the Jewish whore in the international brothel in the unspeakable war against all of them—against Raya and Winokur and his father and himself and . . .

"Yes, if we had met a few years ago I would have taken you to Scotland. You would have liked everything there but the food. Everything. And the dogs. You would have seen the sheepdog trials, where they pen the sheep in a beautiful uncanny way. The dogs stalk, then rush, then sit. They carve out the terrain one sector at a time until the sheep have nowhere to go but the pen."

She wasn't listening; he knew this. She was hunched over her cup and he watched her hair, blue-black in the afternoon sun.

Chalfin was wrong. Raya was listening—she heard every word he said but she could not comprehend this thing, this Scotland. She could not understand the way he talked in front of her. He never seemed to speak what he felt. He always spoke other words that were mysterious, words that she could not understand.

"But Jerusalem is *home*," he said with heavy emphasis, trying to fuse the word "home" with all philosophical truth. But he seemed to fail, and the word sounded to his own ears as merely a safe dwelling.

His Jerusalem now was her body. Her body was the mystical center. He saw sweat on her forehead, just under the hairline. Was she too hot? Uncomfortable? Did she want more

124

coffee? Was she hungry? It occurred to Chalfin that he had never heard her complain; she had never said a word about physical discomfort.

He wondered what his father would say to her if the three of them were here now, together. He wondered if his father, when young and poor in Whitechapel, had ever gone to places like The Trunk.

"And you must take care of yourself," she said quietly.

Chalfin laughed. He had never expected from her a pronouncement of concern. "I will. But I'm not the one who is playing a dangerous game."

"But all men are dangerous—and subject to danger."

"All?"

"Yes, all."

"Even me?"

"Even you." She reached across the table and pulled his hand to her lips. A moment later she was gone.

Chalfin reached Winokur's flat in half an hour. He sat down in a chair that faced Winokur at his desk.

"He was there, last night, with Raya," Chalfin said without expression, as if the words were of no import whatsoever.

Winokur pushed some papers to the middle of his desk, sat back, and smiled. He said, "So."

"She's doing well."

"Then why do you look so pale?"

Chalfin shifted around in his chair. He knew that Winokur had gathered he was fond of Raya, but what else could he possibly know?

"I had no idea I was pale."

"But you are."

"The sun," Chalfin said vaguely.

"The sun?"

"The sun."

"But the sun is good for you!" Winokur left his desk and went to the window, throwing up his hands in exuberance. "Just as Cairo is good for you. You didn't know that I love

Cairo, did you? But I do. It reminds me of a Polish city—any Polish city. In Cairo and Warsaw, women mean little. I mean the chase after women. They are bought and sold. Unless wives or daughters, they mean nothing. In Cairo, bread is everything. Bread is first. So, Cairo has truth. For in the world, bread is first. When you are hungry, my young friend, a woman means nothing."

Chalfin merely nodded. When Winokur was in a philosophical mood it was useless to speak. One just listened.

For a moment putting a fatherly hand on his shoulder, Winokur said, "Do you want to know why the girl is in no danger?"

"Yes."

"Then I will tell you." Winokur returned to his desk. "Because this man—what is his name—Dinton, or Quinton, is an amateur. He gives parties every other night. He transmits from a set that is never moved. He uses an old-fashioned cipher. You understand me? This man is not a professional working for the Nazi apparatus. He couldn't be. They wouldn't allow such behavior, such open solicitation of information at parties, such, such . . . everything."

"Then whom does he work for?"

"You are missing my point. He is sending information to the Nazis. But I don't think he's doing it for money. Not even for gold."

"Why, then?"

He is a believer. He believes that fascism is the hope of his world. He believes what the old ones believed: only fire and blood will make a new world. Only fire and blood."

"She might in any case be in danger."

Winokur made a deprecating gesture with his hand. "Jerusalem told us to collaborate with the British. This stupid little exercise is nothing. The British don't need us. They make a gesture. And believers like Quinton don't know how to operate. They are very good soldiers, but very bad spies. They don't know what they're doing. She will be in and out of the house before he can read his morning portion of the Führer's gospel."

Chalfin leaned back in his chair. What Winokur had said made sense.

Late in the evening, the dwarf slipped a folded piece of paper into her hand. He had been waiting outside the curtain, and when she emerged he made a face, hopped on one foot, handed her the paper. Raya was tired; too tired, she felt, to read anything. It had been a surly night at The Trunk. Fights had broken out every hour. Whiskey had been spilled on the floor. Voices were louder than usual. By now she quickly recognized such nights in their early stages—and she chose older men as customers; they finished quickly and they were always satisfied.

But she was tired.

Finally, she unfolded the paper: "Please come to my house. Now or later. The party will continue all weekend. Please come."

The note was signed *Brian Quinton*. He had written his address beneath the name.

Raya went back into her room, pulled the curtain, and sat down on the bed. She could leave The Trunk at any time. No one cared. She was free. There were other whores in Cairo.

Oddly enough, she wanted to go to this party. The desire had nothing to do with the mission she had accepted. The word itself, *party*, was intriguing. The word defined the sort of event her mother had often spoken of. A place, a time where men and women walk about and talk to each other. Everyone looks beautiful. Everyone desires everyone else. No one acts according to the desire.

She lay back on the bed. Where was David? What was he doing? What was he thinking? She sat up and tore the note into shreds. She slipped out of The Trunk and hurried to her apartment. There she found the dress, folded carefully between two small woven rugs shoved under the bed. It had lain there for years, intact. A long scarlet evening dress with lifted shoulders and a low square neckline. Silk, that rustled as she pulled it on, then turned slowly in a circle as though waltzing. Her mother's dress. It fit Raya perfectly.

She stepped onto the balcony and looked down. The street was silent, the children asleep. She gazed hungrily at the familiar buildings. She knew all the people who inhabited these buildings and she knew which buildings they inhabited. She was at home here. But David was right: this is not home. She left the balcony, glanced in the mirror, and began her journey to Brian Quinton.

Occasionally she stumbled over the floor-length gown. The walk seemed interminable. She traversed streets she only vaguely remembered, or did not remember at all. After a while the landscape changed; the houses were larger and set further apart. Suddenly an immense house appeared, settled deep into a curve between land and water. She was amazed to perceive that the house was actually in the water. She had seldom looked at the river; it was too much a part of Egypt. Lights dazzled from all the windows, throwing brilliance onto the dark street.

A massive, ornamented brass knocker graced the door. She knocked. Once. Twice. Nothing happened. From inside the house came the sound of myriad voices.

She knocked four times more.

Suddenly the door swung open. Raya took an instinctive step backward. Standing in the doorway was the most beautiful woman she had ever seen! Tall. Thin. A tiny cross glistening at her neck.

"Who are you?" said the woman.

"Raya."

"*Raya,*" said Carla Boudine, lingering over the syllables as though to extract from them some meaning, preferably absurd.

"He asked me to come," explained Raya.

Carla laughed in recognition. "I'm sorry. I didn't realize.

128

You mean you're from there." And she pointed outward into the night, into the large undifferentiated Arab quarter. "Brian is choosing better," she remarked. "The last one had a tail."

Finally she made a gesture of invitation, and Raya entered the house.

"Do what you're supposed to do," advised Carla, "but conserve your energy. Brian's weekend parties truly last all weekend." And then she walked away.

Raya was alone among at least a hundred people. A hundred people were confusing. The house was confusing. Where did the rooms begin and end? Was there any end to the house? The men did not resemble the men she saw in The Trunk. Many looked like David, or like Colonel Malorange. The women were so beautiful. They walked so easily.

She took a tentative step down into the first room. Trays of food and drink were passed to her. Men greeted her, said a few words, moved away. Most of the guests spoke English, a few spoke French, some others, Italian. Hardly any men were in uniform.

Soon she began to relax. The laughter all around her was enlivening. The men were not those desperate men she usually met. They did not wear strange grins.

Her assignment seemed far off and vague. There was a book somewhere. Her promise to find it now seemed meaningless.

She saw Quinton. In a dark blue suit. His shirt was startlingly white. He waved, then came across the room to her.

"Raya," he said, extending both hands.

She took them both.

"I'm glad you have come. I'm very happy."

His attitude seemed to Raya simply that of a friend. He held her hands without a trace of sexual feeling. It occurred to her that he had not invited her to this party for himself.

"I've never seen you looking so lovely," he said.

His fingers played with the fabric of her dress.

"And your mother must have been lovely, also," he whispered.

Raya stiffened. Again, he seemed to know more about her than she had told him. Again, she had the feeling that he somehow anticipated her actions and her words. She changed the subject.

"You have a wonderful house."

"Oh, there's more, much more. You must walk around. You must meet all the people."

He kissed her on the cheek. He walked away.

Raya moved into another room and sat down on a soft, deep sofa. She closed her eyes and ears to the babble all around. In fits and starts she dozed, woke, drank something, dozed again. She had no idea of the time, and the time seemed unimportant.

Then a beast was chewing her arm. A large beast, from the river. Speckled scales encircled his neck and his teeth were covered with scarlet silk. As he chewed she felt no pain.

The dream dissolved. She awoke with a start to find Quinton kneeling beside her, his hand on her wrist.

"Raya," he whispered.

She sat up and looked around. The lights had been dimmed. She heard music.

"You were sleeping." He seemed concerned for her health. "Can you stay for the weekend?"

"Yes."

He patted her hand. They watched the people moving slowly through the room. He remained kneeling beside her. She wondered if dawn was close.

"Did you eat? Did you drink?"

"Yes," she said again.

He rose to his feet. "Come with me for a moment."

He led her by the hand through the house. The house now seemed peaceful. Those who had had too much to drink were asleep. In sleep they were not dissolute but peaceful.

They passed through an archway into another part of the

house. They went through a large kitchen and then down a hallway. Off the hall were rooms that looked like rooms—they had doors.

"The sleeping quarters," Quinton explained.

They entered a small study. Raya saw books neatly arranged in a tall bookcase. She stared at the books as Quinton opened a chest and took out of it a small wooden box.

"I must take care of you," he said, "for your efforts. I must make sure you receive at least what you would have earned at your regular employment." He dropped some coins onto the table.

Raya simply stared at them.

"Please, they're yours—take them," he said.

She obeyed, but felt uneasy.

"It's more than you make in a year of paper money at The Trunk. The coins are yours because you've been kind, and dependable, and because you are here this weekend."

She dropped the coins back on the table.

"No, take them," said Quinton. He gathered the coins and pushed them into her hands. "Don't you understand? They are gold."

Suddenly he stepped behind her and placed his hands on her shoulders. Then he slipped them down the front of her dress, pinching her nipples. He pulled her savagely against himself so that she felt the thrust of his knees into the back of her thighs. And then he stepped away. He stood quietly in the half-darkness.

"Two thousand years ago, coins were the only means of exchange. It was good then to be bought and sold. To buy you, Raya, I would have presented you with a round flat coin that had been designed and executed by an artist. Made of the most valuable substance on earth. Then, you see, you were worth beauty and metal—beauty and value. But now— ah, Raya. Now they buy you with paper notes, with British pounds and Egyptian pounds and French francs."

Raya slipped the coins into her purse. She knew they were valuable. In her world, the most valuable inheritance that could be passed from generation to generation was gold coin. Not clothes or paper money or jewels or books or wisdom. Only gold. It was the death-bed gift from God.

It would be nice, she thought, to present a gold coin to David. To wrap it in a soft linen cloth and give it to him. But no—David didn't want a gold coin. He wanted a book. It might even be in that bookcase. She realized that if she stayed the weekend she wouldn't be able to meet David at the café. But he had said that to miss one day was fine; only a second absence would lead him to think she was in trouble. Only the second absence.

Quinton had been saying something to her. He repeated, "Can you help me, Raya?"

"With what?"

"I want you to be nice to a man."

"Not to you?"

Quinton laughed. "So you *can* be coquettish!"

Raya had never met a man who alternated so quickly between violence and gentleness. One minute he hurt her, and the next it seemed that his whole world turned on her smile. Where had he come from? Whom had he loved? She thought that David and Winokur were wrong: Quinton could have no connection with men who machine-gunned Jewish children. No, it was not possible. She would tell David it was not possible.

"If you stay here," said Quinton, "I will bring him."

She smiled. They faced each other, smiling.

"I'm sorry about that lecture on economics. If that was what it was."

"Thank you for the money."

"But you have earned it." He went to the door, then turned and said, "What will you do with it?"

"Save it for my children," said Raya.

"And will they know how you came by it?"

"No."

"Would you lie to a child, Raya?"

"To my own."

He made a gesture toward her as if to touch her again, but he stopped himself. "The man's name is Akenfield. He is attached to the British legation in Turkey."

"His first name?"

"I don't remember," said Quinton. He turned quickly on his heel and left the room.

Raya went to the bookcase and pulled down the largest volume she saw. It was bound in leather and the pages were thick and grained. *Napoleon in Egypt.* She flipped through the pages but found no underlining. She looked for a moment at a drawing of French soldiers on the march, then replaced the book.

Now she took down *On Heroes and Hero Worship* and leafed through the pages. One was underlined. She felt a strange excitement. She began to search the book carefully. There seemed to be no other marks.

"What are you reading?"

Raya looked up.

The man closed the door behind him, walked to the table and turned the book so that he could read the title. "Quinton didn't tell me you read Carlyle."

Uncomfortable at being caught with the book, Raya replaced it on the shelf. She remained at the bookcase, some distance from her visitor, and looked at him. Middle-aged. Snow-white hair parted in the middle. Thin. Hunched, like David. One hand was slipped into the pocket of his dinner jacket. She wondered why so many Englishmen did not stand straight.

"And he didn't tell me your name," said Akenfield.

"Raya."

"Are you here often?"

"No."

Nor am I." He carefully unknotted his tie.

133

Raya stepped a little further away from him and began to undress slowly. For the first time she really looked at the room. There was a bed against one wall covered in blue velvet with black tassels that just touched the floor. The pillows were plump and fluffed. There was an immense armchair. A chandelier.

"Do you live in Cairo?" she asked.

Her own words startled her. She never asked a customer any questions. She never spoke to customers. But Raya was not ready to work. The red dress, the evening, the gold coins, the books—all that had compromised her professionalism. Or was it something else? Was it David? Was it getting harder and harder each time because of him? Because she loved him.

She sensed that Akenfield was undressing too slowly; her whore's wisdom picked it up. He folded his tie too carefully. He slipped out of his jacket too awkwardly. It meant that he was scared, or it meant that he didn't want to be with her. There were a thousand motives that this reluctance could signify. It could mean impotence or disgust or anything she treasured in her customers because it meant brief contact.

Quinton had said that Akenfield had been in Turkey. Many years ago her mother had told her that her father was in Turkey. Raya slipped out of her dress and folded it carefully. Her purse, with gold coins, lay on the table. Coins for her children. Children? Her hands lingered on the red silk dress. Could she still have children? Would David want children? Why not? All Englishmen did. And all Jews.

As he undressed, Akenfield was talking about how he had met Quinton and how much he liked him. The more he talked the more slowly he undressed. Why did these men use her when they didn't really want her? Why did they pay for what they didn't desire?

"And where did you and Quinton meet?" he asked.

"In Cairo."

"Yes, but where?"

Raya did not answer. She walked to the bed and pulled

back the cover. Her toes curled around the tassels. She looked up at the bookcase. So many books! A hundred, two hundred, perhaps more. How could she possibly inspect all of them? And what if there were other bookcases with other books in other rooms?

He continued to remove his clothing, piece after piece, seeming to reflect upon each, as though something substantial had been taken from his body. Finally he stood there undressed. His eyes were focused on her but not sexually. He was merely studying the situation of Raya Fahmi. She had forgotten his name. Was it Akenform? Artfield? She had lost it somehow. Not that it mattered—it didn't matter at all. She wondered if Quinton was at this moment thinking of them. She wondered why Quinton had become a pimp.

Akenfield sat down on the edge of the bed. "Were you ever in England, Raya?"

"Scotland," she lied, remembering the sheep dogs. David's sheep dogs.

"A magnificent country."

She hoped he would never move any closer. She didn't want him to touch her. Suddenly she was untouchable. This she felt throughout her body. If he touched her she would freeze; if he touched her she would turn to wood—impenetrable, unyielding. The feeling astonished her. For more than a year she had worked in The Trunk—she had whored, avoiding only those who seemed too dangerous. She had done whatever anyone asked her to do. And she had felt nothing—not despair, or revulsion, or pleasure. But this man . . . she didn't want him. Her hands were trembling. She had made a promise to David; she had promised to find the book; to find it she had to please Quinton; to please Quinton she would have to please Akenfield. Yes, Akenfield—that was his name.

Suddenly he touched her ankle.

"Do you like Scotland?" she said, trying to revive his disinterest. If only he wouldn't touch her!

135

"Oh, very much."

"Tell me why."

He removed his hand from her ankle. "Because it is a country that is really a fairy tale. No hunger, no tanks, no flames. Just a few bucolic valleys set in beautiful rugged hills. Of course, there are industrial towns and factories, but even the workers don't seem to know they are workers."

She searched for a question, for something to keep him talking. "Is your family there?"

"I have no family."

"No wife?"

"No."

"A brother? A sister?"

"None."

"Will you return to England?"

"When?"

"When the war is finished."

"It will never be finished," he said mildly.

"Never?"

"Never."

She turned onto her stomach. He stroked her back, her bottom, her thighs. She was afraid he could feel her utter stiffness. "Do you come to Cairo often?" she resumed.

"Yes, often."

"Do you speak French?"

"Indeed."

She had run out of questions, she could think of no more. Her mind went blank. He was kissing her back. She turned over quickly and moved up on the bed. His face registered surprise.

She had had too much to drink, perhaps. The room was blurred. Akenfield's skin was an eerie white in the incomplete light. He looked very young. He looked very old.

"Is something the matter?" he said.

"No."

She could not understand her own feeling. It seemed

impossible for her to . . . He kissed her breast. She moved toward him. Their faces were very close. She saw lines of age at his eyes.

On the table was the gold. Quinton had paid for her with beauty and metal. As he had said: beauty and metal. He had paid so that this man could enjoy himself. The thought was sobering and slightly frightening. She pulled his face into her breasts, holding him, keeping him there, to pay her debt.

She heard footsteps pass the door. Then voices. They faded away.

She relaxed. Her untouchability vanished. This was just another man between her breasts. She could do it as she had always done it. She could do it. Men were poor stupid creatures whose only talent was to murder each other. Stupid creatures (but for David). David. David, someday, would be between her breasts every morning, every evening, someday.

She pushed Akenfield away from her breasts, holding his face. She could go through with this because there would not be many more. It was near the end. They would not be able to buy her anymore. All the faces of the past were extinguished. She caressed his face. Soon it would be extinguished.

Akenfield was nervous. He couldn't understand this whore. She was on a string, swinging back and forth.

Raya put her hand between his legs and laughed. They were all the same down there. All the same. Would David ever be the same? Would it ever end with David? Would David ever be simply stiff and hard and the same?

Akenfield thought she was mocking him. He pushed her hand away and swung his legs over the edge of the bed. This unsettled Raya—she had to make him happy. She pulled him back, saying soft, poetic, loving words in Arabic. He didn't know the meaning but he could grasp the tone.

"Listen," she said suddenly.

"I don't hear anything."

"The river."

Yes, he thought, there was a sound, an ineffable sound.

"Listen," she repeated.

He pushed her down on the bed and his hands moved all over her and he kissed her breathlessly.

"Listen." She turned her face toward the wall. The Englishman entered her. She looked at him, thinking, Why do they always close their eyes?

It was over in a second. Akenfield rolled off her, cursing.

"I wanted it to last longer," he said.

She laughed and touched his face tenderly. These men were so sad. So sad. Stupid and sad.

He walked to the middle of the room and stood there for a moment vaguely. Then he went to his clothes, found a cigarette, and lit it. After a few puffs he said, "Will you be here tomorrow?"

"Yes."

"I mean *here*, in this room."

"I don't know."

"Do you find me undesirable?"

She didn't know what to say. She said nothing.

He rephrased the question: "Do you find me tolerable?"

"Yes."

He put out the cigarette and began to dress. Slipping on his trousers, he said, "Are you Quinton's woman also?"

"Why do you ask?"

"Ah, you are."

"What does it mean to you?"

"Nothing. Nothing at all. I think it's absurd to fall in love with whores." He brushed his white hair back with his hands. "But then again, it's very good to fall in love with whores."

"Why good?"

Akenfield laughed. He walked across the room and kissed her on the tip of her shoulder.

"Do you mean that if a man loves me, he loves me because I am a whore?"

138

"He loves you because you are dark and beautiful and your breasts are large."

"No," she smiled, "they are not large."

"Heroes have large breasts. You have read Carlyle. You know that."

"You said it was good to fall in love with a whore," Raya persisted.

"I don't know why I said it."

"Do many men fall in love with us?"

"Many?"

"Two? Twenty? One hundred?"

"Millions. It is a disease of civilization. Didn't you know that? It is the way we move what is between our legs up to our heart."

Raya flushed and was unable to speak again. When he left, Raya slept.

Late in the morning she awoke—frightened, sitting up abruptly, staring at the unfamiliar room. Then she remembered and sank back down. She saw the red silk dress, folded; she saw the purse with gold coins inside. She fell asleep.

Waking again, she saw a woman. The woman said, "Do you remember me?"

Raya nodded, sat up in bed.

"Here," said Carla Boudine, and lay a bathrobe on the bed.

"Thank you."

"I was rude to you last night. Forgive me. I know who you are now. My name is Carla."

Raya slipped into the robe without exposing any part of herself to Carla.

"I'm often rude to everyone, so don't take offense. I'm even rude to our mutual friend, Brian Quinton."

Raya felt uncomfortable beneath the woman's careful gaze.

"There's a bathroom in the hall. When you're ready, join us in the kitchen. I promise you one of the great delights of wartime Cairo: the famous surgeon, Dr. Quinton, unable to stitch a real wound, will be operating on an omelet."

With that remark she left the room.

Raya waited a moment, then went down the hall to the bathroom. Everything had been provided for her: soap, towels, comb, brush, mirrors, powder, perfume, and flowers.

Loud laughter led her to the kitchen, which was large and open at both ends. Several people were seated at a massive table. She didn't see Akenfield, but saw Quinton at one end of the table, standing with a recipe in one hand. On the table before him was a large bowl and a platter of immense tomatoes. He noticed her and called out, "Raya!" When she came to his side he put an arm around her shoulder. Everyone applauded, as though she were the assistant chef.

Raya flushed. She felt pleased, happy. There was a glow, a warmth in the room.

Quinton, in bathrobe and surgeon's mask, announced magisterially, "I will now break the eggs."

Again there was applause. Quinton released Raya and, one at a time, broke fifteen eggs.

"Now I will beat them" he declared. He did so amid noises of encouragement from the crowd.

"Now I will pulp the tomatoes."

Carla Boudine pounded the table. "No! Just slice them. Don't pulp them."

Quinton assumed an offended air. "The recipe, madam, says to pulp them."

"Slice them." She was emphatic.

He turned to Raya. "Will you corroborate this?"

She looked at the recipe, which said to pulp the tomatoes; then she glanced up at Carla, not at all certain that she wanted to contradict her.

But Quinton had already begun to pulp the tomatoes with a mallet. Juice squirted onto himself, Raya and several nearby persons. Some groaned, some laughed. Some ducked.

When the omelet was cooking safely in an omelet pan,

Raya sat down. Coffee was served. Jokes were exchanged. Finally they all ate the omelet.

After breakfast Carla Boudine took Raya on a tour of the house. "My career with Quinton is rather sporadic," she said, opening the sliding door that led into the master bedroom. A glass wall faced the river. "When we sleep together, we sleep here."

Carla Boudine sat down languidly on the bed. Raya, looking out on the Nile, felt that the woman was watching her again. There wasn't much traffic on the river—a few scows, a few fishermen. The river, the men, looked dirty and sullen and tired.

"I'm curious about something, Raya."

Raya turned to face her.

"I know what you are," Carla continued, "and I know he has an affection for you and for others like you. It fascinates me."

Raya was no longer listening. On the far side of the bed was a small night table. Two books lay on it, one on top of the other. A folded shirt half hid them. She must look at those books. Her eyes roved the rest of the room. A glass case held some papers, but no books. There were no other books in the room.

Carla was saying, "Does he visit you often?"

"No."

"But he does visit."

"Yes."

The conversation was awkward, even for Carla Boudine.

They left the room, Raya carefully noting the path. She would have to find her way back alone—if not this evening, then at the next invitation to the house.

It was almost one in the afternoon. She could still dress and meet David, but she decided to stay. She would go tomorrow, Sunday, and from the café she would go home.

The women parted at Raya's room. Raya put on her red silk dress and returned to the main part of the house—the

141

series of sunken rooms. A few servants who were cleaning took no notice of her. The guests had departed.

She was still tired and so went back to her room. Memories of Akenfield disturbed her. The house and the guests were foreign to her. She had no sense of being in a royal or wealthy household. They had all enjoyed themselves at breakfast; they all did exactly what they wanted to do; but there was an unease about the house. At least The Trunk was not confusing. Raya opened her purse and touched the gold coins. Probably David was sitting in the café, waiting for her. Perhaps he had already guessed that she was at Quinton's place. Perhaps he had gone to The Trunk and asked the dwarf. Perhaps he had gone to her apartment and known then that if she wasn't home and wasn't at The Trunk she must be here. With Quinton.

Late in the afternoon the guests began to arrive again. Raya moved among them, watching, smiling, exchanging remarks. Quinton, in a deep blue evening coat and pale yellow silk shirt, waved at her from across a room. She raised her hand slightly in response and smiled. More and more people came into the house. The crowd was thicker than the night before, as was the noise and the smoke. Everyone seemed to be drinking more rapidly.

Suddenly Quinton was by her side, slipping his arm under hers. She knew the meaning; she knew what he wanted. Raya returned to her room.

The man was younger than Akenfield, and less subtle. Quinton was doing him a favor which he would accept quickly, without conversation. She didn't ask his name. He didn't ask her name.

After him, there was another, and then another.

She thought, I am earning my gold.

After the fourth, she walked down the hall that led to the master bedroom, to the books. But Carla Boudine was standing alone in front of the door, smoking. Raya turned back.

In the hall was a heavy-set woman with a lovely round face. A different body, the same purpose. They nodded at each other. Two whores for hire.

She was glad that Quinton seemed to have forgotten about her. She sank down in a corner and sipped a drink that she couldn't identify. People sat down beside her, spoke to her, patted her arm, and left. She closed her eyes and thought of David. Of Scotland and Jerusalem. She thought of the red silk dress and thought of her mother. It was a revery of exhaustion.

Suddenly she heard Quinton's voice and opened her eyes. He was talking to a group of men just a few feet away. He was angry. He opened and closed his fist as he spoke, accenting his words with venom. Finally he slammed his fist into an open palm for emphasis.

The gesture startled Raya. Her spine straightened, her neck tightened. She had seen the gesture before; she knew the gesture. Quinton with the mallet, pulping the tomatoes. She remembered, then, that in the recipe "pulp" was circled.

The sound woke him. He sat up, flailed in confusion at the pillow. He shook the fuzziness out of his head. Had something fallen? Outside? Inside?

There was the same sound again. Now he knew that someone was at the door. He glanced at the bureau where, in the top drawer wrapped in a soft rag, lay a Beretta. He left the bed unarmed and opened the door.

"Raya," said Chalfin softly in disbelief. Raya, in a red silk dress, her face flushed, a parcel under her arm—how like a dream she was at his door.

She walked past him into the flat. She smiled at him, but he felt her sense of strain. He said, "Are you all right? Where have you been?"

She sat down on the bed and opened her purse. Gold coins fell like emblems onto the white sheet.

"For you, David," she said.

143

He stared. "Where did you get them?"

"From Brian Quinton."

He went over to the bed, sat down next to her, gathered the coins together, and put them back in her purse.

"I waited for you today. When you didn't come I thought you might be there."

"I was there," she said simply.

She lay her head on his lap. Her hair was damp from the night and seemed blacker than ever. He kissed her hair, keeping his lips there, keeping them there.

Abruptly she left him, moved to the middle of the room, and turned like a dervish so that her dress flared. He saw that she wore nothing underneath. She laughed with laughter unlike any he had heard from her before.

"I found it, David. I found it."

He looked at her incredulously. He wasn't sure of exactly what she was saying.

"The book! I found it. There, on the bed. In that bag."

He peeled away the paper and stared at the ragged, softcover cookbook. He opened it to the first page and saw that it had been printed in 1931 by one of those British institutes that used to inhabit Cairo. The book purported to present excellent and inexpensive menus for the families of British officials, teachers, functionaries, etcetera, using ingredients that could be purchased locally, in Egypt.

He flipped randomly to another page. A recipe for lentil soup. Two words on the page had been circled: *salt* and *drain*. In the right-hand margin was a single set of three letters: FAK.

Recipe after recipe revealed the same pattern: two words circled, one an ingredient and the other an activity; three letters adorned each margin.

It was an incredible stroke of good fortune. She had succeeded sooner than anyone would have thought possible. She had gone there and simply stumbled upon it.

"This must be it! Raya, this must be it!"

She nodded in fierce agreement.

144

There was no time for congratulations. Winokur had to see it, Malorange had to photograph it, and Raya had to bring it back quickly.

In a state of exhilaration they walked to Winokur's flat. Winokur greeted them in a frayed robe and Chalfin stared at his feet—pipestems, thin rails of bone.

Carefully, almost reverently, he looked through the book, recipe after recipe, page after page. when he was finished he turned back to page one and went through it all again, this time making notes on a pad.

Finally he said, "Maybe."

"It has to be the cipher," said Chalfin. "What other explanation is there for the circling and the letters in the margins?"

Winokur smiled. He went over to Raya and patted her on the shoulder. His medal of honor was thus bestowed.

"I will bring this to Malorange. He will know what to do with it. Then you must put it back where you found it. Do you understand?"

"Yes," said Raya.

Chalfin could see that the excitement of the search and find was wearing off. She seemed utterly tired.

"It will be brought back by courier in a few hours. He will wait across the street from Quinton's house. You will pick it up from him early in the morning, four hours from now," and Winokur looked at his watch, "at six o'clock. He will know who you are. Do you understand?"

"Yes," said Raya once again.

Winokur seemed to become absorbed with the untied cord of his robe. "And will you be going to Quinton's place," he asked in a kindly way, "next weekend, for his next party?"

Raya visibly stiffened. She looked at Chalfin, silently asking the answer. Then she looked back at Winokur.

"No," said Chalfin. "Her assignment is over when she returns the book this morning. She has done what we asked her to do."

145

"But it would be safer, I think, if she does return. At least for another weekend or two. That way there will be no suspicion."

The room was filled with silence.

Chalfin nodded to Raya. Winokur was right, he knew. It would be safer.

Winokur approached Raya and took both her hands in his. "I must tell you what we are doing. We are all Jews here. And you know the old saying, 'Only two kinds of people sleep well: the dumb, and the wise.'" He smiled at her. "It sounds better in Yiddish."

He dropped her hands and began to walk slowly about the room, talking as he walked, his accent growing thicker. "You are there because in a few weeks the British Army will attack Rommel. Quinton is sending messages to Rommel. The British Army will attack in force to the south, through the Quattara Depression, because no one thinks it can be done. We wish to make sure that Rommel believes the Army will attack to the north. Very simple. So, we ask you to go there for a little while longer. So, we ask you to be more brave. Be brave. We are with you and you are with us."

Then, with a sad wave of his hand, he dismissed her. She left the flat quickly. As soon as she was gone Chalfin exploded in a fury: "Why did you tell her anything? And why did you tell her a lie about the direction of the offensive? What was the bloody point of saying anything?"

Winokur ignored him and paid a visit to his coffee corner, sniffing beans, cleaning the grinding equipment. Finally he walked to the window and stood there, fiddling with the cord of his robe.

Chalfin, watching Winokur's move like a predator, eventually calmed. He was waiting for the moment when Winokur would speak.

Winokur let nine minutes go by before he spoke.

"On Tuesday morning, in the market, the big market, will be a beautiful woman. Her name, I have been told, is Carla

Boudine. Very beautiful. A companion of Quinton. She goes to this market on Tuesday to buy ripe tomatoes. You will go to this market, and you will stand next to her, and as you are looking at tomatoes you will tell her that the whore, Raya Fahmi, is working for the British, and that Quinton must be careful; then you will leave."

Chalfin, standing tall and straight, locked his knees to brace against the storm of weakness which was beginning to beat him down. He stood, and then he crumbled.

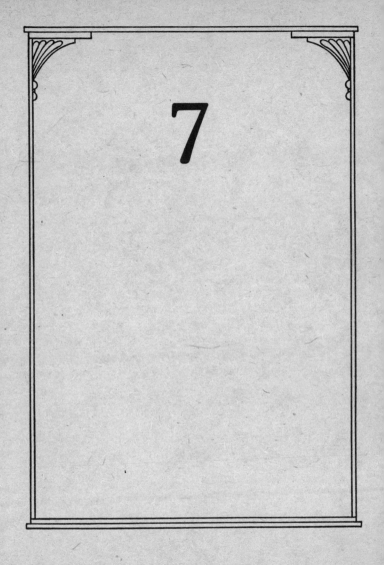

7

Chalfin lay on his bed, fully clothed. He had been on his bed for more than a dozen hours. After walking out on Winokur without speaking (without replying by so much as a gesture), he had gone directly to his flat, to his bed.

The late-morning sunlight streamed into the room. His shirt stank from dried sweat. From time to time he drew an imaginary line with an imaginary pen on the wall beside his bed.

He was still utterly weak. He began to speculate about Raya's mother and her mother's mother and so on and so on. He tried to visualize the long succession of her past. It was a lunatic tableau: with Moses out of Egypt, with the exiles to Babylonia, with the traders of Spain and Portugal, with the victims of the Inquisition to North Africa, and thence to Turkey and Athens and the Lebanon, and finally to Cairo. Or was it another way? Another passage?

Winokur's order could not be dealt with in his head. There was a sound outside the door. Someone must want to come in. That meant nothing to him. Nothing at all. A man's voice called out his name. Was that his father's voice? Chalfin sat up. Was his father at the door? He walked to the door and opened it.

Winokur lunged past him into the room. "You should never leave without saying good-bye. It is bad manners, even in our business."

Chalfin closed the door and sat down on the edge of his bed. Then he got up and splashed water on his face. Then he sat down again and looked steadily at Winokur. Winokur's shirt was white, short-sleeved, open at the collar, he noted.

"Never," said Chalfin. "Never, never, never."

Winokur leaned against the chest of drawers, smiling.

"Never," said Chalfin.

"So, you really do love the whore. I thought you were too smart for that."

"If I did not love her, nevertheless I would not betray her. She's working with us. We asked for her help, and she obliged. Now you want to murder her."

"She won't be murdered," Winokur corrected him. "I doubt that anything will even happen to her. They'll pressure her a little. Then she will tell them what she knows and they will throw her back onto the street, like a fish."

David stared at Winokur blankly.

"And besides, it is done every day," he continued. "You give a courier the wrong information and then you make sure he is caught. It's a British game, and a Russian game, and a German game."

"Raya Fahmi is not a courier."

"True. She's a whore."

Chalfin leaped off the bed, his hands clenched in the air. He came to a halt six inches from Winokur.

"David, are you going to hit me?" he asked sardonically.

They watched each other.

"You must listen to me, David, because what I tell you is true. I'm sorry you have fallen in love with this woman. I'm sorry I must ask you to do this." Winokur's tone was almost passionate. "But I *must* ask you and you *must* do it. You know that. You have given up your life. We have all done the same. We no longer have a right to certain luxuries." He circled Chalfin, lighting a cigarette. "Love is a luxury. Like a visit to a beautiful ski resort. It exists for the moment, and perhaps for the next moment. But you and I are in something that has to do with eternity—with thousands of years past and future, and with corpses. The bodies our brothers. One day I will be sacrificed. One day you will be sacrificed. Now it is her turn."

Chalfin was unable to answer. He gestured with his hand through Winokur's cigarette smoke.

"I think you will carry out the assignment in the market tomorrow morning. She is a tall beautiful woman who likes tomatoes. Just tell her what I told you to tell her."

Winokur shut the door loudly behind him. He liked to remind David that the world was in a state of war.

She dreamed she was a child again, holding her mother's hand. They were walking through a large garden filled with beautiful trees and flowers that hung from baskets. Nothing was actually planted in the earth. Her mother was speaking in a voice so low that Raya couldn't hear the words, which she very much wanted to hear. They sat down on a stone bench. Suddenly a fine mist filled the garden, enveloping them. She turned toward her mother, who was weeping.

Raya sat up in bed. She saw the red dress hung over the chair. Then she saw Quinton.

"You are beautiful when you sleep," he remarked.

"I dreamed about my mother."

He came to the bed and sat down beside her. "Was it a good dream?"

"No."

He pulled back the sheet and touched the hollow of her throat. "Did you enjoy your walk last night?"

"Oh, yes."

"Weren't you afraid to walk alone at that hour?"

"I have nothing to fear."

"Where did you go?"

"I walked along the river."

He kissed her throat, his lips pressed against her for a full minute. She stared at the ceiling. She could sense that he did not want her as he had wanted her in The Trunk. She felt no threat from him, and no triumph over him.

Then he kissed her eyes, like a mother kissing the eyes of her child, thanking God for the gift of sight. She recalled, suddenly, the photo of the naked people about to be shot.

He left her abruptly. He walked over to the red dress hung on the chair and smoothed out a fold in the silk. He looked back at her. "Do you love anyone, Raya?"

"Yes, I do."

"Is he Egyptian?"

"Yes," she lied evenly.

"And when you leave The Trunk you will marry him. And have many children. And the males will be circumcized. And live in a house with a wall and a vegetable garden. Yes?"

She would not answer. She watched him rearrange her red dress on the chair. "And you, do you love?"

"Yes."

"A beautiful woman?"

"No, a thing."

"What thing?"

"There is no word for it in Arabic or English. There is no word for it in language we know."

She saw that he had become sad, and he no longer looked at her.

"Will you stay with us again next weekend?"

"Yes," she replied. "I will."

"Good. There shall be more gold, so your life may become more pleasant, more quickly." He left the room.

Raya pulled up the sheet and tried to fall asleep again. She was tired and would have to work that night. But she couldn't sleep. Maybe it was the excitement—the triumph she had shared with David. Or maybe it was the odd sensation on her eyelids where Quinton had kissed her.

Chalfin spent the day in his room, thinking first of a bicycle trip he had once made through Wales, and a four-day drunken collegiate spree in London, and other bits and pieces from his English past.

Then the questions commenced, like pieces of sugar placed on aching teeth. He must be calm and analytical. Winokur had said it must be done. Why? Winokur himself had also said that this offensive was not the war—the war was in Europe, a thousand-mile front. The Nazis would not be broken because what is left of the Afrika Korps is destroyed by Montgomery's offensive. It is the Russians who will break the back of the beast. Winokur himself had said that the entire Quinton escapade was meaningless, a stupid little operation in a stupid little war. Why throw Raya away for that?

It was too little to throw Raya away for, too stupid, too meaningless, too unimportant. One betrayed a loved one only if there was cosmic significance. If the death of Raya somehow could cause the death of Hitler, he would gladly slit her throat. The thought took him back. No, for nothing and for no one would he ever hurt her. For nothing. For no one. For nothing. For no one.

He felt himself sliding, inexorably, into the trap of reason. If one believed in Jerusalem reborn and the destruction of the German beast, and one knew that the former could not occur without the latter—then everything must be done to accomplish the latter. And that "everything" meant big and small, absurd and meaningful, for no one really knew the ultimate conclusion of events.

He was falling down the slippery sides, falling all the way down. There is no difference between big and small, here. He didn't know what would happen. He couldn't know. He didn't know what the whole thing meant, he couldn't know.

He had reached the bottom. The bottom was like a pane of glass. He would kill himself for what he believed in. Therefore, he must be prepared to kill others. He would accept his own betrayal, calmly, therefore he must be able to betray others. That it was a woman he loved meant nothing.

The logic was like a winding sheet. It could crush all the juices out. No one could or should withstand that logic; no one could or should withstand necessity. A thousand therefores, a thousand major and minor clauses, and no matter what was thought . . . no matter what was conjured up . . . no matter how many times the face and head and body and arms of Raya Fahmi danced on his tongue—there was no way to sneak out.

So he spit her out.

As midnight closed, he simply knew that he would betray her. The betrayal existed, massive and concrete as a city. He could as easily level Jerusalem to the ground as he could not obey Winokur's order.

At one in the morning he opened a bottle of Spanish brandy that he had carried with him from Jerusalem. He dug the cork out of the neck with a knife, and poured into the bottle cap, using it for a glass. He drank off the bottle rapidly, then began to arrange all his belongings on the bed. The pistol, the clothes, the books, the comb and razor. He stepped back and stared at these items as though seeing them for the first time. Sweat poured down his face. Was he preparing his own obituary? All those authors: Hopkins and Marvell, Nietzsche and Schopenhauer, Virginia Woolf, Thomas Hardy, Jack London, Isaac Babel, Moses Hess, and Shestov—what were they telling him?

Chalfin picked up the Beretta. He checked the mechanism. Why shouldn't he die? Betrayers should die. But how and when? When and how? He flung everything off the bed.

I have to see her again, he thought, or at least be somewhere near her.

He loaded the Beretta, slipped it into his belt, and left the flat. He walked very fast, sometimes breaking into a run. When he reached The Trunk he hovered at the door, unable to go in.

"Inside, go inside," said the dwarf, tugging at his arm and making obscene noises. Chalfin shoved him away and crossed to the other side of the street.

What could he say to her? He began to pace. What could he say?

He would go in and sit down at a table. She would come to him. They would walk together to the small room. He would undress. She would pick up the sponge. Then he would press the pistol into his head and pull the trigger.

It was true. If he saw her he would kill himself. If he saw so much as her profile he would blow his brains out.

If only he could hold her. If only he could watch her hair.

He turned and walked away. The brandy now made his legs leaden. Beggars slept in the shells of burned houses. Why not? Chalfin stepped into the charred remains of a kitchen, took off his jacket, and lay down. He held the Beretta in both hands and stared up at constellations he could not identify.

"Naharak sa'id!"

Chalfin leaped up, weapon poised, eyes blinking in the morning sun.

The old man who had wished him a good morning muttered when he saw the gun and moved off, picking his way over the rubble.

Chalfin looked at his watch. It was time.

Shaking sand and dirt from his clothes, he began to walk toward the market. There was a slight buzz in his ears. His sense of distance was inaccurate.

In the ramshackle market, the merchants were arranging their fruits and vegetables. Chalfin strolled among them. He stationed himself beside the stand with the largest tomatoes, and waited. The market was filling slowly with shoppers.

Wearing a shawl, carrying a large straw basket, she strode

157

into his line of sight. Very tall, very beautiful—yes. She paused at the stand and checked the tomatoes, turning each one over, searching for imperfections.

Now, he thought. *It is time.*

She chose one tomato after another, filling her basket.

I must move now.

His mother, he remembered, made him kiss a crust of bread before throwing it away. He had to kiss it and say, "God, forgive me for throwing bread away."

Chalfin walked toward Carla Boudine.

The man was hurting her, moving into her as if he meant to kill her. His hands were pressed into her face, his nails piercing her skin. Suddenly he called out a name, or a curse—she couldn't understand what he had shouted. He rolled off her, stood up, and looked at her with disgust. He grabbed his clothes and backed toward the curtain.

He put on his clothes in a hurry, and vanished.

Raya began to dress slowly. The word he had shouted had sounded something like *Teeko.* Perhaps it was the name of a woman. Or a place. Or an uncle, or a pet goat—or no name at all. Raya hesitated before leaving the room. She looked down at her hands, which were trembling. Impulsively she put them into the basin of water she used for her customers. And she drew them out quickly, as though she had been burned.

Raya kept close to the wall that night because The Trunk was too quiet. When the place was noisy it was safe, and the guests drank and talked and bought women. But when it was quiet, when the revelers could hear each other, there was danger. The Trunk was much too quiet now. Silent. She could hear a chair scrape, she could hear a glass drawn across a table.

"You will find no customers along the wall."

Raya turned toward the voice.

"Moussa!" she cried out, and rushed to the corpulent man seated alone. "Moussa, Moussa!"

She flung her arms around him. He patted her on the head, his face lit with a sublime and appreciative smile.

"You must sit, you must sit," he suggested.

Raya sat down across the table from Moussa and extended both hands, which he grasped in his own. "It has been so long!"

"As long as you have been here," he said.

"You look very well."

"I am like the sun."

"Yes, the sun!" She pressed her hands into his, then sat back in her chair. It was Moussa who had arranged this job for her in The Trunk. It was Moussa who had said that one must live, one must sell, and one must always sell what the other person wants to buy.

It was Moussa who had pointed out to her that she was starving, and that there was no one in the whole city of Cairo who cared, or who would give her a single crust of bread. Not the Jews, not the Muslims, not the Copts, not the Europeans.

"Wait here," she said laughing, and suddenly rushing away, back into the room area. She returned in a few minutes, her face sad.

"I have none left, Moussa."

"None of what?"

"Those pieces of linen you gave me when I came here. White, with the red birds, the ones you told me to give to my best customers so they would remember me, so that every time they wiped the sweat from their face, they would remember the pleasure I gave them. They're all gone now."

"Have you prospered here?" he asked.

"I have saved."

"Good. When you save enough, you can leave."

"Why have you stayed away?"

"I have much to do. The Europeans tire me. They make large requests."

Then Raya told him that she had met a man whom she loved. Then she stopped talking. They sat in silence, enjoying

159

each other's company. To Raya he looked exactly the same as always—a bit sadder, a bit rounder, a bit more resigned, but the same. And the kindness was still inside him, a great ball of kindness like the sun, that warmed all those he circled.

Moussa pulled a large white handkerchief with a border of red herons from his pocket and wiped his forehead ritualistically.

"I have brought someone to see you," he said. As he observed her frown, he held up a hand. "No, not that. This is an old friend."

"Who? Which old friend?"

"You must think."

"I don't know, Moussa, I can't think who it is."

"He is waiting for you outside. He has not seen you for many years. He has been in Beirut and Paris, and other places."

It could not be. Moussa was lying. There was only one person she knew who had been to Beirut and Paris: the man her mother had said was her father. Raya brought her hands up to cover her face.

Moussa looked at her sadly. He stood up. "We will walk outside together."

Raya remained as she was, hands over her face.

"Come," he urged. Then, as she simply stayed there, he put his hand under her arm and helped her rise. "Come. He cannot wait too long."

She followed Moussa toward the rear door. Who will be there? Why had he come? Did she really have a father? Why was her mother dead? Why? What? Where? When? The night air on her face made her dizzy. She stood beside Moussa, just outside the door, breathing deeply.

"He will be here in a moment."

Her mother had said it would be dazzling—his coming—like a flash of silver in the night sky. Her mother had said he would come back with jewels and rugs and foreign fruits. Raya was no longer afraid; she wanted to meet him; she wanted David to meet him.

The blow fell at the base of her neck. Her hands stretched out to meet the ground. Just before the world went black she saw the face of Moussa Tmai—detached, but nevertheless sad.

Chalfin was scuffing at the floor with his shoe. Winokur rummaged haphazardly through Raya's belongings. Chalfin walked to the balcony and stared down at the street.

They had been to Quinton's hospital, then to his house, and now they were in Raya's flat. Gone, all were gone. Vanished.

"I told you he was not a professional. He got frightened, he took his wireless and the whore and he ran. He won't get out of Cairo."

Chalfin was not listening to Winokur. He was listening to himself. *God, forgive me for throwing bread away.* That was all he heard.

"Malorange will find them quickly," said Winokur with assurance.

Now, thought Chalfin, now—fling yourself down. It would be quick, and good. How good it would be not to think. The head would hit the cobblestones. I would feel nothing. Only oblivion. Raya's neighbors would form a circle around me and stare.

They would say, "Here is the man who made a decision. Here is the man who followed the logic of the event. And look at him. Look at the fool. He is dead. Squashed."

He turned to face Winokur and said, "I want to leave Cairo."

"You can easily be transferred back to Jerusalem."

"No, I want to go over."

"You mean, David, you want to die."

"I want to fight. I want to kill Nazis. I want to act. Europe! Not Cairo!"

Winokur sighed, and sat down on Raya's bed. "Every night," he began, looking sadly at Chalfin, "thousands of airplanes drop thousands of heroes on Occupied Europe.

161

They bring weapons, radios, messages—who knows. It is all futile. They really do nothing. They simply die. The British drop Poles, Yugoslavs, Hungarians, Danes, Frenchmen, even a few of their own. They are not prepared to fight Hitler yet, so they feel they must do something. These flights go on and on to oblivion. On and on . . . without stopping . . . parachutes raining down on Europe. For nothing."

Chalfin said, "I want to go over."

Winokur jumped to his feet and shouted, "Then you'll go! I'm tired of babying you. We will drop you into Salonika to find Jews, and there you can fall in love with a Greek whore."

"When? When will I go?"

"When, when, when. Tonight. What about tonight? I will drive you to the airfield myself, right now. You can spend a few hours preparing yourself. We will drop you tonight."

Winokur waited for his words to sink in. He leaned forward on the balls of his feet, as if expecting Chalfin to finally pull back, to say that "tonight" is too soon.

But Chalfin said nothing. He could not understand Winokur's sudden acceptance of his own dream. He could not allow himself to question motives or twists or turns or subtleties—the goal was in sight.

They left Raya's flat, and an hour later they were driving north in a small, groaning Ford. They did not talk. Winokur was agitated. He shifted gears with a vengeance. Occasionally he said something in a vehement Yiddish. Once he pulled the car off the road and asked Chalfin to reconsider. Chalfin saw no reason to reconsider, or to move, or to speak, or to reflect.

The airfield, just outside Alexandria, consisted of a landing strip and a large hangar, both heavily camouflaged. They were stopped at the hangar's entrance by a man in civilian clothes with a tommy gun, who quickly recognized Winokur and passed them through.

"Wait," said Winokur, then vanished behind a crumbling wood door. Chalfin waited. The hangar was crammed with boxes, parachutes, weapons. He recognized a stripped-down British night bomber—the only plane in sight.

The sound of laughter came to him from behind the closed door. At least he thought it was laughter. He seemed to have lost the ability to discriminate. It might be someone weeping. He looked up and saw that the guard with the tommy gun was watching him.

Winokur came through the door and closed it behind him. He waited for the guard to leave. "It is all set," he then said.

Chalfin nodded.

"His name is Henri, a French Jew, from Marseilles, I think—he is very dark. He will see you shortly. He asked if you were a radio operator. I said no. He asked if you could strip weapons. I said no. He asked if you could speak Greek or Yiddish or German. I said no. He asked my why you are going. I said, to die. He asked who had authorized you. I said I had. He owes me a favor so he agreed. He will brief you. You will be dropped. Then make contact, then take out a few adventurers, or at least get them to the partisans. He will tell you the route. The plane leaves tonight. I'll write a letter to your father and hold it until you die. If you survive, I'll tear it up. If I never hear from you again, I will wait six months, and then mail the letter."

Chalfin could not imagine the contents of that letter. What would Winokur say? "Dear Mr. Chalfin: Your son died in the service of . . ." No. Winokur would write a parable, one of his delicious Polish/Yiddish philosophical knots, and then end it with a flourish—"By the way, your son, David Chalfin, was shot to death in a Greek village. The bullets, nineteen of them, entered the throat and head. He did not suffer." Chalfin realized that Raya would not be spoken of—not a word, not an inkling. But how could that be?

Winokur turned and stared at the plane. Turning back to Chalfin he raised his hands as if to question something—anything: the planets in orbit, the bees in hives. Then he shook his head.

"You had better go," said Chalfin.

Winokur embraced him, and said something incomprehensible in Yiddish. He released Chalfin a moment later and walked away, out of the hangar.

Chalfin stationed himself by the door to wait for Henri. It occurred to him that he was a virgin—a perpetual virgin who had been raised never to understand, and thus always to betray. That was why Winokur had agreed to send him, and why Henri had agreed to accept him. They couldn't withstand the joy of letting a virgin jump among Nazis.

The guard returned with his tommy gun, bringing Chalfin a tin cup filled with milk, a slice of white bread, and three olives. Chalfin took the food. His voice broke as he thanked the man, and he was ashamed.

She turned in the darkness, noting a stench of river. Every part of her body ached. Darkness surrounded her. Something seemed wrong with her neck. Slowly her eyes focused, grew accustomed to the darkness. Her wrists were roped together. The rope circled her neck, her knees, her ankles.

Where was Moussa? Where was her father? Was she in The Trunk? The room was small. A beam of light slid under the door. Raya started to cry, struggling against the rope. From outside the door came the sound of voices, blurred voices.

When the door opened there was light, and she saw the shapes of people in the doorway.

"Cut her loose," someone said.

A figure bent over her and roughly pushed her around, untying the rope.

She fell forward when freed, then stood up.

"Light the lamp," someone said.

She closed her eyes as the room became bright. She heard the sound of a door closing.

"Well, Raya."

She opened her eyes to see Brian Quinton, standing leisurely, one hand in his pocket. "Where am I?" she asked.

164

"On the Nile."

"In your house?"

"No, another place. But wherever you are on the Nile, it cleanses. You should know that."

"What happened to me?"

"You were knocked unconscious."

"Why? By who?"

He stepped toward her, brushed back dark strands of hair from her forehead.

"Why am I here?" she asked nervously.

"To talk, Raya, just to talk. We have always talked well together."

He seemed the same man but a different man. He was looking at her differently.

"I'm frightened. I want to leave."

"Soon. Soon."

"Can I have water?"

He brought her a cup of water, which she drank greedily in two long gulps.

Then she looked at him and said, *"Thank* you."

"You should not have trusted them, Raya. You should not have trusted any of them. The tall Englishman told us. He told us that you are not as you appear."

He is lying, she thought. She rubbed her wrists and ankles to restore circulation. He is lying.

"This Englishman is tall and thin. He told Carla Boudine all about you—in the market, as she was choosing tomatoes. He was wearing a suit and a white shirt without a tie, and a Beretta was tucked in his belt. She says he is a polite young man. She says he told her a fascinating story. He told her you are working for the British.

She seemed to collapse. He took her arm and steadied her. *David,* she thought. It was all she could think.

But she could see him telling, speaking, she could see him among the tomatoes. His eyes were half shut so she could not see their color. There was a smudge of dirt on his cheekbone.

He was grinning. A wide grin. He was laughing at her and mocking her. She could see the crease in his brown suit and she could see that little hollow on the side of his neck where she had kissed him.

"Tell me exactly what you did, what you were told, whom you reported to. And why you did it. Then, Raya, you can go."

She shook her head. She could not understand what had happened.

Quinton reached into his pocket and brought forth a pistol. The dark gunmetal contrasted sharply with his red hair. "They made a fool of you. You are too fine a woman to be made foolish. Tell me what you know. Then go in peace."

Peace. Raya could not imagine what peace was. She knew it existed, somewhere, in a different city. There could be peace when the sun was shining and the weather was cool and there was enough bread and milk for all. But as for the thing itself—that she didn't know.

"*Abadan, abadan,*" she said. Never, never. It had come from her without thought. It meant nothing. It meant everything.

The shot rang out. Instinctively she reached down to catch the flow of blood from her thigh. She screamed, and the sound seemed to flow out toward the river.

8

The wine was gone, and also the anchovies and the biscuits and the canned fruit. Tomlinson's face was a livid red, and the skin peeled, and his eyelids were cracked. He was still pulling the rotting corpse by a rope. From time to time he stopped and brushed the flies off the Italian's eyes and ears and uniform. The flies were a plague.

They reached the river, and Tomlinson could make out the lines of the city. He slid the Italian into the water, holding the rope tightly, and watched the corpse float in the dirty brown river. When he thought the Italian was clean he pulled him out. Then Tomlinson jumped in himself, standing rigidly as the water swirled around him.

He climbed out and lay down next to the Italian on the baked mud of the shoreline. "Tomorrow we will go in, Pietro. I will take you to the woman, and she will make you the happiest man on earth. She is dark. Her hair is beautiful. She

169

rarely speaks. Why should she speak? Oh, she will like you, Pietro. You rarely speak."

Tomlinson went on chatting to the corpse as he cleaned his automatic weapon and carefully checked the mechanism.

Suddenly he became morose. Pietro could not be presented to the woman in his condition. The remaining buttons of his tunic were dull with dirt, foul with grime. Tomlinson began to clean the buttons. He scraped away the desert with his nails, spat on the buttons, rubbed them with the back of his arm. Soon they were shining, and even the design was visible.

"Now you can be presented," he said, and rolled the corpse away. He put his head in his hands. He had forgotten Pietro's ears—probably they were full of sand. There was so much to clean. Tomlinson dozed.

A smell woke him. He quickly loaded the weapon, raised a finger to his lips and cautioned Pietro to be silent. A strange smell, of animals somewhere beyond the bush. He crawled toward it, crawled a hundred feet, and peered through the brambles.

Walking in single file were a woman, a boy, and three donkeys. Tomlinson stepped in front of them, weapon raised. The woman grasped the boy in her arms. Tomlinson fired two short bursts at their feet. Dirt covered them all. The woman was screaming. Tomlinson suddenly lost interest.

He went over to one of the donkeys, stood before it, and returned its stare. For a long time they looked at each other. He is the saddest thing on earth, thought Tomlinson, even sadder than me, even sadder than English cows.

He led the beast away, deaf to the curses of the woman.

He brought the donkey to Pietro.

The donkey looked down at the corpse.

"You will carry him into Cairo," said Tomlinson to the donkey.

The blood she tasted was her own blood. She had brought it up from her leg with her hand, and it tasted strange on her lips, like good meat that had been cooked wrongly. There was a blanket over her head and she knew she was in the back of a car, and the car was moving. It bounced and jerked and the pain rose and subsided, and when the bounces were greater the blanket moved and she could see the night through the side window.

She knew she was going to die soon. She knew that Brian Quinton would place the gun against her head this time.

Her eyes ached, even more than her leg. She brought her hand to her mouth again, using the small finger on her right hand to taste the blood.

A face seemed to reach down from the blanket. First the face was David; then it changed, became older, paler. She reached out, instinctively, and the face vanished against the blanket.

The car swerved and she was slammed against the seat. She regained her balance in spite of the pain. If I am going to die, she thought, I must die happy, joyous.

She remembered when her mother had been joyous. Years ago. Raya was small and she was holding her mother's hand and standing in a crowd of people outside the synagogue. Suddenly the doors were flung open and men walked out, holding scrolls high above their heads. They walked slowly through the people, who sang, danced, and clapped. And Raya's mother, still holding her tightly, had pushed through and leaned over and kissed the scroll. And her face was flushed and her eyes danced, and Raya had been frightened.

The car swerved again and this time Raya cried out from the pain in her leg. Seconds later she felt the fist smash down onto the blanket and onto the side of her neck. She fought to be joyous. She fought her pain and fright. She tried to remember her mother's face, but it was futile.

The rough blanket lay on her. Where was David now? She asked herself. What had she done wrong?

"It was your Samuel Johnson who said it—something like: 'Port is good for gentlemen, but if you wish to be a hero, you must drink brandy.'" Henri smiled and passed Chalfin the bottle.

Chalfin couldn't remember the quote, but he believed the Frenchman, and drank the brandy. Henri had given him the "heroes course": six hours of instruction. Chalfin had learned the terrain of the drop zone; he had learned the names of the people who would meet him; he had learned the escape routes. The lessons were all verbal. Henri identified a place, a part of a weapon, a name, and Chalfin repeated it. Name and repetition, hour after hour.

Henri's face had been a blank. He trained Chalfin the way a dog was trained—without emotion. There had been no training in the use of a parachute. Henri said it was better to know nothing. All you had to do was stand up in the plane, hook the ring, and jump. If it opened everything was fine. If it did not open, it did not open.

They passed the bottle back and forth until it was empty.

"Sleep for an hour or two. The plane will take off around midnight. Now I must find you some hero's clothes."

Henri returned shortly with a pair of rough cut trousers, a dark wool shirt, a black peasant's jacket, heavy brown shoes.

"Put them on before you sleep, so you will learn to love them. Leave your clothes on the ground—we will burn them tomorrow."

Chalfin nodded and began to undress.

"There will be others jumping with you," Henri said, "with different missions. It would be best to say nothing to them."

Then the Frenchman stepped back and raised his hands, as if to tell Chalfin it was impossible to say good-bye in any formal sense; that he understood life and death in certain situations but he could understand nothing now. Henri vanished.

Chalfin stretched out between two wooden crates. The trousers chafed his legs, the jacket was too small. He wondered why the Frenchman had quoted Samuel Johnson. Lying there, Chalfin tried to recall anything he had read by or about Johnson. He remembered that Johnson would some-times, in the midst of a gluttonous meal, suddenly leave his seat, kneel beside the table and loudly recite the Lord's Prayer, then return to his seat. And Johnson had once hit a venal bookseller on the head with a book, sending the man sprawling. That was all he could remember.

He turned and pressed his face against the concrete floor. It was cold and damp. More, I must remember more about Johnson. But he had lost the memory of Johnson, and in its place came Raya. He ground his face into the floor, wanting to break the bone. Sitting up, he noticed a figure standing about twenty feet away in the hangar. Too dark to see the person clearly. Then there were two figures, whispering. Finally they walked away.

He was alone again. Touching his face, he realized that he had been crying. He wiped the tears on his sleeve.

Now there were audible voices in the distance and he could see the occasional flash of a cigarette being lit. The heroes were gathering. He sat there, waiting to be called. In the silence it was bearable. But when there was noise, the furies would descend—visions of Raya hurt, Raya savaged, Raya bleeding. And Raya screaming. That was the worst, Raya screaming.

Suddenly a flashlight beckoned him. A line had formed, and each in turn received a parachute, then gathered their weapons and packs. The plane had already been pushed out into the field. Chalfin followed his comrades. Their packs, chutes, and maps were carefully checked before they climbed inside the plane.

On the inside the plane had been stripped. They sat four on each side, on the floor of the plane, their backs pressed against the slight curvature of the sides.

There was no light. No one spoke. The engines sputtered, then took. Chalfin leaned forward as the plane started down the runway, and when it rose he exhaled his breath joyously. It had all come down to this—to his flying there to kill them.

Everything was now solved, paid off, clearly defined. There was no future now, only a past. There was nothing to think about. No reason for chagrin or hatred or regret. He was going *there.*

The plane flew low out over the Mediterranean, very low. Chalfin's eyes were becoming accustomed to the strange light in the plane. The face across from him was Slavic, encased in a leather hat, with heavily whiskered jowls. The man stared back at him.

Chalfin wanted to say something profound to the man. Something about the beauty of them jumping together from a plane into an alien land to kill Nazis. Something about being dropped from the sky, carrying a glittering truth. The man stared fixedly at Chalfin, as if the focus gave him balance.

The plane droned on. Chalfin began to feel a numbness, a distinct lethargy. It was good to be lulled like this. It suppressed the image of Raya.

"Fighters! Fighters! Fighters!"

The low, hoarse shouts came from the cabin. Chalfin understood nothing. Again the shouts came.

Splintering, hissing, metallic noises exploded all around him. His head slammed against the side of the plane and then he pitched forward. Monstrous sounds broke his head into pieces. He looked up. The Slavic face was gone. Bits of flesh and fabric and bone were scattered around jagged holes on the opposite side of the plane. Again, the sounds came.

Sister Charlotte crossed herself quickly in the half-lit corridor. The act was intuitive at the moment she saw the woman. A most beautiful woman, standing in the corridor, dressed in utter simplicity and elegance. Sister Charlotte always crossed herself in the face of death, or life, or beauty.

"Can you help me?" asked Carla Boudine.

"If I can, I will."

Her face is particularly beautiful, thought Sister Charlotte.

"I am looking for Brian Quinton."

174

"But he is gone," said Sister Charlotte.

Yes, she thought, gone. And, in a sense, Sister Charlotte was relieved because the death of the British officer had become a canker in her soul. She could not absolve Quinton of responsibility. She was not prepared to absolve him. She was not able to stop thinking about him. The reality of Quinton was something neither her experience, her training, nor her piety had prepared her for. She could deal with saints and she could deal with thieves; alas, Quinton was none of these. He was the mystery that her faith could not touch.

"Where has he gone?"

"We don't know. He simply didn't arrive. We sent someone to his house. He is not there. And his office has been cleaned out."

"Are you sure?"

"Yes. Come. I will show you."

She turned and walked down the corridor, Carla Boudine following. Then she opened the door to Quinton's office and turned on the light. She extended a hand to evidence the emptiness.

She looks so forlorn, so sad, thought Sister Charlotte. Why did this stranger suffer so over the loss of their physician? Then she flushed, realizing that this woman must have loved him. It is from the heart, part of the heart. Oh, she remembered. She remembered what it was all about.

"And no one knows?" asked Carla Boudine.

"No, no one. He is simply gone. You may look if you wish," said Sister Charlotte, gesturing toward the desk. Ordinarily she would not let a stranger investigatge hospital property. But this was different. This was a higher calling.

Carla Boudine hesitated a moment, then moved quickly. She opened each desk drawer. She opened the file cabinet. Nothing was left of Brian Quinton. She faced Sister Charlotte. "Who did this?"

"We don't know. Someone came and emptied the office, but we don't know who."

"Someone has to know something!" She kicked a discarded bottle of ink across the floor. "Someone must know something!"

"Maybe he will be back tomorrow," said Sister Charlotte, although she didn't believe this. No man would empty his office if he wished to return.

"Do you know him well?" asked Carla.

"Not well. He was a fine doctor. A fine doctor." She thought it was fitting that such a mysterious man would be loved by such a beautiful woman.

"You know, of course, that he was a very Christian man." Sister Charlotte smiled, and lowered her head.

"Yes, a very Christian man," continued Carla Boudine, "and that is why I'm looking for him. I wish to give him a Christian gift, the kiss of peace." She opened her small purse and held it toward Sister Charlotte. All Sister Charlotte could see in it was a small brown revolver.

The plane had bellied onto the sea and then disintegrated. Five men had exited but only three were still afloat, their arms clutching a wooden box that had been so fastidiously nailed it was still waterproof. Chalfin's weapons were missing and so were his shoes and most of his clothes. For many hours he had felt headless. He heard the lapping of the water, he saw his comrades, he felt nausea and pain, but there was nothing to process these sensations.

When lucidity returned he first reasoned that he was, indeed, in the wine-dark sea. He was in it, clinging to a piece of wood. His second thought was that a whale would swallow him, like Jonah. Like his favorite Bible picture book, of the tall thin man sitting morosely in the bowels of the whale, waiting to be spat out.

Then he began to explore himself, to see what had happened to him. Nothing was really the matter. All his limbs seemed intact. There were intermittent chills and pains in the joints of his fingers from clinging to the wood. He looked over at the other two men. One was wounded, his blood mixing with the sea. His eyes were open, but looked only straight ahead. The other man appeared to be sleeping. Humming noises came from his throat. Chalfin called out to them, but there was no response.

The sea washed over them and pushed them up, swirled around them, and shook them out. One moment he couldn't breathe and the next moment he rode high on the water in a dizzying spiral.

In the first predawn light, the wounded man slipped away. He had been there, and then he was gone. Chalfin felt no remorse, no sadness, nothing. Now there were two, and one wooden box. His comrade opened his eyes with the dawn. Chalfin stared at the deep creases in the man's face—furrows that might have carved initials in an unknown language.

Chalfin wondered which of them would die first. Who would sink first, slipping from the box, slowly descending? Better to sink than to die of thirst. He wasn't afraid to die; he was afraid of the journey, of falling thousands of feet down. The sea was so deep! He would fall for days, months, years. He would fall, already dead, feet over hands, mouth agape, down and down and down. And as he fell all his limbs would eventually separate from his body, until he was just a nameless thing falling.

A wave took him under and swung the box around. When he surfaced still clinging, the sun was in his eyes, making noises. The sun was bursting with sound. He shook his head and clung even more tightly to the wooden box.

The box shifted in the sea and he spun around again. Then he saw the low-slung ship. The claxon horn was from the ship. It boomed out over the water. It was a British ship, and Chalfin could see the boat being lowered.

No, he thought, I'm not going back to Cairo. "Never!" he shouted to his uncomprehending comrade. The small boat puttered toward the survivors. Chalfin heard the sound of English and it sickened him. They were very close now.

Someone threw a rope and his comrade grabbed for it. They hauled the man aboard, then came toward Chalfin.

He pushed himself away from the wooden box. He was not going back. He was going to complete his mission. But he seemed unable to swim. Another rope was thrown. Hands grabbed him. They were pulling him back ... back ... back. ...

9

A sliver of light, and then something cold came on his face. Chalfin pushed himself up, his arms flailing. Someone pushed him back down. Chalfin opened his eyes. The face was familiar. It was Samuel Johnson. He blinked and turned his head away.

It was not Samuel Johnson. It was the Frenchman, Henri. Chalfin laughed. So it had all been a dream. He was still in the hangar, waiting. He sat up again and his hand groped for the weapon. No weapon. He looked around wildly, trying to cement his optimism. Henri gently pushed him back.

Then Chalfin heard a familiar voice.

"Some men find it very hard to die. They try and they try but they can't. Like certain beautiful women who cannot get married. They are beautiful, they are wise, they are good in the kitchen and good in the bedroom, but they can't get married."

Winokur sauntered over and peered at David's face.

"Where am I?"

"In the hangar. The same place you took off from. And now you are back, compliments of the Luftwaffe. We have lost a plane, thirteen out of fifteen men, thousands of pounds' worth of equipment. But you, David Chalfin, are back, and safe. In fact there is nothing the matter with you. But tell me, why did you fight those men who tried to save you?"

"I don't remember fighting," he lied. He did remember. He remembered not wanting to come back. He remembered the English voices from the English boat. He remembered fighting the hands that pulled him on board.

"Did you think it was a German boat?" Winokur persisted.

Chalfin did not answer. He lay back and closed his eyes. His fingers touched the edge of a cot, probably Henri's bed. He must be in the room where Henri and Winokur had first consulted.

"I had started to write a letter to your father. A terrible letter." Winokur reached over and pressed Chalfin's shoulder. "Sleep. Henri will care for you. Sleep for a few hours."

He could hear mumbling between Henri and Winokur, then the sound of footsteps leaving the room. He opened his eyes and looked at his hand—the skin was white and creased from the Mediterranean.

In a few moments Henri returned. "Can you sit all the way up, my friend?"

David raised himself to a sitting position. Henri propped a parachute pack behind the small of his back.

"Eat this," said the Frenchman.

A bowl of warm cereal, laced with honey. He wolfed it down with a wooden spoon, then licked the sides of the bowl.

"Now, tell me what happened," said Henri.

Chalfin began to recount the events from the moment the plane took off. He told Henri everything he remembered, even the smallest details. He was astonished at his own recall, and by the dispassionate way he spoke, as if it had all happened to some other English Jew.

When he had finished, Henri said nothing for a long time. Finally he said, "We will walk around the room a little. It will help you sleep."

Chalfin took Henri's arm and stood up. Immediately his legs gave way under him. Henri prevented his fall.

"Take a step."

Chalfin gathered himself, took a step, and felt bruising pain up and down his body.

"You will hurt a little, but nothing is broken," Henri assured him.

Chalfin took another step, and the two men slowly circled the room, arm in arm. When he was led back to the cot, Chalfin was sweating and breathing hard. Pain had gone from one part of his body to another—it had simply changed places.

Henri came back with a cup of tea. Chalfin drank it burning hot, and the sweat poured off him.

"Now you will sleep," said Henri.

And he did sleep. He slept for thirteen hours. When he awoke, Winokur was standing beside the cot, smoking a cigarette.

"How do you feel?"

"Better, much better."

Winokur threw him a bundle of clothes and watched while Chalfin dressed. Soon he became a little unsteady and sat down on the cot again. He had broken out into another sweat.

"In a day or so you will be back to work."

"No," said Chalfin quickly.

"Maybe a week."

"I want to go back to Jerusalem."

"Why?"

"I want to go."

183

"The war is here."

"I want to fight or not to fight. Not what I had to do here."

"Spoken like a true Talmudist." Winokur laughed.

"Can you arrange it?"

"If you wish."

"Quickly."

"If you wish."

Chalfin lay back on the bed. He wanted Winokur to leave.

"But there is something you must do before you go back."

"What do you mean?" said Chalfin.

"Pay a visit to Raya Fahmi. It is the polite thing to do."

Chalfin stared at the ceiling. He must not react. He must exercise control. He must understand the words he had just heard. He studied the ceiling. Poorly constructed, he thought. He held up his hand, still somewhat white and creased.

"She was shot in the thigh. A flesh wound. And they threw her out. She says she told them nothing, but she probably told them what we wanted her to tell them. Another little deception as to which way Montgomery will move. Add up a thousand of them and Rommel will be waiting for a ghost. So you see my young friend, it turned out as I said it would turn out. A little blood and a little pain. She's in her apartment, sleeping. Quinton has not been caught yet—but our friend Malorange will find him."

Chalfin turned on his side, facing the wall, away from Winokur. She was alive! To hell with their stupid little deceptions. His hands were trembling and he thrust them into the blanket. She was alive! Alive! Alive! He felt a triumphant surge of power in his hands and rolled over so that he faced Winokur.

Winokur said, "But you can go back to Jerusalem when you want."

As suddenly as it had empowered him, the triumph vanished. In its place came impotence, crumbling his body. He could not possibly see her. He could not look at her or speak to her. He had loved her and he had sent her to her death.

"Don't you understand?" he screamed at Winokur. "I betrayed her. Don't you understand?"

The effort of speech made him limp. He lay back, trying to catch his breath. Winokur was smiling at him. Chalfin shut his eyes.

The yellow-haired Slavic whore in The Trunk was called Helene. That wasn't her real name, but all new whores in The Trunk were called Helene; even Raya had been known as Helene for a while. It was a tribute to the reputation of French whores. This Helene had come from Alexandria and before that somewhere in French West Africa and before that, Warsaw.

Now a child lay on top of her, a British soldier. He smelled bad, from fear and from need. She loathed all of them, but she loathed this sort the most—the young ones with shocks of brown hair falling over their eyes, and the start of decay in their teeth. This sort tried to prolong it. She felt as though she were under an insect whose tentacles were out of control.

He was making noises. She stared past his shoulder at the wash basin, the table on which it sat, and the chair beside the table. There had been worse times. Everywhere. He touched her face but she brushed off his hand. There had been worse times.

She heard a sound outside the curtain. Then the curtain was pulled aside and people entered. She froze suddenly, the heel of her hand slamming against the forehead of the young soldier. He cursed her and rolled off.

Helene sat up. Both she and the soldier stared at the corpse sitting on the chair and at the tall angular man holding the corpse. His clothes were in shreds and he carried a weapon in one hand.

Helene stared in disbelief at the corpse. Its face was skeletal, stuffed with fleshlike netting. Its stench was overwhelming.

Tomlinson patted his friend on the shoulder, leaned over, and whispered into his ear. Then he walked over to the bed and studied the two figures. He was particularly entranced with the naked young soldier and he pressed the gun against his knee. The young soldier shrank back against the wall.

"I have come a long way," said Tomlinson.

Then he walked back to his friend, spotted the washbasin on the table, dipped the sponge in the water, and began to wash the corpse's face. When he had finished, he washed his own. He turned to face Helene.

"Where is she?" he said.

Helene paused. How did one talk to such a person? Finally she said, "Who?"

"The lady who was here."

"I don't know who you mean."

"You know! You know!" Tomlinson screamed. He moved suddenly to the bed and kicked the mattress with such force that Helene fell off, landing heavily on her side. She pressed her face to the floor. The madman's ankles were inches away from her shoulder.

"The one with the dark hair."

Now she knew: Raya. But Raya hadn't been here for days. No one knew where she was. Helene stared at the corpse, perceiving it now with clarity. It seemed to represent what she aspired to.

His foot crunched down on her hand. She cried out in pain and rolled over. "I don't know! She has not come in."

Tomlinson began to pace the room with his head down. Occasionally he glared at the whore and the young soldier. He muttered as he paced, swinging his weapon against his side. "We can wait . . . why can't we wait . . . why shouldn't we wait . . . it is possible to wait . . . if we wait she will come. . . ."

"She has not been in. She has left," said Helene.

The young soldier reached out carefully for the blanket and wrapped it around himself.

Helene's eyes were fixed on the corpse. Why shouldn't he get on top of her?

Tomlinson went to his friend and apologized. "Pietro, I'm sorry, but we will find her. It will take a little time, but we will certainly find her."

Now the room was filled with the fetid stench of the corpse. Helene felt no revulsion. Her eyes met Tomlinson's. "I don't know when she will return," said Helene.

Tomlinson nodded, shouldered his weapon, and lifted Pietro from the chair. A moment later he left the room. The curtain billowed gently in the air.

Quinton's house was shuttered. No light, no sound, no movement within could be discerned. Carla Boudine watched the house from a distance, as she would have watched an unconscious person; she waited for the moment of awakening. But it seemed that the house was overwhelmed by the river.

She had waited too long, she knew. She could have killed him that first night. She deluded herself into thinking that she was playing with him. It was not that. It was his bloody charm. She had deluded herself into thinking that she had merely been waiting for the right time. No, she had not killed him for that most pathetic of reasons—a bed.

She turned away and looked up at the night sky. Egypt was upon her again, as it had been when she was a child, when she had first identified its power.

Cairo and Alexandria were cities, but not cities such as Paris, Rome, Berlin. They seemed to have been put down, suddenly, in the middle of a porcelain saucer. And the cities rolled from one end of the saucer to the other, absorbing design. And yet, in a moment, all the design might vanish. What had enthralled Carla was the precarious nature of these

187

cities. Thousands of years old, yet on the edge of extinction.

She began to walk slowly along the water, thinking of Quinton and of what she believed in. It was Egypt she believed in. When all the dross was shaken away, it was Egypt she believed in. But not a whore's Egypt, not an Egypt touched by Europe. An Egypt free to return to its deserts and its holy men and its *fellahin*.

"Carla Boudine."

The voice had come from behind her. She did not respond.

"Carla Boudine."

She turned and saw Quinton's flunky, Moussa Tmai, huffing along after her. She waited for him with impatience and contempt. She thought: He is probably sifting the mud of the Nile for Quinton.

Moussa approached, panting, wiping his forehead with a large handkerchief. He shrugged apologetically. "Pardon me for interfering with your revery."

He was everything she hated in the old Egypt. He could be bought for a hair from the tail of a donkey, if ten such hairs could make a broom. "What do you want?" she asked sharply.

"I have a message for you. Brian Quinton says he is sorry you will not get the chance to kill him."

Carla took a step backward.

"He says you should not seek vengeance for the death of Colonel Quaffid. The man was a fool, and is now in Paradise."

She raised her hand instinctively—as if to strike the ugly man. The hand froze in midair. Then it began to tremble. The river was turning cold. The river was all around them. Quinton knew!

She stared at Moussa as if to pull the lie out of his face. But Moussa did not budge. He was not lying.

Quinton knew! He knew even when he was making love to her; when she could have slit his throat at the moment of

188

orgasm so that vermin like Quinton would never again destroy an Egyptian like Quaffid.

Quinton had known all the time—while her husband still didn't know that he had married a woman of the New Egypt.

How could it be? How could that confused, degenerate, European fool have possibly known?

She had lived two lives so perfectly. She had broken her consciousness in half in order to help the New Egypt. When the time came, when all the whores and killers and traders and Europeans had left the city, then she could let the grand and beautiful Alexandrian woman drown in the Nile.

"Tell your master," she said softly, "that we will exterminate him. If not me, someone else. Tell him that we are not interested in European wars. Tell him that he is filth."

Moussa Tmai shrugged even more apologetically. Then he drove a knife through Carla Boudine's ribcage, piercing the heart.

She fell forward, and her horror of touching that man was greater than her horror of dying. Moussa stepped back as she slid to the ground. He kicked her body into the river.

10

It had taken all his courage to get there. Now, standing just outside her door and staring at the guard Winokur had provided, he was unable to proceed.

The guard, a short, thick-set man with blond hair and an easy smile, was dressed in civilian clothes. He moved constantly back and forth from the landing to Raya's door. He opened his mouth to say something, but Chalfin silenced him with a gesture. Chalfin didn't want her to know he was there. It would be bad if she knew. But everything was bad. After several minutes had passed he said, "You can go. Winokur knows."

The man nodded. He moved off lightly down the steps, into the street.

Chalfin put his ear to the door. He heard nothing. Longing to hear something, he pressed his ear against the wood. He was desperate to hear her walk, or breathe, or cough. The door was open. He had only to turn the knob and walk in. That was all he had to do. She was there, lying on her bed, with a bandage, Winokur had said, around her thigh. A bandage.

Abruptly he sat down on the stairs, his body filled with weakness. Since he had left his recuperative cot in the hangar, this weakness would appear, stay awhile, then vanish. Wherever he was, whatever he was doing, he simply had to stop and rest. There was no pain, it was not unpleasant. It was just there.

I have come this far, he thought, and I will—I must—walk through the door. Walk in. Make an apology. Leave.

But he sat still. Odd that she was on the other side of the door. She seemed to be in a different country. She seemed to be walking somewhere, thousands of miles away. He tried to remember the last time he had seen her. Where? When? There was a red dress. That was all he could remember.

Chalfin rested his head in his hands. The red dress had been turned into red blood. Raya had been shot. Shot. Winokur had said so. Shot in the leg. The vision of her blood flowing made him lose equilibrium. He leaned against the wall.

When I walk through the door I will make a joke about her leg. He tried to think of something funny. Line after line was dredged up and thrown out. Nothing was funny.

He changed his approach. An aphorism, a philosophical aphorism, à la Nietzsche. Something like . . . something like . . . He thought of nothing.

He would be a clown, yes, that was it. He would slouch like a tiger, hop like a kangaroo, bark like a dog.

He would be silent, for there was nothing to say.

He would do this, say that—his mind was a jumble of absurdities. Still he sat on the stairs.

Was this cowardice? Why couldn't he walk through a door and see the woman he loved? Betrayal is a fact of life. A rock-hard fact. He had committed a betrayal. Someday, perhaps she would too. Chalfin stood up and walked to the door. He turned the knob quickly, as though it were hot enough to sear his fingers. He passed into the room and closed the door gently behind him. But he could not look at her. He knew where the bed was, and he couldn't turn his face toward it.

Raya had awakened when the door closed. She looked up lazily, expecting to see the familiar face of the guard. She saw David Chalfin, standing with his head down, hands clasped behind him.

"David? David? Is that you?" She swung her legs over the bed. "David?" She stood up, in a white blouse and a white bandage. She crossed the room and stood in front of him.

They stood that way for several minutes without speaking.

Then she put her hand under his chin and shoved his face up sharply. She saw that he was frightened.

Her hatred was sudden and uncontainable. She looked around for a weapon—steel, glass, anything. But there were only her hands, and she raked his face, and her nails drew blood.

And then she walked back to the bed and sat down, and she began to sob, leaning forward, holding her leg which throbbed.

Finally she looked up again to see him still standing there, his face covered with blood. He seemed to be saying something. She couldn't hear him.

She did not hate him now. She could never hate him again. She looked down at his blood on her nails.

"Do you want me to go?" said Chalfin.

How was she to answer?

"I don't want to go," he said.

Chalfin walked to the bed and sat down as far from her as possible. "I don't know what to say to you. I don't know how to look at you. I can't bear my shame."

"Shame," she said, wondering why he had used the word.

"There's nothing I can do, I understand that. I made sure you would be tortured and murdered. I betrayed everything there was between us. I sent you to hell. I murdered you."

Chalfin looked down at the bandage around her thigh. He reached out, but did not touch her—his hand hung in the air. Now he could look at her. He watched her face. Her eyes. Her mouth. Her hands that seemed to want to touch him.

"I told them nothing," she said.

"It doesn't matter," Chalfin said. The success or failure of Montgomery's offensive did not depend on one lie, blurted out under torture. He had betrayed her so she would blurt out that lie. Now, only the betrayal loomed large.

"It matters!" she shouted.

Chalfin said slowly, "I did it, Raya, because I thought there were larger things."

She ignored this. "At first I didn't believe it was you. But then I did believe, and I couldn't understand. You must have done it for a reason. You must have done it for those people in the photograph. But I am one of those people in the photograph now. You made me one of the people in the photograph."

Raya suddenly grabbed Chalfin and held him as though he were a child, and spoke softly to him in Arabic. He let himself be held as a child. She had taken him back—that was all that mattered. She had cast off his betrayal. He could stay with her now, held like this, for years. Everything seemed coherent. Everything seemed to have been designed toward this point. Everything had been undertaken and suffered in order to arrive here.

When she awoke, he was standing near the open door of the balcony, drinking a cup of tea. The room was flooded with moonlight; he stood half in light and half in shadow. It was strange to wake up and find the man she loved in her room— a man who was not a danger. She sat up. But he was a danger. If he had betrayed her once, he would betray her again. She wondered if the English find it easy to love and betray at the same time. No, it was not that. It was because what they say often has nothing to do with what they mean. She had learned that in The Trunk.

"David."

He turned, and lifted his teacup. "Do you want some?"

"No."

"Does your leg hurt?"

"Very little."

"I was thinking about when we can go back—to Palestine. I've already told Winokur I'm going back."

"What is it like there?"

He laughed. "It's funny to hear a Jew ask what Palestine is like. Well, there are long-haired prophets running around, and there is a brisk trade in locusts and honey. Some eat the locusts raw, some eat them cooked. As for me, I boil them, coat them with honey, and eat them with a knife and fork."

"What will we do there?" she asked.

"I'll be a clerk for the Agency, until the war is over and we're free. Then we'll find the ugliest, most godforsaken spot in Palestine and we'll go there and farm."

Chalfin began to pace the room, telling her about soil and crops, describing communal farms. Raya listened but his words meant nothing to her; what mattered was the enthusiasm. She could understand an enthusiasm for space. She could see herself in a wilderness, surrounded by miles of clear dry emptiness. No one there to touch her.

He said abruptly, "Will you miss Cairo?"

"I don't know."

"What is here to miss? You can find the same bazaars in Jerusalem and Haifa. You can hear the same languages."

"I'll go with you whenever you want."

"A week at the most. A week!" he exclaimed.

She loved to see him happy—how he moved his hands, how his face brightened from its usual sober tone.

He put down the teacup and went over to Raya. He took

her hands and kissed the palms. She stared at the scratches on his face.

"We'll be married in Jerusalem." He embraced her tightly until he remembered her leg. "I'm sorry."

"It doesn't hurt."

They made love like thieves. Each of them careful. They could give only what they thought the other capable of. They made love slowly. They made strange sounds. Jerusalem was hovering above them. They made love out of need, with no thought of pleasure, no thought of ecstasy. They made love to annihilate Quinton and The Trunk and the betrayal and the doomed airplane flying low over the sea. And they succeeded.

"Look! Look!"

Raya sat up and the morning sun almost blinded her. David had just come through the door, waving a piece of paper and a small set of keys.

"Here. Come here." He was at the balcony, pointing down with one hand and holding up the keys with the other. Raya took slow stiff steps to the balcony.

"Do you see it?"

Looking down, she saw a battered gray motorcycle with a sidecar.

David laughed and kissed her. "Winokur delivered it. His note says it's ours for a few days. I haven't seen a good British motorcycle in two years! And look at the sidecar. You will sit there like a potentate and I will chauffeur you about."

"I've never ridden in one." The thing looked threatening.

"Then get dressed. Now. I will take you for a ride."

Raya dressed slowly, careful not to brush her leg. As she dressed David talked about his old motorcycle, the one he had in England.

As they walked down the stairs she held his arm, and then he helped her into the sidecar. The engine turned over on his second kick, and the machine moved off.

He had no idea where he was going. He kept to a low speed, carefully following the traffic. Raya's fear soon vanished and she leaned forward, laughing and pointing out the sights. Chalfin felt himself moving into a hypnotic wonderland: the slow throbbing of the cycle beneath him and the colors and sounds that washed over them. Once, a sharp piece of loose cinder block jolted them, and Chalfin remembered the shuddering plane, and he ducked instinctively. Then he smiled shyly at Raya.

An hour passed, and another hour. They didn't stop, they moved on and on. They were in Old Cairo now, where the Coptic churches hid in courtyards. He could see that Raya had closed her eyes. The wind was whipping her black hair.

They turned north again. I am like Sir Francis Drake, thought Chalfin, circumnavigating the world of Cairo. Then, suddenly, watching Raya, he decided on a gift for her. Turning the cycle northeast, he increased his speed, hoping to reach his destination before she opened her eyes again.

When he stopped the cycle she opened her eyes on the squat ugly building that housed The Trunk.

"I thought you'd like to say good-bye to it," said Chalfin. He pointed to a jagged paving block in the middle of the street. "Say good-bye by stoning it."

Before she could say anything he was off the cycle, picking up the large stone. He made as if to throw the stone through the front door of The Trunk. Raya laughed, and shook her head: no, she didn't want to throw the stone. Chalfin began to walk back toward her with the stone.

The street exploded around him. Bullets churned up the stone, flinging bits and pieces high into the air. Screams. Curses. Bodies running and falling. He looked down the street in confusion. Raya was standing up in the sidecar, waving to him. Chalfin ran the other way, to the shelter of The Trunk, and the bullets followed him, tattooing the ground at his feet. He hurled himself against the door and it gave, splintering. He fell heavily inside.

The firing stopped. He could hear only moans and shouts. He peered out and saw the street littered with bodies, some still, some crawling. Raya was still standing up in the sidecar. He stepped out of The Trunk and waved.

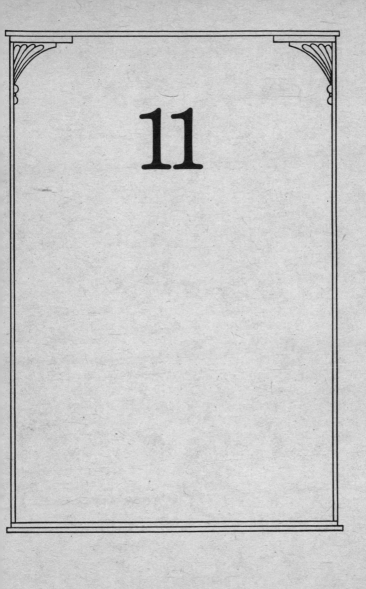

11

"**Y**ou are talking like a fool," said Winokur, his voice hard, unyielding, daring to be contradicted. He was leaning forward over his desk with a look of utter purposiveness.

"It was me they were after."

"Who was after you? Who? Someone shoots up a street in Cairo. Dozens of people are hurt or killed—but you say *they* were after you."

"Yes, that's what I say."

"Were they waiting there for you?"

"Yes."

"But you told me that you didn't know you were going to The Trunk. You thought of it suddenly."

"I can't explain how they knew I would be there."

"You should have stayed in bed a lot longer after they fished you out of the water. You are thinking like a fish . . . a fish."

Chalfin stared out the window. He was exhausted. He was still frightened. His clothes were filthy.

"I saw them."

"You *saw* them?" Winokur pushed his chair back away from the desk, and folded his hands behind his neck.

"For just a minute, before I started to run. There was a strong sun but I saw them, down the street, two of them and a donkey. I didn't see them clearly, but I saw them."

"Exactly what did you see?"

"One was a British soldier."

"How do you know?"

"I know."

"But how?"

Chalfin shook his head and turned away to look out the window. He heard Winokur throw something on his desk. Winokur was disgusted. He didn't know why he thought it had been a British soldier, but that was what he believed. It was something one knew. The way one knew from someone's expression that someone else had died. It was that kind of knowing.

"Can I talk to Colonel Malorange?"

"I haven't seen him in days," said Winokur.

"Can I contact him?"

Winokur got up and walked around his desk to stand before Chalfin. "Do you think Colonel Malorange tried to assassinate you?" he asked in astonishment.

Then he went back behind his desk, shaking his head. "Go back to Palestine, David. With your woman. You wanted to go back and I have already cleared the transfer."

"I want to speak to Colonel Malorange."

"Why, in God's name, would British Intelligence try to exterminate you? Would you please explain that to me?"

"I don't know. I don't know if that is the case. But I feel there is a connection. A British soldier tried to murder me. Malorange is British. Malorange has British soldiers under his command. Malorange probably hates me."

"Why? Because you're an English Jew who gave up England? God, David, you are talking stupid."

"I just want to see Malorange once more before I go back."

Winokur began to beat his fist on the desk in a demonic rhythm. "No. You will not see Malorange. No. You will not talk to Malorange. No. No. No."

And then, suddenly, as though ashamed of his outburst, he spoke softly. "It has been a difficult time for you, David. You must understand that. You must understand your own strength, and lack of it. Go back to Palestine. Rest. Think. It will be a very long war."

Chalfin wanted to speak, but he couldn't. He wanted to tell Winokur that yes, he was weak, and tired, and frightened, but he had to see Malorange anyway. He wanted to tell Winokur that logic had nothing to do with Cairo—and they were all in Cairo—and intuition was more potent than logic. But he loved Winokur and he didn't want to anger him more. The older man smiled. Chalfin felt ashamed. "I will go back," he said.

"We can leave tomorrow," said Raya.

Chalfin heard her, but made no response. He simply watched her move about the room.

"Winokur thinks I'm mad," he said abruptly. "He says it was a random shooting."

Raya bent her head in remembrance. She could not forget those people shot down; she could not forget the blood.

"They were after *me*," said Chalfin.

She didn't know whether he was right or wrong, and she didn't care. The reality was that they had almost killed him.

"I want to find out *why*," he added.

This didn't make sense to Raya. If someone was trying to kill you, you ran from the killer or fought him. It was pointless to find out why the killer wanted to kill. There are those who kill. It is as simple as that. It is the way of the world. There are killers and saints and whores and physicians and dogs and cats and sunbeams. She went to Chalfin and kissed him on the forehead.

"I asked Winokur if I could question Malorange. He refused." Chalfin lapsed into silence. Then he resumed, "But don't you see, Raya, what Winokur is really saying is that I'm too unimportant to kill. That no one would go to great lengths to kill me. I'm too impotent to be murdered. Too inconsequential. Too pathetic."

"What do you mean by 'pathetic'?"

"Imagine a dog who is dying of thirst. The dog comes to a fence. It can smell water. It knows that behind the fence is water but it doesn't know how to get to the water. The dog is pathetic."

"And you are that dog?"

"In a way."

"Where is the water?"

Chalfin buried his head in his hands.

The word "pathetic" she must remember. And she must remember the image of the dog who cannot get the water it needs to live. Why can't it get the water? Because it isn't smart enough or strong enough or fast enough. But there was more. What exactly? She watched the man she loved. She could not imagine him "pathetic." The word continued to intrigue her. What the word finally named was the men who bought her body. It was a word for them. She was the water and they were the dog, and the fence was the money they paid her. But they were still thirsty. Yes, that was it. They were worse than the dog—more pathetic—for they still died of thirst. The water did not save them.

What had Brian Quinton said when he gave her the gold coins? Something about beauty and value. Better to be bought with gold than to be bought with paper. Something like that.

Then David's arms were around her. She turned in his grasp, momentarily startled, assuming it was someone at The Trunk.

"I have to find out," he said.

She felt his heart beating rapidly.

"It is something all the Maloranges must learn. Thou shalt not shoot Jews anymore. The Eleventh Commandment. There, Raya, I have given the world the Eleventh Commandment."

He slowed down, kneading his hands: "I will find Malorange and I will find out. Then it will be over. If I'm wrong, I'm wrong. But I must find out—and give him this new Commandment. Then we can go to Palestine."

She put her ear against his chest and heard his heart beating. Closing her eyes tightly, she saw him running across the street, chased by bullets. Now his hands were under her robe. She saw him throwing himself against the door of The Trunk.

"We have time," she whispered to him. But she did not know what she meant.

Moussa dipped into the vat of coffee beans and pulled up a handful. He sniffed the beans thoughtfully, closed his hand and shook them around, then sniffed the beans again.

"I told you they were excellent," said the skeletal figure, Ribeiro. He was dressed in an amalgam of styles, and grinned widely, showing a jagged cavern of nicotine-stained teeth.

But Moussa did not accept Ribeiro's judgment on one handful alone. It was common practice to cover the top of the vat with choice beans, while below lay beans no coffee drinker would want. He took off his jacket and folded it, noting a spot on the lapel. He stared at this spot and shook his head mournfully. Carla Boudine's blood.

Ribeiro took the jacket from Moussa. "I will take out this spot for you," he said consolingly. He found a small bottle in a cupboard and shook a few drops of clear fluid onto the stain. Then he spread the jacket out to dry.

Moussa returned to the coffee beans. He thrust both arms

deep down into the vat and pulled up two handfuls. The beans were merely a little greener. "Good," he said.

Ribeiro put on his grin.

"What else?" asked Moussa.

"Preserves." Ribeiro gestured toward the back of the dingy storeroom. Moussa followed him happily. Preserves were gold. The British would pay anything for preserves. They would sell their mothers, their fathers, their children, their Queen, for preserves.

Ribeiro hovered over a large crate, smoking furiously. Then he proceeded to open it, cursing in a language Moussa did not know. The jars were lined up like disciplined soldiers, a thick cover of dust over the lids. Moussa plucked one up and blew away the dust. Strawberry preserves!

Moussa admired the beautiful glass jar. Jars always intrigued him. He found it astonishing that millions of glass jars had caps that fit perfectly. Now he gave the cap a little tug but it did not move. Ribeiro seemed to bow and took the jar. He leaned forward, holding the jar against his stomach, and gave the cap a violent wrench. He handed the open jar back to Moussa.

"Ma'la'a," said Moussa, signaling for a spoon.

But Ribeiro could not find a spoon. Finally he pulled a long splinter of wood off a crate and handed it to Moussa, who dipped it into the preserves. He found that the strawberry preserves were delicious. He ate nearly half the jar. Then he gave it back to Ribeiro.

"It will take some time, but there will be no problems," said Moussa, sure of his ability to sell the preserves and the coffee.

"And perhaps you would like to see some soap?" said Ribeiro.

Always open for merchandise, Moussa nodded.

Ribeiro carefully unwrapped a bar, crackling the paper. "It is fit for a god," he said rapturously, pushing the soap under Moussa's nose, "and it makes froth."

Moussa took the soap and sat down on a carton. He knew

about froth, those glorious white bubbles. Yes, this was gold, he realized. Gold. "How many bars?" he asked eagerly.

"Five thousand."

So many bars of soap, thought Moussa. So many people who want soap that will froth. Had Carla Boudine loved soap? Did all beautiful women use soap that frothed?

Moussa glanced at his jacket. Indeed, Ribeiro had removed the stain.

Chalfin hesitated as he reached the street. He was going to find Malorange—that was decided—but he suddenly understood that he could not confront the man with an accusation. He had nothing to go on. Someone (probably a British soldier) had tried to kill him. In some radically intuitive sense he felt that Malorange was behind the attempt. This did not make sense. Nevertheless there had been an attempt.

Chalfin began to walk. He would make a joke of it, throw it on the table, and watch the man's response. If there was no response he would probe further. Did Malorange know about his abortive jump into Greece, he wondered. What kind of dossier did British Intelligence have on him? And why, why did he hate Malorange so intensely? He had hated the man on sight.

Chalfin made his way into the other Cairo, which he knew quite well. When he had first arrived from Palestine he had spent his nights in the bars and clubs that fanned out from headquarters. Any bar was a sanctuary from loneliness. He could drink and listen to the voices and once in a while he would meet someone he knew from England. Malorange, he knew, would be in one of those clubs. There was no place else to go. There was nothing else to do. If he was relentless he would find the man.

He went first to Blakey's. Frequented for the most part by field officers, the place had always hosted a scattering of intelligence personnel. You could spot them easily: they were consistently the most raucous. After long months in bizarre situations performing absurd acts, any semblance of normalcy made them aggressive and funny and prone to falling under tables.

Blakey's smelled good. It smelled of leather, and Chalfin despised himself for liking the scent. When English Jews desired to become gentry, they naturally gravitated toward horses. And Chalfin's family had been no exception, and Chalfin had always despised the milieu—but now he liked the scent of leather. Where did this leather come from? There was no cavalry here; they used tanks in North Africa.

He ordered a gin and tonic at the bar. The thought came to him that Malorange would not have authorized a murder unless he, Chalfin, had compromised an operation. He slid the drink along the burnished bar. Nice to drink here. The bar was a thing of beauty. But what operation had he compromised? None that he could think of. With respect to Raya and Quinton he had done exactly what he had been told to do. He had betrayed Raya. But that was done under orders, and Malorange didn't give a damn for Raya. Chalfin spun his glass. Interesting. What if Malorange had been a customer in The Trunk? What if he was attached to Raya? What if the attempt was his way of getting her back? Interesting, but not productive.

He turned on his seat and looked around. A slow night. Just some ordinary soldiers gathered in pairs and trios. Chalfin could read the patches, identify the branches, isolate the brigades. There was no one here of interest to him.

The White Nile was next. It occupied the back of a once plush hotel that had been taken over for administrative offices. The White Nile was spacious and one could have dinner. The bar twisted and turned around two walls. Chalfin ordered a drink and began to circulate. His confidence suddenly vanished. What a ridiculous way to find someone. Perhaps Malorange spent his evenings alone playing solitaire. Perhaps he was in Alexandria. Perhaps he was near the front. And how was he to know?

210

This was all Winokur's fault. Winokur could have put him in touch with Malorange immediately. Winokur should have understood that one might want to find out *why* one is gunned down on the street. And he had been machine-gunned. And Cairo had been a disaster from beginning to end. He had emerged a fool at best. He had wanted to fight and all he had done was procure. But this would be his finale in Cairo. He would find Malorange. He would find out why those bullets had followed him down the street. He would know the truth.

Chalfin went into bar after bar, trying to find someone who knew Malorange.

No one knew Malorange. Or no one would say he knew Malorange.

As the night wore on he began to think of Raya. He desired her more as the hours passed. And as the hours passed his nihilism and disgust increased until virtually every conversation, every attempt to get information ended in harsh words or a fight. He began to mock those he sought information from, and they, in turn, mocked him.

The gin and whiskey were rapidly destroying his sense of balance. He staggered into a new bar.

"Get out of here, you drunken ass," said the bartender.

Chalfin knew it had been a donkey. Now he was a donkey. A donkey had been with that British soldier who tried to kill him. Had to have been a donkey. And he was a donkey. He left the bar.

Out on the street he hallucinated that bullets were landing at his feet again. He danced grotesquely to avoid them. When all this was over, would he forget the Jewish Agency, forget Raya, and remember only the bullets?

Now he was back where he had started—Blakey's. The bartender gave him a long hard look. Chalfin touched his own face; nothing the matter with it—it was still there.

He ordered whiskey and thought of the name *Malorange*. He had been thinking of the man, now he would think of the

211

name. For in the name was . . . Mal meant bad or rotten in some language. So, the man was a rotted orange. No, that was unfair. His skin was rotten but inside was the health of the killer. Malorange. Le Grand Orange. Orange Blight. Blightorange.

Chalfin tried to invent a limerick, but he couldn't find a word to rhyme with orange. "What rhymes with orange?" he asked the bartender.

"Purple," said the bartender, pouring out another whiskey.

Chalfin tried to decipher what he considered to have been the philosophical remark of the bartender. How did purple rhyme with orange?

"If purple rhymes with orange, what rhymes with Malorange?" He put his hand on the bartender's arm.

"Colonel," said a voice from the side.

Chalfin spun around on his seat. A heavy-set man with two days' growth and a rumpled tunic was staring into his face.

"Colonel," the man repeated, "and fool."

"I must speak to him!" Chalfin knocked over the whiskey with his elbow.

"I would imagine that a great many people wish to speak to Colonel Malorange."

"Will he come here?" Chalfin asked excitedly.

The man regarded Chalfin as though he were demented. "What do you want from him?"

"I have to find Colonel Malorange."

"You won't find him here. Malorange dropped out of sight a year ago."

"But I saw Malorange just last week!" Chalfin suddenly realized that he had been shouting.

The stranger took his drink and went to the other end of the bar. Chalfin was shaking with confusion. He couldn't recall what he himself had said, nor what had been said to him. Finally he ran out of the bar into the street and pressed himself against the wall of a building. He took very deep breaths—

inhaling, exhaling, inhaling, exhaling. The fog and nausea began to clear. What the man had said was that Malorange was not in Cairo. Malorange had vanished a year ago. Chalfin stopped breathing. The man was crazy. For Chalfin had seen Malorange at Winokur's.

His fury overwhelmed his drunkenness and he reached for his pistol. But he didn't have it—he had left it with Raya. No matter. He would accomplish this without a pistol. He leaned into the wall. An hour, a day, a week—he would wait for that man. He slid the belt off his pants and held it in a loop in his hands. Sour sweat drenched his clothes. This is the end, he thought, of my career as a victim.

He wondered if Raya was asleep.

As the man came out of the bar, Chalfin noted his limp. He followed the man into the first turn.

Now, he thought. Now! It will be very easy. What is violent is always easy. I must not make the wrong move. I must not be soft, or sentimental, or sloppy. I am going to hurt him, quickly and efficiently.

Chalfin slipped the belt around the proffered neck and pulled it tight with a savage jerk. The man gave a muffled scream. Chalfin threw him to the ground, face down.

"Now tell me about Malorange. Tell me where I can find him."

Chalfin loosened the belt so that the man could speak, but he began to fight and Chalfin pulled it tight again.

The man's face was a cipher. It puffed up and then contracted, and then puffed again. The eyes seemed to recede into pouches.

"Malorange," Chalfin whispered. He knew that he wanted to kill the man. He loosened the belt.

"I told you what I knew," the man said hoarsely. "Malorange was in my section. He was sent out on a mission a year ago. I don't know where. They say East Africa. No one has seen him for a year."

213

Chalfin slipped the belt off his neck and helped the man sit up. Then he kneeled down beside him. He felt weak. The violence had been sucked out and suddenly he felt no enmity at all toward this man. He kneeled beside him: "Listen. My name is David Chalfin. I spoke with Malorange last week. We were as close then as you and I are now."

"You didn't speak to Malorange." The man massaged the back of his neck.

Chalfin held out his hands in a form of apology. He was offering to help the man to his feet. He was offering to neutralize the attack. The oddity of what he was being told had wrapped him in benevolence. The man waved off the proffered hands and got to his feet, alone.

"Did you *know* him?" Chalfin pursued, slowly.

"Not well. You know these dons—difficult to understand."

"Malorange, a *don?*"

"Ah, I see you have not heard of the great Malorange. The war saved his career. He had spent, I understand, ten years searching for the identity of the Dark Lady of Shakespeare's sonnets. To no avail." The man suddenly laughed. "What did you say your name was?"

"David Chalfin."

"Mine is Craig Harvey. This week." He shook Chalfin's hand with enthusiasm. "After seven brandy and sodas, I even like strangulation." And he moved off unsteadily.

Chalfin stood rooted in the alley. He played with his belt. He was suddenly and acutely aware of the astonishing revelation. He tried to push back the enormity of what he now knew.

The man who was supposed to be Colonel Malorange; the man who had sat with Winokur and himself, who had planned with them and conspired with them—that man was *not* Colonel Malorange!

He could not be Malorange. He could never be Malorange. Because he had never heard of Lopez, the physician executed by Elizabeth. How could an Elizabethan scholar not know of

214

Lopez? Or Essex? And the real Malorange was an Elizabethan scholar.

The revelation shamed him; it seemed to suck his confidence away; it seemed to strip him of his clothes and his strength.

They had been taken in by a total fraud. Winokur and himself had been conversing with an imposter. But how could that man have fooled Winokur? Who was he? Why was he?

Cairo seemed to wrap itself around Chalfin. He was chilled and he was frightened. He slid the belt into the loops of his trousers.

They were piled right up inside the hospital entrance: thirty-six boxes of chocolate—Nachtigal! One box was different from the others—it had been beautifully wrapped and beribboned and a note was pinned to it "For Sister Charlotte."

Overwhelmed, Sister Charlotte stood there, staring at the boxes, shaking her head in absolute awe. Thirty-six boxes of Nachtigal! It was like finding a new Shroud of Turin. She counted the boxes again, which were stacked six by six. She had the sense of being inside a beautiful store window during Christmas week.

Of course, even in the hospital there were thieves, so she would remove the chocolate from public view. In four trips she carried the boxes to the safety of her office, and she was breathing heavily when the job was done.

Her box, the one for her alone, rested on the top of her desk. She sat down and waited to be restored. She napped a little in her chair. Then, waking, she opened two of the regular boxes and took them along with her to the wards.

I will give one piece of chocolate to each patient, she thought, certainly not more than two. That way it will last for days. And so she paused at the beside of every patient able to eat chocolate, and beamed as she dramatically unwrapped them. She either handed them to the patients or, when necessary, popped the chocolate directly into the patient's mouth.

In the material world, chocolate was the greatest proof, she thought, that God loved his children. It brought joy, it overcame grief, it gave men a common, harmless addiction. So she thought, but never said.

When she was too tired to continue her rounds she returned to her office and again napped in the chair. She woke, smiled at the box of chocolates on the desk, and fell into a half-sleep.

There was no doubt about it, she mused, the chocolates were from Brian Quinton. He knew she would distribute them in the wards. And he had beautifully wrapped one box so she would know it was for her. It was his way of telling her that she was obliged to vanish, but he would always keep the memory of the hospital close to his heart.

Then she was ashamed of her arrogance. Quinton had more likely been reunited with that beautiful woman who was searching for him, and they were once again lovers. He had sent the chocolates simply to be polite.

She shook her head, suddenly, and bit her lip. And the horror of the situation weighed on her. He had sent the chocolate because he had murdered the soldier; to show her that he knew she knew, and would be silent. He had sent the chocolate to solidify the conspiracy.

Sister Charlotte opened her box carefully. She folded the beautiful wrapping paper and the ribbons, and stored them in the desk for future use. Slowly, she ate three pieces of chocolate. It had all become too much for her. Much too much.

They found Sister Charlotte in her office, sitting at the desk, nine hours later. The strychnine had contorted her mouth into a lopsided grin.

Raya was in that limbo between sleep and wakefulness, and Chalfin was watching her absent-mindedly. A cool breeze came in through the balcony. He realized that there had been no mistake, that the stranger must have been right. Chalfin now remembered precisely the conversation with the so-called Colonel Malorange. He had been baiting the Englishman. He had spoken of the Earl of Essex and of Lopez, and of the portrait of Essex in Woburn Abbey. The man had not known any of this. Yet the real Malorange was an Elizabethan scholar. He had been searching for the Dark Lady of the sonnets.

Raya moved languidly on the bed. Who, then, was the man who called himself Malorange? And why was he in disguise? Raya moved again and he felt a deep sexual longing. He turned away to look down at the darkened street.

Suddenly he turned back to Raya and looked at the white bandage on her leg. What if it hadn't been a British soldier gunning him? He had seen in that fleeting moment a soldier with light hair. What if the hair had really been red? Quinton, it was said, had red hair.

He needed something to do with his hands. This clarity was oppressive. But there was nothing to do with his hands. In a street filled with gunfire and death, Raya had simply remained standing in the sidecar as though she were immortal—or as though she knew the bullets would never touch her.

The clarity was receding, leaving obscurity. He must have taken a wrong turn in his reasoning. He had moved away from sanity and accuracy. He had begun to think like a madman. Too many hours in too many bars. He walked over to Raya.

She opened her eyes, said softly, "Come to bed."

He leaned forward and kissed her shoulder, then straightened up and stared at the white bandage as though it were transmitting signals of grave consequence. Why would they let her live? If she had talked they would have killed her. If she didn't talk they would have killed her anyway. There was no room for a simple flesh wound.

Chalfin walked back to the balcony and recalled the scene.

Raya had been standing straight up in the sidecar. He had started to run. Chalfin now felt sick to his stomach. Suppose the three of them—Raya, Quinton, the false Malorange—were in concert, with himself and Winokur to be annihilated.

Color drained from his face and strength from his limbs. He wanted to pray, but wasn't certain he could still pray. "It cannot be," he whispered to the street.

But all roads led to Raya. Each turn, each fork led to Raya. All roads led there, and he felt very ill.

He went to the bed again and sat down beside her. In her half-sleep she snuggled close to him. The black hair wreathed her face, accentuating her beauty. Her breasts gently rose and fell. He wanted her.

The greatest horror in the world, he realized, was a beautiful whore. He had always been certain about her beauty. It could be measured. There were yardsticks. Beauty was not speculation, guesses. Beauty was beauty. Her nose, her breasts, her neck, her eyes. Yes, don't forget that. There are her eyes.

She opened her eyes. "David."

He was speechless, his face chalk-white.

"What's the matter?" she asked in alarm.

Chalfin pushed her head into the pillow. "Tell me what happened. I want to know exactly what happened with Quinton."

"I told you," she said, laughing nervously. She brushed the hair away from her eyes.

"You told me nothing."

"It happened so fast. Brian Quinton asked me about you and your friends. I didn't tell him anything. He shot me."

Chalfin got up and began to pace the room.

"David, what is wrong?"

He faced her: "I want to know what he was wearing. What you were wearing. What the furniture was like. His exact words. How you got there. What you felt. What you said to him—each word, each pause. I want to know what you did the morning before. Where your body was dumped. The first thing you thought of when you regained consciousness. I want to know if he touched you. I want to know what you were thinking when he pointed the gun at you. What you felt when the bullet went in."

Chalfin had been shouting, and now, when he stopped, he seemed to stagger. Catching himself, he stood like a soldier.

Raya was staring at him, half reclining on the bed.

"Did you hear me? I want answers."

"I told you. I said nothing. I revealed nothing."

It all seemed too clear and too terrible. "You're lying to me, Raya. You signaled them from the sidecar, outside The Trunk. You were waiting for them to kill me. You wanted them to kill me."

The words poured out of him. He felt he could continue to speak for days; as if he could make ten thousand accusations; as if there was no longer anything in the way of truth.

He lifted his hands in a gesture of confusion. "But why, Raya, why? Why in the name of God are you with them?"

"You are talking foolish, David. Come here. Sit down."

In a sudden rage he put his hands around her throat. He would choke the life from her filthy Nazi body. Her beautiful eyes would be gone. He wanted nothing left of her, nothing. And then, suddenly, he let go. He kissed her again and again. He staggered backward.

So what if he killed her? What then? He couldn't kill her enough. What if he killed each section of her, and buried her, and mutilated her?

No, he thought, no death. Not here. I am going to run from her, he realized. I am going home to Palestine. I'm going to run. And he did.

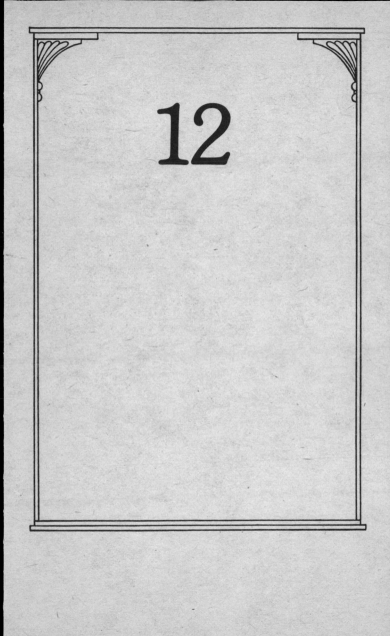

12

Palestine. Two white strings, eighteen inches apart, seemed to stretch into eternity. They were supported by sticks. David Chalfin commenced digging between the strings. He was digging what would ultimately be an irrigation ditch. He had a pick ax and a shovel.

When he had first come to Palestine from England, bursting with enthusiasm for the idea of cosmopolitans returning to the soil, he had embraced the pick with fervor. Fifteen, eighteen, twenty hours a day—the joy of killing labor was wholly satisfying. Then, slowly, it had worn thin. But now, once again he used the pick with an approximation of joy. The pick was sanctuary.

It was midmorning. Chalfin held the pick with both hands, brought his arms up, the tool reaching high over his head for a moment's suspension, and then brought it down into the rock-hard earth. He pulled out the pick and repeated the

223

entire sequence. Chalfin was rusty. Now he began to concentrate, and it went better and better, and soon he was swinging the pick easily. He progressed down the lines of string.

Every several feet he lay down the pick and dug out the earth with his shovel. Then he moved on with the pick. There was no reason to hurry. The ditch would take months to dig and he wanted it that way. He wanted to be obliterated in a functional manner, day by day.

Chalfin had visited the headquarters of the Jewish Agency in Jerusalem, and he had told them that he was through for a while, that he needed a rest. And that was all he told them. What he felt, what he knew, he could not articulate. And besides, it was of no interest to anyone else. It was only a little intrigue in a bizarre corner of the world, and it was without clarity. No point, no reason, no clarity. He found it incomprehensible, so why should he speak of it? Only Raya could he comprehend. Raya had been abducted by Quinton. She had been told that he, Chalfin, had betrayed her. In fury she had allowed herself to be turned. She had set him up for the kill. As for the false Malorange, Chalfin hadn't a clue.

The palms of his hands were starting to blister. He let gravity take more of the downswing so that he needn't grasp the pick so firmly. Toward noon he stopped and rested. A woman was walking toward him with a cart of chicken feed. She paused, smiling, and offered him some water.

Chalfin drank, avoiding conversation, and handed back the cup. She continued her journey, and Chalfin watched the cart, which was almost like a child's wagon. Its wheels were bent and unsteady, and the woman pulled it along with difficulty.

He wrapped a handkerchief around one hand and returned to the pick. He tried to increase the tempo of his efforts. I will spend the rest of my life doing this, he thought. My fidelity will be to impossible tasks. That was fine. That was what it was all about. When the war was over he would change his clothes and continue digging. A thousand irrigation ditches dug by

David Chalfin. And when there was a Jewish state, as there must one day be a Jewish state, he would be famous for his ditches.

The pick at its apogee, Chalfin halted. Suddenly he wanted Raya. To see her, to talk to her, to love her. How to proceed from day to day without her? How to forget? The pick dropped from his hands.

If he couldn't touch her again, what could he touch? The loss was unbearable. He could not bear the loss. He had never known such loss. He sat down beside the shallow ditch, looking for another human soul. The woman with the cart had vanished.

Hope dies if the loss is great enough.

Hope was like broken glass. Chalfin was ashamed of his weakness. From the Atlantic to the Volga his brothers and sisters were being systematically destroyed—and he couldn't bear the loss of a woman. He shook his head in despair and shame. Winokur had been right. There is no hope for the Englishman who falls in love with a whore.

"A madman was looking for you. He came here with a gun and a corpse. He stayed a while and then left. I was afraid, but not so much as you might think. I have never seen such a crazy man. He was looking for you so you would be nice to his corpse."

Raya didn't quite understand what Helene had said. A man brought a corpse into The Trunk? And why? She didn't understand and she didn't want to understand. She was sitting with Helene only because it was usual, just before opening, for the whores to sit at a certain table, together. The Trunk was empty but for the five whores at one table.

"What is the fee for a corpse?"

No one could answer.

"What do corpses like?"

"To be bitten," said the oldest in Greek. And at this they all laughed.

225

The conversation was now given over to corpses. They told jokes and true stories. They giggled. Raya listened. She watched the large Nubian clean the floor. He would save his money and then vanish into the tribal south, toward the Sudan. He cleaned the floor under the women just as if they were not there.

"The Germans," Helene was saying, "are good to their women. I know. They pay in coin. They are polite. But sometimes they do strange things. There was an officer, I forget his name. He came to see me once or twice a week. And then he vanished. Two months later he returned. He undressed very slowly. He took off his boots, his tunic, his cap. When he was entirely naked he gave me the money. Then he grabbed his pistol and blew his brains out."

"Why?" asked the oldest one.

"He didn't say why. He just shot himself in the head."

"In front of you?"

"Right in front of me. No one knew what to do with the body."

"The man who wanted Raya could've made use of it. To keep his friend company."

The Nubian had finished cleaning the floor and was now rearranging the tables, aligning them precisely along the walls and at exact right angles in the middle of the room.

"Raya, are you sick?"

She had heard her name but not the question. She continued to watch the Nubian.

"She is sick."

"Tell her to go home."

"Tell her yourself."

Raya put her head down on the table. She missed her mother. Why wasn't her mother here in The Trunk, telling lies?

Someone put a hand on her shoulder. She shook it off.

"She's crying."

"She's sick."

226

"Get her home."

"But she doesn't listen."

Another hand on her shoulder. Again she threw it off.

"What's the matter with her?"

Her mother should be here, facing the door. Raya would tell her about the red dress and the gold coins and about David. And the cipher. And Quinton. Raya would tell her everything.

Someone spotted the white bandage beneath Raya's skirt.

"Look at that. Look."

They all looked. They asked questions. She ignored them.

Raya was not sick. She was thinking with a white-hot continuity. Her future was gone. David Chalfin hated her. She would never see him again. He was gone, her future was gone. There was nothing she could change now. A wall stood between herself and tomorrow. A wall solid as the table beneath her cheek. Raya picked up her head and looked across the room. Her mother was not there. Her mother was dead. And what about her mother's mother? Raya slammed her face into the table. Pain. Pain was good. And what about the woman who gave birth to the woman who gave birth to her mother?

If I'm going to die, to be dead, I want to know where I came from. I did not come from this filth called Cairo. I am here now but I did not come from here. I did not come from those meandering alleys of cries and screams. I did not speak a little of Arabic, English, French. I came from somewhere.

Only when she tasted the salt did she know she was crying. She did not mind crying. The other women hovered around her, not knowing what to say. They wanted to protect her, but from what they did not know. They had no idea what was wrong. They had no idea why she could not respond to their concern.

The Nubian was laying out ashtrays on the tables. He put two on the table at which the women were sitting. Raya picked one up and threw it across the room.

227

Helene retrieved it, brought it back to the table, and kept her hand on it. "Don't throw anything else. Come with me," she said gently, and tugged at Raya's arm. Raya planted herself rigidly, and then, in less than an instant, followed Helene to the back of The Trunk, into one of the rooms.

Palestine. Chalfin lay on a cot, fully clothed. There were twelve other cots in the darkened hut, all empty. He was too tired to take off his clothes; he had no desire to attend the weekly party of farm workers now going on in the ramshackle rec hall. The sounds of song and laughter filtered through the open windows.

His legs ached from the unaccustomed swing of the pick. Why his legs and not his back? The songs he heard were in Yiddish and Russian and French. They seemed to be having a very good time over there.

Chalfin longed for a shower—there was one just outside the room. He wanted to shower. But he lay there.

He had done well with the pick that day, but not too well with the shovel. He liked to swing the pick. He hated removing the earth with the shovel. He had the classic disease of the English bourgeoisie: the inability to clean up.

Sooner or later he would have to write a letter to his family. A long letter. The best thing would be to wax poetic about the farm, the ditch, the parties in the rec hall. Nothing about Cairo.

Finally he fell asleep and dreamt a convoluted dream about an airplane that dropped him somewhere in Europe; Germans appeared in great numbers and he killed all of them, but there was never any blood. No German bled. When he awoke he thought of Raya instantly, and the thought of her obscured the dream. Songs and laughter still flowed from the rec hall, but the sounds were more subdued.

Chalfin sat up and began to unlace his shoes. It was time to brave the shower. Suddenly the steel door of the hut opened. He could make out only the silhouette of a man.

"David Chalfin, I presume. Found at last in the darkest pit of Africa. Near death, emaciated, bereft of hope."

The voice was clipped, sarcastic, and familiar. Chalfin got to his feet.

"However, this doesn't seem to be Africa. It's Asia. Where, exactly, are we?" And here the man began to laugh.

"Matthew!" Chalfin rushed to the door and embraced him. "My God! It's been more than a year."

"Much more than a year."

"But how did you know where I was?"

"They told me."

Matthew sat down on a cot and lit a cigarette. He was young, with a dark complexion and a shaven head. He wore the clothes of a Beirut merchant: an ill-fitting suit of heavy linen forty years out of fashion. Matthew had been Chalfin's closest friend in the Jewish Agency. They were both English, they were both Zionists.

"I heard that you went around a very long bend. And that I had missed you only by hours. I thought it would be nice to see my old friend who had flipped. In England, friends flip all the time. But here?"

"Tell me where you've been."

"South America."

"South America," Chalfin repeated, as though the words denoted a very exotic realm.

"It was warm there," said Matthew. Leaning back on the cot, he stared at his friend.

Chalfin was disconcerted by the stare and looked out the doorway.

"And you," said Matthew, "were in Cairo."

"I was in Cairo, yes."

"You don't appear crazy," observed Matthew.

"I doubt very much that I am."

"Maybe it was just the impression you gave."

"Maybe," Chalfin agreed.

"What did you do in Cairo?"

"What did you do in South America?"

Matthew laughed. He ground out his cigarette and went over to Chalfin, throwing a friendly arm around his shoulder. Chalfin moved aside.

"Too pat, too pat. They sent you here, didn't they, Matthew? This is an interrogation."

"Call it what you will. You leave Cairo in a hurry. You appear at Agency Headquarters. You announce your sudden retirement. And you vanish. Surely you expect people to be curious."

"Then what do you want to know? Tell me. After all, old friends shouldn't be hesitant. What do you want to know?"

"I suppose I'll have to think of some questions."

"I suppose you will."

"But first," said Matthew, "I want to show you something, in the light."

They left the hut and stood under the small electric bulb that illumined the doorway.

"Look here," said Matthew. He pressed a pistol into Chalfin's hand. Chalfin looked down at the weapon. It was terribly heavy, large and ugly. It had the aspect of a small cannon.

"That, my friend," said Matthew with obvious pleasure, "is an American forty-five-caliber pistol." Then he grabbed the pistol and removed the clip. He returned it to Chalfin, who took aim and gently pressed the trigger.

"When it fires," said Matthew, "it takes your arm off."

"As ugly as the world." Chalfin handed back the weapon.

"But it has an interesting history. The Americans developed it during the Philippine Insurrection. It seems there was a tribe known as the Moros, and they continued to overrun the American positions because no single-shot weapon could stop their charge. So this thing was developed. It can blow a hole in you. Ah, the Americans—they have a startling grasp of the real. Wouldn't you say, David?"

Matthew was certainly the same. His shaven head held vast stores of information mysteriously acquired. No one had ever seen Matthew read a book.

Chalfin began to walk away from the hut and Matthew followed. He stopped at the incomplete irrigation ditch and stared at the two white strings, luminous in the night.

"I'm tired and a bit sick. I don't want to work for the Agency anymore. I want to dig ditches."

"Perfectly comprehensible," said Matthew.

Chalfin looked at his friend. What was the content of their friendship? Why, if they were friends, had he not thought of Matthew in so long? But certainly they were friends. Of course.

"There's nothing much to tell, Matthew. Just one of those sad little tales, you know. One of the saddest tales of all. I fell in love with a whore. Raya. I recruited her for an assignment. It was a joint operation with British Intelligence. Of no great importance to anyone—not to us, not to the British, and surely not to the Germans. Things happened. Inexplicable things. And, as it turned out, the whore did not love me at all. And she helped to have me killed. But you see, I am still alive. I still love the whore. So you see . . ."

"I see."

"And that is all there is to tell. Now you can go back." Chalfin kicked at a rock but missed it. He bent down, picked it up, and threw it into the night.

"A whore," said Matthew musingly.

"Yes. Nothing philosophical. A good old-fashioned whore. A few shillings for a few minutes." Chalfin looked down, searching for another rock. "Ah, yes—there is one other thing. This whore, Raya, is a Jew."

They turned, as if on cue, and began to walk.

"So there. That was the information you wanted. The content of my lunacy."

Matthew simply pointed to the rec hall.

"The weekly bash," Chalfin explained.

They reached Matthew's stripped-down Land Rover, part of its body rusted away. Matthew eased himself into the driver's seat. He had obtained what he had come for. There was no reason to stay. He said, "Didn't your father caution you against falling in love with whores?"

"My father never spoke of such things."

"Well. You'll survive, David."

"Yes, I suppose I will."

"May I give you a word of advice?"

Chalfin nodded. "Why not?"

Matthew started the engine and smiled. Chalfin did not care for the smile.

"My advice is this: the next time you tell the story, tell it straight."

"I told you exactly what happened!" Chalfin was furious.

"Yes, but you wrapped it in a cover story. For others, that is fine. But remember, I work for the Agency. No operational collaboration between the Jewish Agency and British Intelligence has yet been authorized. I happen to know this. We exchange a few files, we exchange a few odd jobs, and we may do something together in the future. But not yet. So, be brave. A whore made a fool out of you. You're in good company."

The Land Rover started to pull away. Chalfin stood rooted to the ground for a moment, then sprinted after the vehicle, shouting Matthew's name.

Matthew finally braked. Chalfin caught up to him.

"What did you mean about no collaboration? Exactly what did you mean?"

Matthew wondered at his agitation. "There are no joint operations yet. None have been authorized. None."

"I don't understand!"

"It's all very simple: no joint operations. When you are through with all this rural idiocy, come round and we'll have a drink," said Matthew. Then he drove off.

Chalfin felt as though someone had kicked him in the stomach, and he squatted on the ground like an Arab. The revelation had been too intense, too severe. *Winokur!* Winokur had told him that the joint operation was authorized. There was no joint operation with British Intelligence. *Winokur!* Chalfin squatted in the middle of the road.

He felt an immense exhaustion. In the entire panorama of betrayal and confusion, the notion that Winokur somehow was orchestrating events never crossed his mind. How could it be? Why would Winokur fake a collaboration with British Intelligence? Did Winokur know that the Colonel Malorange who solidified this bogus partnership was himself bogus? The weight of his head seemed to push him into a deeper squat. He could think of his epitaph: "Lo, the man loved two persons, and was betrayed by both."

He tried to think. He tried to remember. There was only a diffuse fog in his brain—images, sounds, smells, but no coherence. Slowly, gradually, some contradictions began to surface; they were pulled out of his brain by his heart—by his hurt.

Winokur had sent him to The Trunk before the meeting with the bogus Colonel Malorange. Winokur had sent him to The Trunk before the mission was even identified.

Winokur had said the entire British offensive was of no importance really in the war, therefore the entire Quinton operation was absurd—yet he was willing that Raya should die to enhance the "absurd" operation.

Winokur had refused to send him on a mission to Europe, had ridiculed those missions, had fought against his going—and then suddenly, in a moment, he had sent him, seemingly on a whim.

And Winokur had let him return to Palestine, without argument because he thought his young friend was burned out; he thought David Chalfin no longer could reason, no longer could respond to events. He thought Raya Fahmi had destroyed him.

Contradictions. Contradictions. Chalfin began to breathe slowly, in and out, out and in.

13

London. The letter lay between the covers of the rich red leather portfolio. Samuel Chalfin had written it a week before, to his son, but had not sent it. And he knew that even if his son had been answering his letters, this particular letter would still not be sent. He had written it on fine-quality paper, with a scratch pen. As he sat at the desk and his fingers played with the end of the paper, he was astonished at his own writing. He didn't know if it was the truth or a lie. It occurred to Samuel Chalfin that what he held in his hands was a letter he had written to himself.

Some ash fell on the desk and he blew it away, then rubbed the beautifully polished wood with his palm to make sure no blemish remained.

He read the letter he had written for the third time.

"Dear David—

"Lately I have been thinking about the past, my past. And suddenly I remembered why I came to England. Oh, I know you think I came here to better myself, like millions of other emigrés, or to escape a land that had always meant death to our people. Even I believe that now. But that really was not the reason. It was a childhood reason. It had lay buried for years. It had to do with a book your Uncle Will once gave me. He was the older brother, so I wore his clothes and read his books.

"It was a very grimy book with big ugly pictures that had a purple tint, and it was all about Launcelot and Galahad and the knights of the Round Table. There were pictures of men in steel clothes, with visors over their face, and they were always traveling back and forth across Wales killing dragons and saving women and searching for something called the Grail, which I never knew what it was, and still don't. Of all the books of my childhood, that was the one I loved best.

"I read it thousands of times. I stared the pictures off the pages. But please, don't think I loved it because of the adventure. The Germanic knights were really more adventurous than Arthur and his friends. No, I loved the book because they were so polite. They were always saying to each other: 'Pray tell, fair knight, whither art thou going?'

"All these men upon their furious war horses were the gentlest souls in Christendom. Don't misunderstand. I did not think that they still existed in England. It was just that England had given them birth. Am I being foolish in bringing this up? Am I deluding myself into thinking that a childhood infatuation is the reason I am here now, and you were once here. Maybe I am not making myself clear. I did not long for Arthur's realm as a child because it was gentle; I longed for it because I felt that if it was gentle, it must be beautiful. Vienna was never beautiful to me. But then again, neither is Liverpool. I am here now and England is neither gentle nor beautiful. I am successful, and I will die here. It is all very strange. As I said, it was just something I remembered after all these years. Please forgive a businessman for his vanity."

Well, thought Samuel Chalfin, it is a very strange letter, and it isn't even a finished letter. A letter must have an ending. But

238

he didn't try for one, because he was not mailing the letter to anyone.

Hour after hour Chalfin lay in the produce truck. It was the last leg of the always backbreaking journey to Cairo; the first leg being a motor launch from Haifa to Alexandria, hugging the land. Neither the length nor the discomfort had any meaning this time.

Winokur. Chalfin conjured up the face of his hero. His hero singing bawdy Yiddish songs. His hero making cryptic but unarguable remarks. His hero in his Merlinesque cave, moving figures back and forth, moving loyalties, making clear that which was once cloudy, making obtuse that which was once naked and apparent.

Winokur was throwing the dice. Winokur had gathered them all—himself, Raya, Quinton, the phony Malorange—and put them in a dice cup, and then he had thrown them out to kill each other.

From time to time on this ride back to Cairo, Chalfin felt positively gleeful. The glee—a form of romanticism—made him nervous. He didn't feel that the great Winokur had betrayed him; he felt that Winokur had merely exhibited another aspect of his unique personality. Chalfin shoved away the glee. Many were hurt, many were dead, and he, Chalfin, might easily have been dead. No, romanticism must be shunned. It had betrayed him before.

As for Raya, he had no idea what she was doing with Winokur. Or why she was with Winokur. Or how.

Chalfin's plan evolved amidst the jostling of produce crates. He would simply follow Winokur until he found the answer. He would track him day and night until Winokur revealed Winokur. *Until Winokur revealed Winokur.* Repetition of the phrase put him into a stupor.

An hour after dawn he arrived in Cairo; twenty minutes later he was standing across the street from Winokur's flat. He felt no fatigue. He stood there without any discomfort, with the sense of keeping an easy vigil.

At ten o'clock, Winokur appeared. Chalfin's confidence and energy vanished. He pressed back against the building wall, hoping to make himself invisible. He wasn't strong, he was weak. He wasn't analytical, he was a frightened fool up against a man he revered.

Chalfin didn't know how to follow a suspect. He found it difficult to watch Winokur along with cars and donkeys and pedestrians. Sometimes he fell too far behind, and sometimes he found himself too close. An hour went by before Chalfin realized that the job would be easier done on the other side of the street.

Winokur was walking easily, looking at stalls, at passersby, at vehicles, and occasionally up at the sky. He stopped at a newsstand, dug in his pocket for coins, and gathered several newspapers. Chalfin felt a sudden remorse. Buying the papers and combing them for significant information had been one of his chores.

Winokur sat down at a café with the papers and ordered a coffee. Chalfin stayed across the street, facing Winokur's back. He watched the man read each paper, fold it, and slide it behind his back, pressed against the chair. When he had finished all the papers he ordered another coffee and lit a cigarette—his first of the morning as far as Chalfin knew.

A fixed purpose kills flies, Chalfin recalled Winokur having said. Well, he had a fixed purpose. They both did.

After a third coffee and another cigarette, Winokur paid his bill and sauntered out of the café. Chalfin followed him back to his flat. When Winokur went upstairs, Chalfin leaned against a wall across the street and began to peel an orange he had picked out of one of the produce crates on the truck. All this tracking had been exhausting but nothing had happened. What if Winokur never went anywhere, if he just took trivial walks day after day? If Winokur never revealed Winokur. If he, Chalfin, would never be able to discover anything. If . . . The orange was dry. He ate it slowly, section by section. Dry. For how long could he follow Winokur? He had nowhere to stay in Cairo, no friends, little money. Two days? Three days? Four days?

Winokur appeared at the window. Chalfin felt sure he had been preparing coffee—then he had paced the room and come to look out the window. Chalfin had watched him do it so many times.

Late in the afternoon Winokur emerged again. Chalfin followed. Winokur's gait was now more purposeful; obviously he was going somewhere. Chalfin followed him north, past the old hotels. He stopped, to Chalfin's astonishment, in front of the Egyptian Museum.

Winokur soon vanished in the hordes of soldiers taking a dab of ancient Egyptian culture. Chalfin moved with them like a barnacle on a ship, occasionally catching a glimpse of Winokur. Room 29 contained papyruses of different periods, plus the tools of the trade such as scribes' palettes—and here Winokur lingered for a while.

In the corridor outside room 34 he lit a cigarette. A group of soldiers joined him, equally forgetful of the no-smoking regulation.

Chalfin concentrated on the artifacts in front of him: a musical instrument, an axe, a small statuette of a mother combing her daughter's hair; a perfume jar from the Eighteenth dynasty in the shape of a man carrying a vase; a small wood tortoise from the Eleventh dynasty with dog-headed pins; sticks, lances, daggers, boomerangs, weights and measures, castanets; a cosmetic spoon from the New Kingdom.

Suddenly he heard Winokur's distinctive laugh. He moved to a case near the corridor and watched Winokur engaging in a heated discussion with a soldier. He edged closer but still couldn't make out their words. He had never seen the soldier before. Were they talking about something of importance or were they talking about tobacco? The conversation abruptly broke off. Winokur proceeded to tour the rooms, Chalfin following. Now Winokur seemed to move with impatience,

241

and he went through the remaining rooms in less than half an hour, then left the museum.

Chalfin followed him home, watched him enter the building, then slid to the ground against a building across the street. There was the problem of sleep. How was he to keep a constant vigil, without sleeping? If he fell asleep and Winokur slipped by him, what was the point of it all?

The soldier in the museum . . . was he of any significance? Should he have left Winokur and followed the soldier? Was Winokur given to starting conversations in public? On any topic?

The hours passed. It grew dark. In spite of himself he napped from time to time. He thought of the sequence of events which had brought him back to Cairo: the abduction and release of Raya, the shooting, the conversation with the stranger in the bar, Matthew's interrogation. He was like a crippled spider scurrying back and forth across a web that held food he couldn't digest. Back and forth he scurried, up and down.

To stop his train of thought he impulsively emptied his pockets, dropping everything on the ground between his legs. An orange, a few dates, some nuts. A penknife, the keys to his former flat, a few coins. Then he cleaned and loaded the Beretta. It didn't have the philosophical bluntness—the lethalness—of Matthew's American pistol. Had Matthew wanted to give that to him? Maybe all he had to do was ask.

Whatever Winokur had done, surely he thought he had gotten away with it. He was sitting up there, reveling in his mastery over the stupid young Englishman. Chalfin put his pistol back in his pocket. The thought that Winokur did not know he was being followed, that he did not know the stupid young Englishman had returned—this thought gave Chalfin great pleasure.

As the night wore on he lay down on the ground, his eyes turned toward Winokur's window, though he could barely focus. It was very odd: in Cairo, an English Jew was watching the flat of a Polish Jew. Chalfin felt a sudden affection for

Cairo, for that enormous hub that now held and supported hundreds of thousands of foreigners. For the city that allowed them all to die in their own way, with their own weapons, at their own appointed times.

"Cairo," Winokur had once said, "is the only city that lays eggs."

More of his chicken imagery. Chicken imagery that had survived Poland, where a chicken that could be eaten was the chariot of Ezekiel, and a chicken that laid eggs was the closest thing to the godhead.

Two *fellahin* paused in the street, stared at Chalfin, and exchanged remarks about him. They were accustomed to drunken soldiers in uniform, but Chalfin gave the appearance of a civilian derelict. When he took out the Beretta they passed on.

Winokur appeared at the window, staring out onto the street. Chalfin aimed his pistol at the compact figure. It was possible. With one shot he could destroy Winokur. He lowered the weapon. What, exactly, was Winokur's crime?

He stayed at the window for what seemed to be a long long time. He is remembering, thought Chalfin. Perhaps he stands at the window every night and looks out over Cairo and remembers the past.

As Chalfin lay there he thought the night would never end. It will never end, it will never end, it will never end. He began to say numbers, magically, as a child, so that the light would come and extinguish the darkness.

Raya hovered over everything else in his mind. He longed to embrace her; the longing was unendurable; he bit his own hand to obscure the pain. Sweat poured from him. His scent was rancid. His clothing chafed his skin.

He looked up and saw that Winokur was gone from the window. Was he asleep again? Or pacing the floor? Making coffee? Smoking? Plotting another unnamed crime?

Chalfin knew where Raya was and what she was doing. She was being bought. Again and again.

He was lying here on this street precisely because he would not be bought.

And what if the bullets had reached him? Chalfin sat up to speculate. Enthralled, he imagined his own funeral. It would be in Cairo. Winokur would be there, and the phony Malorange, and Raya, all in tears. Naturally in tears. They had all killed him.

He ate a few nuts, rolled onto his stomach, and began to compose a letter to his father. *Dear Father.* No, just *Father.* Or no salutation at all? That wasn't possible. It must be *Dear Father.* Chalfin had no paper. He wrote in his head.

Dear Father: I am lying in an alley in Cairo, but I am in the best of health. Across the street is a building, in the building is a flat, in the flat is a man. I am waiting for the man to lead me to a certain solution.

No, that won't do.

Dear Father: I am lying in an alley in Cairo with a loaded Beretta. I am here because I fell in love.

No, no, no. Too sudden an opening. He glanced up at Winokur's window.

Dear Father: Thank you for your last letter. I received it a long time after it was mailed, because I am no longer in Palestine. The Jewish Agency assigned me to Cairo. The work is not difficult, but boring.

No, that won't do. No.

Dear Father: A few days ago I was machine-gunned outside a brothel in Cairo. I survived, untouched.

Dear Father: Today I visited the museum in Cairo and saw many remarkable artifacts, among them an exquisite cosmetic spoon from the New Kingdom.

Dear Father: Did I ever tell you about my immediate superior, Winokur? A remarkable man. I am proud to serve under him. He is smart, cynical, brave, and above all, wise. I think he is the history of East European Jewry writ large in one small man. I would die for him. He came from Poland. Probably there is much blood on his hands, but as he would say, it is all fascist blood.

244

Dear Father: I loved a whore. I betrayed her. Then she betrayed me.

Dear Father: As an occasional university lecturer on the perils of high finance, did you ever run across a scholar named Malorange? He was working on the Dark Lady of the Sonnets problem.

Dear Father: I am tired and frightened and hungry. I am lying in an alley in Cairo, waiting for a man to reveal himself.

Dear Father: I miss you. I miss England. I miss all the slaughtered Jews.

Dear Father: Do you remember that vacation in Scotland?

Dear Father: I am proud of the fact that I have discovered one truth . . . which, for some reason, escapes me at this moment.

Dear Father: I think I despise you and your friends and what you stand for because you have no contradictions. Now, consider my contradictions. I fell desperately in love with a woman who has been bought by hundreds of men. If you have some pound notes you can have her. That was the way I had her. With pound notes. But then I moved further—I loved her without money, I worshiped her, I would have killed just to be able to touch her. How is it possible for a sane man to love a woman who is constantly being bought? How is it possible for *me*, whom you know, to love *her*—whom you do not know but can imagine. So, you see, I am a man with immense contradictions between what lies between my ears and what lies between my legs. But that was a small contradiction. I am now waiting for a man who I wanted to replace you. And it is possible that I will have to kill him.

Dear Winokur:

Dear Winokur:

Dear Winokur: When will the dawn come?

Raya's day of derangement had passed. She was working again. Soliciting, collecting, performing. The camaraderie of the whores had also passed. Only Helene kept a wary eye on her.

The memory of Chalfin's accusations was like a sore that never healed. Painful, continually open. But she believed that he had gone crazy, and that one day he would come out of it. She was not without hope.

Seeing the white bandage, her first customer of the night was at first solicitous. Then he was overly talkative. He stroked the bandage. Raya thought he wanted to see the wound bleed through the bandage. He was intensely passionate, and this nauseated her.

Finally he left, and for the first time she cheated the house. In the rear of The Trunk were small wooden boxes, hidden from view. Each box was lettered with the name of a whore. After finishing with a customer each whore would put the money in her box. Later on, at the end of the night, The Trunk would take sixty percent and give forty percent back to the whore. Raya slipped two paper bills into her shoe before depositing the money in the box.

As the night wore on she began to study her body as she performed. None of them usually did this. To survive as a whore they had to keep their heads well away from their bodies. But now she watched herself with genuine curiosity. The way she moved about the tables. The way she lifted her hands. The way her head inclined to one side.

She watched herself under the Oriental merchant seaman. He was young and thin. He seemed almost to be chanting. His eyes were gray, fixed on the wall behind her head. She saw herself move underneath him.

David had said of all those who paid that they were dogs who needed water to live—but no water slaked their thirst.

What did those gray eyes see? What were those sounds that came from his throat?

She watched herself receiving his final thrusts. She watched herself as he rolled away from her. He sat up and looked toward her from the end of the bed.

She wanted to ask, Now that you have had water and are still thirsty, what next?

He picked up her skirt from the chair and ran it through his fingers. "My name is Duc. I am a Christian."

Raya simply nodded.

"My family are not Christian. I decided for my own."

She found his way of speaking attractive, but saw that it caused him discomfort.

"This is my third voyage."

Raya reached for her skirt. He pushed her hand away and continued to caress the fabric.

"What is your name?"

Raya kept silent.

"Does not matter," he said. He folded the skirt and handed it to her.

Raya got off the bed and began to dress. Suddenly he slipped his hand under her blouse. She stood quietly.

"I am frightened of the ocean. And sick all the time. The waves they are very high. Higher than the city. Many ships go down, sink. We saw them. Noise, then red flame, then ship go under the water." He let his hand fall slowly to illustrate a ship sinking.

He is more pathetic than most, thought Raya.

"I have much money," he said, his gray eyes on her breasts. Then he leaped like a cat to his clothes. He gathered a lot of paper bills and put them on top of her fee. "Again," he said.

Raya sat down on the bed.

"Again," he repeated, this time pleadingly.

It was easier than soliciting at the tables once more.

The young seaman undressed her. He was childishly exuberant. She was his finest toy.

This would take some time, she knew, but there was no rush. He had paid for this time. He was talking about his ship again. Where was David now? In Palestine. A vast land, a vast land. She could see him walking across the land. She could see him sitting in a café, drinking coffee. Was he well? She hoped he was well. Perhaps he had gone from Cairo to

Jerusalem. Jerusalem, the city her mother had always talked about. But she had made fun of it. People went there, she had said, to pray or to die. And her mother had refused to pray and had never believed she would die. Jerusalem. A beautiful name. It must be a beautiful place to die.

The young Oriental was kissing her arm. His gray eyes now seemed almost black. He kissed her arm, her shoulder, her neck.

"I am happy," he said. Then he entered her.

Raya could no longer watch her own body. The curiosity was gone. Gone as well was the sense that he was pathetic. He wasn't pathetic, he was hateful. She hated him. She desired to tear out his gray-black eyes.

He is in Palestine, she thought. She brought her hand up onto the young man's shoulder. It was a loving hand, for David Chalfin.

Winokur kept to the same pattern: a morning walk and then a walk in the afternoon. Chalfin continued surveillance. The place from which he watched Winokur's flat was littered with orange peels.

In the morning, Winokur bought the papers and had coffee in the café—the same newsstand, the same café. In the afternoon he went for a stroll through the Azbakiya Gardens. He gazed upon each shrub as though it might contain the world's wisdom.

Chalfin followed him back to his flat, then glanced at the alley which seemed to be home. The idea of another night there was horrifying. He had no option. Tonight he might compose letters to Matthew. The next night to Raya. And the following night to unknown soldiers in France, England, Germany. . . .

He arranged himself for the evening, back against the wall, legs outstretched. The next morning he would have to buy fruit and bread, and a container to keep water in. Night came down. Chalfin got to his feet and began to walk the small space of the alley. Around the perimeter, across the diagonals, up and down, back and forth. He counted his steps. On the four hundred and fifty-fourth step he glanced over his shoulder and saw Winokur on the street. Smoking. Wearing a cap. Chalfin pressed himself against the wall and waited.

Winokur seemed to be enjoying the night. Smoking, looking around contentedly. Then he took off in a hurry, tugging on his cap as he walked. When he was nearly out of sight Chalfin followed. Night made things difficult. No crowds to hide in, no workaday bustle to assure anonymity.

Winokur kept the brisk pace until he reached the river. Here he paused and lit a cigarette, then looked behind him, as if to check on whether he had been followed. But Chalfin had anticipated the smoking break, and he successfully hugged a building. Winokur finished his cigarette and walked on at a slow pace, following the river. This part of the river was unknown to Chalfin. Derelict houseboats, crumbling shacks, and antique Arab fishing boats lined the shore. People carried pails and nets and baskets suspended between poles. The only European Chalfin saw was the one he was following.

Winokur stopped before a barge that sat a few yards out on the river, connected to shore by a ramp. He paced back and forth. He stopped again and looked all around. He seemed to listen, to wait for a cue. Then he walked down the ramp and vanished through a door.

Winokur was in the barge. Everything was in the barge.

If Chalfin went down the ramp they would hear him immediately. He took off everything but his trousers and put his pistol in one of his shoes. Then he rolled up his pants and slid into the water. It was cold and it was filthy. He breast-stroked around to the other side of the barge. His feet touched the slimy wood just below the surface of the river. Directly beneath the lighted windows he could hear the sound of laughter.

Suddenly he was afraid. He looked out upon the river. The river could swallow him. It could swallow every trace of David Chalfin. He was also afraid of what was inside the barge. He was also afraid of the slime.

The lapping of water against the barge seemed to him explosively loud.

Chalfin shoved aside all his fears. He pulled himself up onto the ledge and peered through a window. What he saw left him without equilibrium.

Winokur and Quinton! Drinking from paper cups!

He fell back into the Nile, turning to escape the tide. Slowly he worked his way back to shore. Slowly he climbed ashore. Blessed are the heroes, they shall inherit the earth. By collaboration. He tried to lace his shoes. Blessed are the Jewish heroes, they shall happily drink with Nazis. He was very cold and very wet. Obsessively in the darkness, he cleaned and recleaned his Beretta. He waited. Half dressed, he waited for Winokur.

Winokur walked down the ramp an hour later. He strolled a hundred yards along the river's edge and then turned into a street. Turned, as well, into Chalfin's gun.

Chalfin lay the tip of the barrel against Winokur's forehead. He cocked the weapon. He delighted in the sweat that appeared on his hero's face.

"David, what are you doing?"

"Holding a gun to your head."

"When did you come back?"

"Now. I came back now."

"Put that stupid thing down."

Chalfin pushed the pistol harder into Winokur's bone. "Tell me again," he said softly, "how brave you were in Poland. How you fought the fascists tooth and nail. Tell me again."

"David, put the gun down."

"What about the *real* story? Perhaps you survived by selling your friends. Perhaps you survived by a little collaboration. Not much. No, not much. Just a little. A very, very little."

Winokur burst out laughing. "Do you think I was collaborating with Quinton? Remember our mission, David. To get the cipher, catch him, and turn him. We did it. He's ours. He's transmitting what we tell him to transmit. Oh, God, did you

250

think I work for the Germans?" He laughed uproariously.

"There was no mission. No mission. Matthew told me. The Agency never authorized any joint operations with the British. You're lying, Winokur. Lying."

Winokur drove his knee into Chalfin's crotch. Chalfin fell forward, holding on to the gun. He saw Winokur running. The pain lunged from his crotch to his gut. He forced himself to stand. Winokur was vanishing. One foot. The other foot. He could walk. One foot. The other foot. Jogging. Running. Running the pain out. Winokur was just ahead of him now. Closer. He could see his hero's collar.

Winokur stumbled, then fell to the ground. Chalfin kicked him in the face. An open gash, bleeding. Chalfin kneeled down and wiped away the blood with his sleeve. In a frantic whisper he said, "Do you want to live? If you want to live, tell me. If not, I will kill you now. I swear I will kill you."

Winokur said something in Polish.

Chalfin clawed at his open wound. "If you want to live," he shouted, "tell me. Now and in English. Who are you? What have you done? Why have you lied?"

Winokur whispered: "The future."

Chalfin straightened and stared down at the bloody face. Winokur's reply was incomprehensible.

Winokur repeated: "The future. The future." And then: "Lenin. Kamenev. Martov. Stalin. One Red World."

No, he could not comprehend that. He would not.

Winokur was screaming now: "For the future, David, so that you will never see another Jewish baby blown to pieces, or another Polish baby. . . . Do you understand me? I do everything for the future. For the Soviet Union. For you and that whore of yours."

Chalfin stared at the blood-splattered hero. God is a gypsy. Winokur, the Soviet agent, with Quinton, the Nazi operative, dancing together in the light of the Cairo moon. Winokur, the heart and soul of the Jewish Agency . . . the man who will lead the ingathering. . . . A Soviet agent! He didn't know what to do, how to respond. He didn't know whether to laugh or cry or dig the gun butt into the open wound. No, it could not be dealt with now. No, not now.

He turned away from Winokur, the Beretta light in his palm. He would act. That could be comprehended. One Nazi would die. He began to trot toward the barge. The pain was gone and he felt a hundred feet tall. When all was said and done, a Nazi was a Nazi, and Quinton was there. He had seen him. His feet took the ramp voraciously. When he kicked the door it flew open. Brian Quinton stood in the middle of the room. Chalfin raised the Beretta with a sense of exquisite pleasure.

"Well, David Chalfin," said the red-haired man in the middle of the room. "It appears by the state of your clothes that you have spoiled our little game. I'm Malorange. Colonel Malorange. Why don't you put that weapon down?"

The body of Carla Boudine lay tangled in moonlit weeds on the shore of the Nile. Her face was swollen but still beautiful and the eyes were wide open.

Tomlinson approached her carefully. He nudged her gently with his boot, and when there was no response he pulled her feverishly to the shore and cleaned away the weeds and mud.

She is more beautiful than the other one, he thought, and she seems kinder. This woman from the Nile was truly fit for his friend, Benito. This was Benito's mate.

It was the best of fortune. He had despaired of Benito's fate. The woman from The Trunk had been unfaithful. She had not waited. And that was why he had machine-gunned her and her lover. There must be fidelity. Oh, there must be fidelity. Oh, there must be fidelity.

He started back to the tethered donkey, to tell Benito the good news.

He never reached Benito. The sky seemed to explode on the horizon line. Tomlinson threw his hands over his eyes. And then, following the light, he heard the low rumble of the guns. His feet could sense the tremors in the earth.

Slowly he sank down until his face was against the ground. The rumbling continued—pulsing louder and softer.

His hands went over his ears, and then from the ears back to the eyes, and then back again—desperately trying to push the noise and light away.

They were coming again. They were coming to get him. He could smell the petrol and the burning rubber and the flayed flesh. He could feel the white hot rivets as they careened through the inside of the tank, cutting through bodies and fabric.

Something was wrong with his head. The pain was shooting up through his eyes. He started to crawl away from the sounds and the lights. His fingers pulled him along, his fingers grabbed and clawed and propelled him. Then he was up—running unsteadily toward the river.

He tripped over the body of Carla Boudine. He screamed. It was a corpse. He turned away from her and saw the donkey staring at him. Tied to the donkey's back was another corpse.

Tomlinson started to laugh. He was surrounded by corpses. Who were they? Who had they been? He could see what was left of their faces in the flashing lights.

He didn't know how he had arrived there—with the corpses. His corpses.

The guns were now synchronized with his own heartbeat. Every beat brought a beat of fear. He untethered the donkey and pulled it toward the river. He gathered up Carla Boudine in his arms and they all staggered to the water line.

There was safety there—across the river, on the east bank. When they came—when the Beast came, it would not be able to cross the river.

Ten yards. Twenty yards. They were crossing to the east. Until they came apart—arms, legs, hooves, ears. Apart, then down, down under the Nile.

It is a game, a lie, a way to stop me. Kill him, Chalfin thought.

"The guns," said the red-haired man. "That means Montgomery is moving. Well, it's all meaningless now."

Chalfin's finger was still on the trigger. The thumb which cradled the pistol was trembling.

"No doubt, Mr. Chalfin, you've seen a picture of me as the good Irish doctor, Brian Quinton, who, in his spare time, transmits the Eighth Army's most important information to Rommel. But, as I said, my name is Malorange. And, in fact, I'm English like yourself."

"I'm a Jew," said Chalfin, moving to his right, carefully.

"Yes, yes, I know. Would you care to put the safety on that weapon?"

Chalfin ignored the request.

"I am Malorange, Mr. Chalfin. Believe me. I am Colonel Malorange of British Intelligence."

"And I am Lopez," said Chalfin.

"But, as you well know, Lopez is dead, more than three hundred years dead. In the Elizabethan days, Mr. Chalfin, it was very dangerous for Sephardic Jews to make unpopular diagnoses, particularly if they were court physicians."

Chalfin put the safety on the weapon. He tried to relax, to let the motor run down, but his breath came in sharp short bursts. The man in front of him *was* Quinton *and* Malorange. Winokur was lying bloodied on the street. The man in front of him was Colonel Malorange, the real Colonel Malorange, the specter, the don of the Dark Lady of the Sonnets, the real Malorange.

Malorange smiled, gently.

"Some time ago it came to our attention that a Russian agent had infiltrated the intelligence section of the Jewish Agency here in Cairo. Strange, we thought. Why would the Russians go to the trouble? We are allies, all of us. Strange.

"Winokur was that agent. His associate, not affiliated with the Jewish Agency, was a man called Neurath. Our curiosity was aroused.

"So we gave Winokur two choice pieces of bait: a lone,

fascist sympathizer transmitting secrets to the Germans; and a Jewish whore who had serviced him. I, of course, was the fascist Brian Quinton. It was a role I had carefully constructed. And the whore's name was Raya Fahmi.

"He took the bait. Then he proceeded to enlist you in the battle. The man whom you thought was Colonel Malorange, was his associate Neurath.

"You did well. You recruited the whore. The whore found the cipher because I wanted her to find it. Winokur proceeded to capture me and turn me—a bona fide Nazi wireless operator to play with.

"Winokur ordered me to transmit to the Germans as much as he knew of the actual plans of the invasion."

Chalfin shouted back: "Do you expect me to believe that the Russians want Rommel to break the back of Montgomery's offensive?"

"Of course not. The Russians wanted the Germans to show Montgomery that they knew enough to stop it . . . that they knew how and where the British would be coming. The Russians wanted this offensive never to occur."

Slowly Chalfin was discerning the contours. He listened.

"The Russians don't want this offensive. They don't want the Allies to commit any more men or materials to North Africa. They want a second front in Europe, now. The Red Army is battling for its life against the Wehrmacht and the British are playing tactical games with a depleted Rommel. That, you see, is their reasoning. That was why Winokur came to Cairo."

Malorange paused to listen as the rumbling of guns intensified. Then he added dryly: "They do have a point, you know."

Chalfin stared at the thin line of red hair that seemed to join Malorange's eyebrows.

"By the way, I hope you didn't kill Winokur. After all, he is our ally."

"He's alive."

"Good. Very good."

Then Chalfin said with slow deliberation: "Tell me why you tried to kill me."

"But my dear Chalfin, we didn't. What would be the point of killing you? You were no threat to us. In fact you performed all your tasks perfectly. We know that someone machine-gunned the street. We have a description of the assailant and it seems to fit the description of a rather lunatic tank commander who deserted. If I recall, his name is Hopkinson or Tomlinson or Arlinton. He is quite mad. He was last seen traveling about with a corpse."

Malorange smiled and shrugged, as if to apologize for the madman.

"We also know you were beaten and robbed in one of the stall streets. I suspect that was your friend Winokur. Perhaps he just wanted to check that you were not sending any letters or dispatches that would compromise his operation."

"And Raya Fahmi? Is she with you?"

"The whore? God no, she's just a whore. An associate of mine informed us of the existence of this Jewish whore. It was a fortuitous coincidence, something that fit quite nicely into our plans for Winokur. I visited her as Quinton, and both of these facts were thrown to Winokur and Neurath. We speculated he would use someone in the Jewish Agency to recruit a Jewish whore. You. Then, after she obtained the cipher, Winokur engineered her betrayal. Merely to get rid of her. Winokur thought I would kill her, but I didn't wish to. The woman is simply one of those unfortunates. She knew nothing, except what you and Winokur told her. I understand that Winokur also tried to liquidate you; on an absurd flight to the partisans. Winokur is bright and imaginative, but sometimes a bit heavy-handed."

Ashes. Chalfin could taste ashes and cinders in his mouth. Shame, weariness, and remorse obscured his vision like a blanket. He had cursed her and struck her and deserted her for nothing. The nothing of a supposedly brilliant intuition. His existence was wholly cretinous. How could he continue to . . . He looked up and saw Malorange's face wreathed in the light of the distant guns. He could search that unfathomable face forever, without results. Physician. Scholar. Spy. Murderer. The Dark Lady of the Sonnets and the bullet in Raya's thigh.

Malorange was saying: ". . . One of those rare cases in which both causes are just. Winokur made a fool of you. And we made a fool of Winokur. But, surely, someone has made fools of us all."

"Exactly who?" asked Chalfin.

"Oh, someone. Or something. One doesn't know. Perhaps one doesn't want to know."

Chalfin could feel Winokur; bloodied, limping along the river, going back to his source of light. He could feel the man thinking, thinking in Yiddish.

The onset of the guns produced an unprecedented quiet in The Trunk. Soldiers and civilians stayed at their tables, seeming to be no longer drunk, but reflective.

Mud-splattered Chalfin had been unable to find a table to himself, and was sitting across from a British soldier. The soldier ignored Chalfin and wrote busily on a piece of paper. His face was round and unmarked, almost well-fed, almost angelic. Perhaps he's writing a poem, Chalfin thought. Perhaps he's writing a poem that will be in the first postwar anthology, with a preface by Auden.

Raya was nowhere in sight. To ease his vigil, Chalfin ordered brandy; when the bottle came he did not drink. He waited. From time to time he glanced at the British soldier writing on the paper—short, passionate strokes with a stubby pencil.

He poured a glass of brandy. He did not drink. He felt an odd sense of well-being. He felt an almost sublime clarity now that he knew he had been wrong every step of the way, that he had misjudged every act, misinterpreted every bit of evidence. He felt, also, an odd sense of strength in the fact that Winokur had duped him, totally, from the beginning. He felt defined—irrevocably defined—as the man who had been beaten, squashed, lied to, by Winokur. He felt that Winokur had saved his purity, his resolve, his allegiance. Winokur and Malorange were whores. Raya Fahmi and David Chalfin were just children.

Finally, he stood up and walked stiff-legged to the rear—to the third curtain on the left.

With his foot he opened the curtain an inch. He saw a corpulent man on top of Raya Fahmi. He saw her face, her eyes staring vacantly at the far wall.

No, he could not watch that. He turned away.

Watch it, David. Watch it, said a voice crawling through his head. *Watch it.* He turned back and watched. This was the required penance. A very light penance. No burning of the palms, no slaughter of the calf, no forced marches. Only watching, perceiving, knowing. And what did this mean to Raya Fahmi? She had been betrayed, shot, passed around like a salamander. Salamander. He was watching a fat predatory lizard on a beautiful salamander.

He watched. He listened. The sounds, too, were penance. His eyes and ears took up the scene. All penance. All of it. He was watching Europe, that he knew. He was watching centuries of beauty, truth, and light in their denouement. He was watching the fat man on top of the whore.

Poor Winokur, he thought suddenly. Poor Winokur who had hocked his considerable soul to Moscow instead of Jerusalem.

Now the man was dressing, and Raya lay on the bed. Chalfin pulled out his Beretta. He watched the fat man dress.

The man came through the curtain.

"Was it good?" Chalfin asked, pressing the gun's barrel into his neck.

The man's eyes opened wide.

"Did you pay her well?" Chalfin asked.

The man stammered in some language Chalfin did not know.

Chalfin abruptly lowered the gun. He was here to see Raya, to take her to Jerusalem. The fat man lunged away. Chalfin passed through the curtain.

She was sitting on the bed. "I knew you would come. I knew you would come. I knew . . ."

He sat down on the bed and she lay down with her head in his lap. There was nothing he wanted to say, nothing at all. He circled her head with his hands. He kissed her eyes and her throat. He wanted to gather her up, just gather her, without guile or lust. Just gather her and go home.

Raya said, "We are going to Jerusalem."

He nodded.

"To die there," she said.

Yes, Chalfin thought, we will die there. And we will have children, and read books. And one day we'll meet Winokur there and drink Polish vodka, and he will tell our children stories.

"I like the Jews," said Colonel Malorange. He was staring through a window of the barge into the river. "But they are often confused about just who their friends are. Do you agree?" He turned to face Moussa.

Moussa nodded his agreement. Rarely did he disagree with Colonel Malorange. And rarely did he understand him. Malorange seemed to kill people unreasonably. And Moussa was a man who believed, above all, in reason.

"And because they have this confusion, they are often sloppy."

Malorange paused to contemplate all the perils—political, psychological, philosophical—of sloppiness. He shook his head once in dismay.

"Winokur will try to exit from Alexandria. Other routes would be too slow. Perhaps he will meet Neurath there. And then, who knows? Moscow? London? Finland? Istanbul? Who knows? He's imaginative, and it will be a long war. Kill him, Moussa, in Alexandria."

Moussa acknowledged the order with a slight nod. Malorange turned to look out on the river once more. It had been exhausting. So many little tricks to trap one man. Very exhausting. And poor Carla. Beautiful Carla. The Dark Lady. But Carla was political. She had played and lost, though there was nothing wrong with her vision of a New Egypt. It was her time that left much to be desired. As for Reggie Cornell—that was most regrettable. But it had been necessary to kill him at the time in case Winokur wanted or searched for real proof that Brian Quinton was a fascist. For only a fascist would kill an English war hero.

Malorange noticed the thick dust along the window ledge. Poor Sister Charlotte. She had to be dispensed with in case it was ever brought to light that a physician named Brian Quinton was really a British officer, and said British officer had murdered a genuine war hero merely to establish a cover. War is entirely monstrous.

Malorange glanced over his shoulder. There was Moussa with a jar of preserves, and a silver spoon poised in the air. They both smiled. Small pleasures were to be particularly treasured in times of war. And besides, Sister Charlotte, who was now with her God, always approved of sweets.

FROM THE

NICK CARTER

KILLMASTER SERIES